Julie Wassmer is a professional television drama writer who has worked on various series including ITV's *London's Burning*, C5's *Family Affairs* and BBC's *Eastenders*, which she wrote for almost 20 years. She lives in Whitstable and is well-known for her environmental campaigning.

You can discover more about the author at juliewassmer.com

MURDER ON THE PILGRIMS WAY

Pearl receives a surprise birthday present from her mother, Dolly — an early summer break at a riverside manor house that has been recently transformed into a gorgeous hotel: the newly named Villa Pellegrini. *Pellegrini* — the Italian word for 'pilgrims' — reflects the fact that the building lies on the old Pilgrims Way into Canterbury, and Pearl is looking forward to the break, not least because DCI Mike McGuire has been neglecting her due to his work. But when she discovers that she's actually booked in for a cookery course from Italian celebrity chef Nico Caruso, she begins to think again . . .

JULIE WASSMER

MURDER ON THE PILGRIMS WAY

A Whitstable Pearl Mystery

Complete and Unabridged

CHARNWOOD
Leicester

First published in Great Britain in 2017 by
Constable
An imprint of Little, Brown Book Group
London

First Charnwood Edition
published 2019
by arrangement with
Little, Brown Book Group
An Hachette UK Company
London

A catalogue record for this book is available
from the British Library.

ISBN 978–1–4448–4002–5

Published by
F. A. Thorpe (Publishing)
Anstey, Leicestershire

Set by Words & Graphics Ltd.
Anstey, Leicestershire
Printed and bound in Great Britain by
T. J. International Ltd., Padstow, Cornwall

This book is printed on acid-free paper

For Berty Taylor and bees

'What chance or destiny has brought you here before your final day?
And who is he who leads your pilgrimage?'

Dante Alighieri, *Inferno*

PART ONE

1

Pearl was listening to her mother, Dolly, on the other end of the phone as she took in the scene beyond her bedroom window. It was late afternoon and the sun had finally escaped behind clouds, the fading light causing the flat sea to appear like a grey steel plate. A few beach walkers were heading away from the outgoing tide and towards the comfort of the Old Neptune — the white clapboard pub that had once been swept away by a surge tide, only to be rebuilt from the reclaimed timbers and to remain ever since, resolutely upon Whitstable's shore, as an integral part of the local landscape.

The old pub's fortitude was a reflection of the defiant spirit of this little North Kent fishing town whose former history was still evident in the network of ancient alleyways that had been used by local smugglers to evade the coast-guard's men. A rebellious spirit continued with more recent campaigns, including one to defend the town's independent shops from the threat of encroachment by chain stores.

Eight miles offshore, the Red Sands Army Fort served as a reminder of the anti-aircraft defence that had housed more than two hundred soldiers in a valiant effort to prevent the passage of enemy planes on their way to London. After the war, it had been duly commandeered by pirate radio stations in the 1960s, when a group of local DJs began spinning Mersey Beat singles in the same bleak quarters in which soldiers had once risked their lives. Now there was talk of the fort becoming a holiday resort, complete with apartments and helipad, demonstrating that one of the town's greatest secrets of success was its continuing ability to adapt without sacrificing its inherently quirky nature.

Pearl watched a group of sparrows as they hopped among clumps of cerise-flowered mallow which grew wild on the shingle together with other plants that had dared to spread beyond garden boundaries. Small shrubs of sage and white Japanese rose had found a home close to yellow horned poppies which vied for attention with viper's bugloss, whose deep blue petals proved so irresistible to bees. Much closer to the high waterline grew sea kale, soon to burst into small white flowers, while the shape of its silvery-green leaves reflected that of the waves themselves.

Reacting to something her mother had just said, Pearl looked away from the window and ran a hand through her long dark, tousled curls as she asked: 'But why on earth does this have to be such a secret? If you won't even tell me where we're going tomorrow, how can I know what to pack?'

Glancing towards the empty suitcase on her bed, Pearl recognised with some frustration that while she liked to travel light it was Dolly who always over-packed, insisting on using any empty space in her daughter's luggage to cram items of clothing she would never get to wear. A trip to the Greek Islands had been testament to that when Dolly had sworn she would need red espadrilles, trainers, sequinned stilettos and even a set of flippers — only to spend the entire two-week holiday happily slopping around in a pair of flip-flops.

The trip ahead of both women the next day was a shorter one — a well-earned week-long break. Pearl had been looking forward to it for months since it was, in fact, a belated birthday gift from her mother. Pearl's birthday was back in February but now in early June, and on the eve of their departure, she was none the wiser as to their destination because Dolly still insisted on secrecy.

'Are we flying?' she now asked.

'You know how I hate air travel these days,' Dolly said dismissively.

'Travelling by boat?'

'With *my* mal-de-mer?'

Dolly's seasickness was legendary and somewhat ironic for the widow of an oyster fisherman, though Pearl herself had inherited her father's love of the sea. She lived in Seaspray Cottage — aptly named since its garden backed straight on to the shore — and her closest neighbour was an old yawl which now lay permanently beached on Starboard Light Alley. Rescued by enthusiasts, the boat was a reminder of another time when ship construction had dominated Whitstable's shores and tall, three-masted schooners had towered over the roofline of dwellings like Seaspray Cottage. In 1870 alone, over a hundred master mariners had been listed in the town, and the trade in oysters, for which Whitstable was famous, had flourished.

These days, yawls were only to be seen during the Regatta, though the local oyster tradition continued in the form of an annual festival, as well as their regular appearance on the menu of Pearl's own High Street restaurant, The Whitstable Pearl. Pearl's oyster bar satisfied the appetites of visitors and natives alike, as the town had burgeoned in the last ten years with fishing cottages becoming gentrified by the DFLs, the town's acronym for the Down-From-Londoners. They flocked to Whitstable at weekends and during summer months to visit seaside boltholes while the old *Favourite* sat moored for ever on the shingle bank beside Pearl's cottage, her bowsprit pointing like an accusing finger at a block of 'new build' apartments across the road.

'At least tell me if I should pack a swimsuit?'

'Questions, questions!' said Dolly. 'Why do you have to know everything beforehand? Relinquish control and see where life takes you.'

'But it may take me to a swimming pool,' said Pearl. 'So unless you want me to go skinny dipping . . . '

Dolly paused before conceding, 'No pool.'

'Shame.'

'But there may be a Jacuzzi.'

'Really?'

'I don't know for sure.'

'Now you're teasing me.'

'And you're interrogating me. Stop playing detective and just go with the flow.'

Pearl sighed to herself, knowing all too well

that, for her, mysteries were for solving, not ignoring. This was the main reason why, at the age of eighteen, she had set her heart on becoming a police detective, only to give up on her basic training just a year after beginning it, when she discovered that she was pregnant with her son, Charlie. Instead of continuing with the career she had always wanted for herself, she had remained in her home town and, over the course of two decades, built up a small but successful business with The Whitstable Pearl. Eventually, the need to revisit old dreams and unfulfilled ambitions had resulted in her starting up a new venture — Nolan's Detective Agency, based in an office consisting of a converted beach hut in her sea-facing back garden.

Pearl prided herself on having solved most of her cases to date, including several murder investigations, in the course of which she had found herself treading on the toes of DCI Mike McGuire. A Canterbury City police detective, McGuire had entered Pearl's life during a case involving a drowned oyster fisherman and had stayed ever since — though far too intermittently for Pearl's liking — remaining as slippery as an oyster in its shell . . .

Pearl was just considering this when Dolly broke her train of thought.

'So, yes, do bring a swimsuit and a few nice outfits,' she said. 'Plus some casual wear for the day.'

'No hiking boots?' asked Pearl, drily.

'Definitely not. Though it *is* an activity break of sorts,' her mother added.

'What sort of activity?' asked Pearl, becoming suspicious.

But Dolly signed off quickly. 'I'll pick you up tomorrow morning around ten-thirty.'

'Wait!'

Infuriatingly, Dolly had already put down the phone. Catching a glimpse of herself in the mirror above her bed, Pearl saw that her face was now creased into an anxious frown. The window pane rattled with a stiffening breeze but outside, the sea was still calm. Though the weather was set fair there was always a chance that things might go awry because summer rarely settled in Whitstable until July came marching in, bringing with it hordes of visitors. At that time, Pearl would never be able to leave the restaurant but for the next few days she was certain that her staff could cope, not least because she had hired a new young chef, Dean Samson, who had proved himself capable of replicating all her most popular dishes — and a few more besides.

It was an uncomfortable truth that Pearl was becoming dispensable — not only at her restaurant but in her son's life too. At twenty years old, Charlie was managing quite well on his own, with a flat in Canterbury and a place at university studying graphic design. If it wasn't for the few evenings he waited table in the restaurant, Pearl might not have seen much of him at all these days. It was indeed a challenge to relinquish control of the business, but with Whitstable's summer season yet to begin, she needed a break just as much as Dolly did. Nevertheless, the phrase 'activity holiday' was

8

still troubling, particularly as some of Dolly's former favourite 'activities' included belly dancing and having once been part of a local group known as the Fish Slappers, whose fertility dances and elaborate hand-crafted costumes had caused a stir at a number of Oyster Festival parades.

The bedroom door opened silently and in padded Pearl's rescue tabby cats to remind her it was feeding time. Pilchard mewed, while three-legged Sprat pressed his body up against the coverlet on the bed before pausing in his tracks at the sight of Pearl's suitcase. Both creatures seemed to eye her accusingly as though aware she was about to desert them. In fact, Pearl had made arrangements for her best friend and neighbour, Nathan, to take care of them in her absence, and knew that he would spoil them as much as he spoiled his own cat, Biggy, who lived in feline splendour with a variety of special chairs and designer fleeces. Pilchard and Sprat didn't do badly either, with a regular diet of salmon and fresh prawns from the restaurant but nevertheless the sight of a suitcase always provoked some concern and Pearl moved quickly to stroke them.

At that moment, the white sail of a small dinghy glided past her window. Pearl herself had been looking forward to spending an afternoon sailing with McGuire, only for him to bail out of the date a few weeks ago, citing pressures of work. She recognised now, in the light of Dolly's words, that McGuire remained perhaps the ultimate mystery — and one she might never fathom — though whether it was the attraction of opposites at work or, as she liked to think sometimes, the fact that he represented the perfect balance to her own passionate nature, she could not be sure. Certainly, in appearance, they looked as though they might have sprung from different tribes, for McGuire's blond good looks were almost Viking while Pearl, having inherited the physical traits of her father's Irish ancestry, was a tall, slim, dark-haired Celtic beauty with grey eyes the colour of moonstone. In spite of all the chemistry between them, McGuire had failed to call to re-book their date and the thought of this rankled for Pearl — almost as much as the lack of information offered by Dolly about their trip away.

Looking back at her suitcase, she decided to get on with the task of packing it, this time with renewed resolve as she selected a few light summery items from her wardrobe. Then her gaze fell on an item she hadn't seen for some time: a scarlet silk dress, fitted and off-the-shoulder. It was one she had yet to wear, having saved it for a special occasion — like a date with McGuire. Hesitating for only a moment, she now grabbed it from its hanger and folded it efficiently before adding it to her case. If the restaurant would not miss her for the next few days, then surely neither would DCI Mike McGuire.

2

Dolly hadn't learned to drive until the age of forty and it occurred to Pearl, as they hurtled along the Blean road in the direction of Canterbury that Friday morning, that her sixty-three-year-old mother might have chosen today to make up for lost time. Dolly was a rebel by nature and her inclination to push all things to the limit extended to her driving — in respect of both speed and safety. Travelling in her little convertible Morris Minor was always a memorable experience for passengers, but on a gloriously sunny morning and with the car's roof down, Pearl tried not to focus on the speedometer but instead to follow Dolly's instruction and relinquish control.

It was quite some time since she had taken a proper holiday. Although she had managed a brief trip to visit Charlie while he was living in Berlin, the break had mainly consisted of a whirlwind tour of sightseeing, interspersed with evenings cooking for her son and his friends, so it had hardly constituted a rest. In truth, Pearl had become so used to the race against time to accomplish all she had to do, that with every mile travelled away from Whitstable, she began to feel she was being released from the natural frantic tempo of her existence.

Slipping on her sunglasses, she leaned her head back, enjoying the warmth of the sun on her face and the wind blowing through her long hair while Dolly sped on, down towards the looming spires of Canterbury Cathedral rising in the distance. The Norman cathedral dominated the landscape, inspiring visitors with the same sense of wonder it had surely conveyed to many throughout the centuries, for the city had become one of the most visited pilgrimage sites in the medieval world after Thomas a Becket's murder, and Chaucer's *Canterbury Tales* had further spread its fame.

Dolly, as yet, had still given up no clues as to the location of the mystery tour. Arriving over half an hour late that morning at Seaspray Cottage, she had managed to find a spot in the car's boot for her daughter's case beside a large parachute bag and numerous plastic bags containing everything from a variety of footwear to a watercolour pad and paints. Her only comments during the journey so far had been to remark on the striking contrasts of colour provided by garden trees laden with clusters of pink cherry blossom or luminous golden chains of laburnum.

Dolly was an artist and in love with colour while Pearl's creativity lay firmly in her cookery. Having long since studied the basic principles of good cuisine, Pearl's own rebellion consisted in shunning further instruction and learning only from her personal experience and experimentation. Her culinary creations were achieved largely by instinct and the results so far had proved successful in terms of the reputation of The Whitstable Pearl — though it was true she had never been able to tempt McGuire to try a Whitstable oyster. He claimed to be allergic to shellfish and in spite of Pearl having explained, on numerous occasions, that many people who are allergic to crustaceans can nevertheless tolerate molluscs like oysters and mussels, McGuire refused to be persuaded.

As she and Dolly now passed beneath the sixty-feet-high West Gate, which stood like a sentinel at the entrance to Canterbury, Pearl's thoughts stayed with McGuire. He would surely be here somewhere in the city, interviewing suspects in a stuffy interrogation room at the police station on Longport, or perhaps taking a welcome break at the South American eatery in Dane John Gardens on the other side of the old city walls. She imagined that the gardens would look special at this time of year and recalled how she had once walked with McGuire in the shade of an avenue of lime trees to a fountain where they had shared their first kiss . . . but the sweet memory was shattered by the sudden noise of Dolly's car horn, blasting the driver ahead of her to signal that the lights had changed to green.

After making good progress along St Peter's Place and on to busy Rheims Way, the flow of traffic began inevitably to slow as cars headed into the shopping centre. Dolly heaved a sigh of frustration but it wasn't long before she found herself at another roundabout where she displayed a moment's hesitation before taking a sharp right turn. This prompted Pearl to ask: 'Are you sure you know where you're going?'

'Of course,' Dolly snapped. 'But grab the map

there in the glove box. We might need it before long.' Dolly steadfastly refused to take instructions from the satnav Pearl had bought her, insisting on the use of old road maps instead — and the services of Pearl as navigator — though that onerous role sometimes also fell to grandson Charlie.

Ahead stretched Wincheap, the road which gave its name to Canterbury's south-west suburb and which ran for almost a mile from the city wall to the parish of Thanington Without. Having found the appropriate page in Dolly's road atlas, Pearl traced the length of road before them, noting how the Great Stour River ran like a concealed artery at the rear of properties whose frontages would have offered no clue to this.

From her mother's car, Pearl glimpsed the old parish church of St Nicholas surrounded by yew trees. One in particular was reputedly more than nine hundred years old, its great age serving as a reminder that yews had been planted in churchyards as signs of everlasting life. Another sign, showing fresh eggs for sale, indicated the way to an old farm at the rear of the church where sheep and chickens grazed on the riverbanks, seemingly oblivious to the stream of traffic.

'We should be approaching another roundabout soon,' warned Dolly. 'And the old Milton Manor Road is on the left, right? I mean, correct?'

Pearl confirmed she was indeed correct, though she would never have known it without consulting the map, and Dolly drove on, leaving the villages behind them as a patchwork landscape began to open up ahead with furrowed fields on either side of the road. Soon, the rolling countryside had become a distinct contrast to the busy Canterbury suburbs and the only building on the horizon that seemed at all recognisable to Pearl was signalled by two tall black-tipped chimney-stacks that rose in the distance like giant matchsticks.

'The old Chartham paper mill?'

'I hope so,' said Dolly, 'or it means we're heading in the wrong direction.' She offered a brief smile before braking, then reversing quickly back up the road. 'You distracted me,' she said. 'I've missed the sign.'

Pearl looked around but could see nothing but open countryside. 'What sign?'

Dolly failed to answer but was now looking keenly from left to right before she gave a sudden exclamation. 'There! Look — the old hawthorn tree.' She spun the steering wheel, making a sharp right turn as the tyres kicked up gravel. A short distance ahead, a set of wrought-iron gates finally came into view — left wide open as though welcoming visitors. Dolly stopped and put on the handbrake, this time exiting the car to investigate a small object she had noticed on the road ahead. She picked it up and it glinted in the sunlight as she examined it.

'How's this for good luck?' She was brandishing a small horseshoe. Tossing it into the rear footwell, she took her place again in the driver's seat before crunching the car back into

15

gear. Smiling at Pearl, she said, 'You know, I have a feeling you and I are about to have a wonderful few days.' Then she drove on.

A few hundred metres along the road, an avenue of mature beech trees opened up to reveal meadows filled with buttercup and rapeseed lying burnished beneath the sun. Dolly's car trundled down into the Stour Valley, where the sight of a tall willow signalled that the river itself could not be far away.

'Almost there,' she said, pointing a finger to the road ahead.

All Pearl could see was a line of tall cypress trees, but soon the roof of a building came into view, then pale rose-pink walls against which the shadows of trees danced in the sunlight. A man appeared, dressed in white overalls, standing on the road ahead to flag down Dolly's car. He gestured for her to turn into an area on the other side of the road where a staid black Volvo estate and a smart silver Mercedes were already parked. Dolly instantly obeyed, screeching to a halt as the man approached. In his late thirties, he was fairly tall and well-built with a head of thick chestnut hair which he took pains to smooth back before quickly turning down the rolled-up sleeves of the white overalls he wore. The house was still half concealed by the row of cypresses, though Pearl could see it was of considerable size, with four gables and eight shuttered windows visible on the upper floor, their ledges lined with terracotta pots filled with red and white geraniums.

'Ah, *just* like the brochure described,' sighed

Dolly. 'A little bit of Italy on the banks of the Stour.' She turned to Pearl. 'This,' she announced, 'is the Villa Pellegrini.'

'Pellegrini?' echoed Pearl.

'That's right. It's Italian for pilgrims, apparently — which is just what we are. Come on.' She removed the car keys and jumped out, moving on to meet the man who was now waiting patiently to welcome them. He looked first at Dolly, then at Pearl, his face clouding with slight confusion for only a moment before he asked: 'Mrs Nolan?'

'That's right,' she replied. 'And my daughter, Pearl.'

The man made to shake hands then thought better of it, quickly wiping his palms down his overalls. 'I'm sorry,' he said. 'I've just been checking the hives.'

'You keep bees?' asked Pearl, her curiosity piqued.

'Three hives in the meadow,' he said, nodding back in the direction of the house.

'I've always fancied keeping them myself,' Pearl confided. 'Perhaps one day I will.'

Her smile seemed to put the man at ease, but before he had time to introduce himself properly, another voice was heard. Silhouetted against the sunlight, an older man was now approaching, limping slightly as he leaned on the walking cane in his left hand. He was dressed smartly in dark-blue trousers, crisp white shirt and a cream linen jacket; a silk handkerchief blossomed from its pocket. His hair was straight and iron-grey, and as he stood before them, Pearl sensed he was somewhat restrained, like a tightly furled

17

umbrella. She judged him to be somewhere in his early sixties though his limp had initially made him appear older.

'Take the luggage in, would you, Robert?' he ordered efficiently, gesturing towards the car keys still in Dolly's hand. Robert took them from Dolly and instantly obeyed, heading off to unpack luggage from the boot of the car. Only then did the expression on the older man's face soften as he looked at Dolly and said, 'I can't believe it. After all these years . . . ?'

'It's certainly been a long time,' Dolly acknowledged.

The man's face broke into a warm smile and he leaned forward to kiss her cheek while Pearl looked on, feeling somewhat out of place. When he turned to her, his blue eyes scanned her face as though searching for something. 'So this is Pearl,' he murmured. 'I should have known she would turn into a beauty. I'm Marshall,' he said, reaching out his right hand to her and as Pearl took it he responded to her enquiring look. 'Marshall Taylor. An old friend of your mother's.'

None the wiser, Pearl looked to Dolly, who stepped forward and rested her hand on the man's arm. 'The last time we saw one another must've been . . . ' She broke off, looking suddenly lost.

'Autumn of eighty-five,' he prompted her.

'Is it really over thirty years since Peter and Lucy died?'

Marshall gave a brief nod then looked again at Pearl. 'I'm sorry,' he said, remembering something. 'You're at a distinct disadvantage because

18

your mother's been keeping this a surprise, right? Come on,' he added brightly. 'Simona's been looking forward to meeting you both.'

He used his cane to indicate the house, but before he had settled it back down on the ground, Pearl saw that it was no ordinary walking stick: it was highly decorative and made of a dark hardwood with a gold collar above which sat the silver form of an owl. He laid his palm firmly down upon it and led the two women back across the driveway towards an area at the rear of the house where several empty loungers were stretched out upon a lush green lawn. A well-kept garden was terraced right down to the river, where the tall willow seemed to be craning to listen to running water. Close to a jetty, a woman was seated at a table shaded by a white parasol, her head bent forward as though she might have been reading. Wearing a sun hat with a pale blue scarf tied around its wide brim, she was facing away and oblivious to anyone approaching until Marshall called out to her. 'Simona!'

Looking back, she now seemed taken by complete surprise but a smile slowly spread across her beautiful face and she got to her feet and hurried across to meet them. 'I'm so sorry. I was miles away. I didn't even realise the time.' Flustered, she checked her watch before catching sight of Robert leaving the house to make his way back to Dolly's car. 'Is the new sign up yet?' she called to him.

'Not yet,' he called back. 'But I'll fetch the luggage up and do it straight away.'

As he moved back towards the driveway, Simona gave her full attention to her guests.

'You must be Pearl and Dolly,' she said, taking off her sun hat to reveal long blonde hair which tumbled down upon her shoulders. She wore a pale cream silk blouse and stylish white lounging trousers. As she offered her hand, Pearl took it and noticed the string of amber beads she wore around her throat.

'I'm so pleased to meet you,' Simona said warmly. 'You know that Nico won't be here until much later?'

'Nico?' asked Pearl.

Marshall broke in. 'Remember,' he warned. 'A surprise?'

Simona smiled at this. 'Oh yes, of course.' Turning to Dolly, she said: 'You've managed to keep it a secret all this time?'

'So far,' said Dolly, 'which is quite an achievement as Pearl's pretty good at solving mysteries.'

'One reason why you have that detective agency, I shouldn't wonder,' Marshall remarked but Simona looked confused.

'I . . . thought you owned a restaurant?' she queried.

'Pearl has both,' said Dolly, proudly.

'Food *and* crime?' Simona declared. 'Strange bedfellows.'

'Well,' Pearl replied, 'I always say that clues to a crime are rather like ingredients for a meal. Put them together in the right way and the results can be very satisfying.'

Simona considered this for a moment before adding, 'Well, you'll certainly have a break away from crime while you're here. Let me show you to your rooms and you can get settled in before the others arrive.'

She led the way across the lawn, up some stone steps and through a door framed by wisteria in full bloom. Once inside, the spacious hallway was refreshingly cool, with a marble stairway rising from a chequered tile floor.

'What a beautiful house,' said Pearl. 'Have you been here long?'

'Less than a year,' Simona explained. 'I was in Tuscany while the renovation was taking place though I came back from time to time to check on progress. Marshall's my godfather. He was supervising the work for me and . . . well, to be honest, I don't know how I would have coped without him. He's been brilliant.'

On the wall ahead, Pearl noticed a striking painting of a middle-aged man. Fair-haired and with sensitive features that resembled Simona's, he was seated in an armchair upholstered in a William Morris print, looking straight ahead as if offering Pearl and Dolly a silent welcome.

On the upper landing, Simona indicated a number of doors on either side of the hallway. 'There are eight bedrooms in all,' she told them. 'Yours is a suite.'

Pearl noted the nameplate on the door. '*Fiammetta*?'

Simona smiled. 'Yes, I've called the rooms after characters from *The Decameron*. Do you know the stories by Boccaccio?'

'I've read them,' said Dolly. 'But a very long time ago.'

Simona went on to explain as she slipped the key in the lock. 'Fiammetta is a very clever, strong-minded and independent lady . . . ' She was looking at Pearl as she added, 'Which is probably very fitting in the circumstances.'

But it was Dolly who, assuming the remark was meant for her, quickly replied: 'Oh yes . . . that's me all right!'

They entered the room and Pearl found herself in a light and tastefully decorated space dominated by a huge four-poster bed. The ceiling beams had been treated with a white wash, together with the floorboards, over which was spread an antique rug in pastel shades. She went straight to a set of French doors which, she discovered, opened out on to a balcony overlooking the terraced lawn. 'Stunning,' she heard herself whisper. Turning, she saw that Dolly had gone through the connecting door to her own room, where she was examining a large Venetian glass mirror.

'Yes, indeed,' her mother called. 'Such attention to detail.'

'Thank you,' said Simona, clearly relieved at the positive response. 'I must admit, most of the furniture has come from my home in Tuscany.' She broke off abruptly before adding, 'Though it's no longer my home, of course.'

'No,' said Dolly gently. 'This is. And what a wonderful home it will be.'

Reassured, Simona indicated a tea tray, set with crockery and a kettle. 'Please help yourselves to tea and coffee. Maria's left a light lunch for us which we'll have once some of the other guests arrive.'

'Maria?' asked Pearl, turning to her.

'My housekeeper,' Simona explained. 'Robert's wife. They were both with me in Italy.' She offered a warm smile. 'I've heard so much about you from Marshall. I'm really looking forward to getting to know you both.' It was at this moment, with the midday sun shining through the window, that Pearl noticed the tiny insect trapped in the largest bead of Simona's necklace — a bee, preserved forever in amber.

Simona left them then, and as the door closed after her, Dolly opened her arms wide and turned a circle before looking directly at Pearl. 'What do you think?'

Sitting back slowly on the four-poster bed, Pearl glanced around the elegant surroundings which struck a fine balance between refined taste and opulent indulgence. 'I honestly can't believe you've managed to find somewhere so perfect.'

'Neither can I,' agreed Dolly. 'As soon as I heard from Marshall that Simona was offering breaks here, I had to book us in.'

'I'm glad you did,' said Pearl, hesitating before checking: 'And we *do* have a whole week here?'

Dolly nodded. 'Precisely.'

Pearl moved back to the French doors, her attention suddenly caught by a skiff moored by the riverbank. A thought came to her. 'Then for a whole week we can do whatever we like. You can get on with some painting and I'll go exploring the river.' She was about to head out on to the balcony when Dolly said, 'Yes, well . . . there probably *will* be some time for that.'

Noting the tension in her mother's voice, Pearl looked back at her.

'Among everything else, of course,' Dolly added.

'What 'else'?' asked Pearl.

Dolly failed to give her a straight answer and said cagily: 'Well, I did mention it was an 'activity holiday', of sorts, didn't I?'

Picking up a brochure from the dressing table, she handed it to Pearl. It bore a striking photo of the Villa Pellegrini on its cover and a brief description of how the house stood close to the Pilgrims Way, an ancient pathway passing through the other great cathedral city of Rochester and across the landscape of the North Downs before descending into the Stour Valley and on into Canterbury. Shot from the other side of the river, the photograph showed the house framed by the lush green weeping willow and canopied by deep blue skies like those of today. It offered a tempting glimpse of a secret hideaway — but then the spell broke and a sudden feeling of apprehension came over Pearl as she opened the brochure's cover and noted the title on the very next page. Reading the text aloud, she added a question mark after the words: '*Cooking with Nico?*'

'Absolutely perfect for you!' Dolly exclaimed.

Ignoring her mother, Pearl quickly scanned the following description: '*A unique opportunity to learn from the experience of the renowned chef . . .* ' She then uttered in an incredulous whisper ' . . . Nico *Caruso?*'

She looked to her mother for an explanation

but Dolly simply said airily: 'A wonderful idea, don't you think? You can hone a few skills and pick up a few recipes for the restaurant.'

'But I don't *do* recipes.'

'Yes, I know,' said Dolly, turning to face her. 'And I'm not criticising your cooking, Pearl, because you're a wonder with food and everyone knows it, but . . . well, you're never too old to learn a few new tricks.'

'From Nico Caruso?' Pearl's mouth gaped at the thought.

'Why not?' asked Dolly. 'It was such a coup for Simona to have bagged him for this. They met in Italy. Simona lived there for years — went out as a young student, fell in love with the place and stayed on. Anyway, Nico's agreed to do a whole season of these weeks for her, but we'll be here to experience the very first one — with a few of Simona's friends.' Dolly was looking thoroughly pleased with herself, but Pearl remained mute, which forced her mother to concede: 'All right, so you're not a fan but frankly, I don't understand why not. Everyone loves Nico. He's talented, charming, popular — with everyone else. And he's also very good-looking, with those dark eyes and that . . . lovely deep voice.' She breathed in as though inhaling any one of a number of designer aftershaves that Nico Caruso endorsed.

Pearl made a sudden realisation. 'I'm here because *you* want to meet Nico Caruso?'

'We'll *both* be meeting him!' said Dolly. 'And, as the brochure says, we can all learn a lot in the next few days. After all, he's had restaurants all over Europe — *and* his own TV series.'

'None of which he has any more,' Pearl said coolly. 'He was made bankrupt, remember? In fact, he's lucky to be doing anything at the moment considering the size of his unpaid tax bill.'

'That's very unfair.' Dolly fired up. 'He took some bad financial advice apparently, and that could happen to anyone. He's a chef not a businessman and a very good friend of Simona's, by all accounts, which is why he offered to help with this whole venture.'

Pearl frowned. 'What venture?'

'The launch of the Villa Pellegrini, of course!' Dolly tipped her reading glasses from her head onto her nose and began reading. '*Hidden away in the Kent countryside, this former manor house on the banks of the Stour has been transformed into a luxury holiday villa where guests can relax while being personally looked after by Simona Cartwright and her team.*' Here,' she continued, 'why don't you read this for yourself before casting judgement?' She shoved the brochure back on to Pearl before picking up her handbag and glancing towards her own room.

'I don't know about you but I'm going to take a shower and then get changed before lunch. You do at least want lunch, don't you?' She gave Pearl an arch look and headed off.

Finding herself alone, Pearl heaved a sigh, conflicted by her own reaction. Looking around the beautiful room, she recognised that the house and its setting were indeed idyllic — and

26

the idea of staying at the Villa Pellegrini was one she would have relished, if only it hadn't included Nico Caruso. She turned a page of the brochure in her hand and found a smiling photo of the celebrity chef. Though he was undeniably handsome with regular features and soulful dark eyes, there was something about him that Pearl found distinctly unattractive; his stylish gelled hair and sharp clothes betraying evidence of the vanity he had always seemed to exude on TV. But, right now, it wasn't Nico Caruso she was most irritated by, but the fact that Dolly must surely have known how she would react to the idea of spending time with a TV personality she couldn't stomach — and yet she had gone ahead and booked them in for this course, regardless. Now it had become abundantly clear to Pearl why the whole trip had remained shrouded in secrecy.

As she was reflecting on this, a knock sounded at the door and Robert duly entered, carrying her case. 'Will there be anything else?' he asked politely.

Pearl softened. 'No, thanks.'

He smiled briefly and made to leave before remembering to add: 'Lunch will be served shortly. And not by Mr Caruso,' he clarified quickly. 'It's been prepared by my wife.' The explanation was offered almost as an apology in the light of a renowned chef gracing them with his presence.

'Maria,' Pearl remembered. 'Yes, I'm looking forward to it.'

Robert appeared relieved by this, but before

he had a chance to respond, voices were heard in the garden below. 'New guests,' he said. 'They've just arrived.'

'Of course,' said Pearl. 'How many people are you expecting?'

'Seven in total — including yourself and Mrs Nolan.' Robert beamed at her, looking slightly stressed.

'I'd better go,' he said.

As soon as he had left, Pearl went out to the balcony and stood looking down. She could see three figures milling about on the steps below. A tall, slender woman, wearing a strawberry-pink boater with a white carnation, was standing slightly apart from the other two guests — a couple, judging by the way the other woman's arm was laced tightly through that of the man beside her. As though sensing that he was being watched, the man glanced up and met Pearl's gaze. In his early thirties, he was attractive, with sandy red hair, smiling eyes and a well-groomed moustache. His partner immediately followed his gaze, taking off a pair of enormous sunglasses before she called up to Pearl in a loud voice — and an Australian accent: 'Why g'day there! Are you staying here too?'

Pearl nodded. 'I've just arrived. My name's Pearl Nolan.'

The woman's broad smile exposed bleached white teeth that looked too improbable for her age. She could have passed for forty but something about her confident manner told Pearl she was, in fact, much older. Her suntanned face was broad and moon-shaped and its open expression showed she was friendly enough. 'Layla Bright,' she said. 'And my fiancé, Steven Sparkes.' She tugged a little tighter on her partner's arm. 'Hyphenate us, and you get the Bright-Sparkes. Geddit?' She gave an uninhibited guffaw, demonstrating that she had yet to tire of what was surely a stale joke.

Her fiancé allowed her to plant a proprietorial kiss on his cheek before he smiled up at Pearl. 'Very nice to meet you,' he offered finally, in a cut-glass English accent.

Recognising it was now her cue, the third guest took off her pink boater, revealing a mop of curly grey hair and a shy smile as she introduced herself. 'Anemone Broadbent.' Though she was in her fifties, her pale complexion was like that of a child — totally unlined and unblemished.

'Anemone. What a wonderful name,' said Layla.

'Beautiful,' Pearl agreed.

'Thank you,' Anemone replied politely. 'People always assume that it refers to the flower, but in fact my mother was a marine biologist and named me after the sea creature.' Seemingly content that she had delivered more than was required of her, she popped her hat back on her head and gave a nervous cough. Steven was still looking up at Pearl — though from curiosity, she thought, rather than because he had anything further to add.

At that moment, Simona appeared, hurrying across from the parking area. 'Please do come inside,' she said to them all, glancing up at Pearl to offer a warm smile before taking her new guests off with her. They followed obediently behind, like a line of ducklings, and Pearl watched for a moment longer as Marshall approached, still relying heavily on his walking cane. He failed to see Pearl looking down from the balcony and entered the house as Robert appeared, ferrying more luggage.

Pearl took a deep breath of the jasmine-filled air, her mood suddenly buoyed by the prospect of spending time at the beautiful Villa Pellegrini with guests whom she was sure she would find far more interesting — and vastly more entertaining — than Signor Nico Caruso.

3

'I must say, this photo in the brochure does not do justice to your gardens, Simona.' Layla Bright was surveying the grounds of the Villa Pellegrini from the open French windows of the dining room where the guests were enjoying a delicious lunch of poached salmon served with lemon and dill mayonnaise. She passed the villa's brochure to Steven beside her and took a bite of a sliver of cucumber that garnished the glass of Pimm's perched in her other hand.

'I think you're right,' agreed Anemone. 'Though I'm not sure any photograph could do it justice. I'm so pleased you invited me to your new home.'

'It's a pleasure, Anemone,' said Simona, 'and I'm only too pleased you could come. It was lovely having you to stay in Italy, and now that I'm back here in England, I'm hoping to see much more of you. That goes for you too, Steven,' she said, before quickly adding, 'and Layla, of course. I've heard so much about you from Steven, it's good to meet you finally.'

'Likewise,' beamed Layla, raising her glass.

Steven looked around him before commenting: 'It looks like a tremendous amount of work has gone into this place. Did you say it had been left practically in ruins?'

'That's right,' Simona confirmed. 'It was originally an old manor house so it was very

English in style. I was lucky to get it because someone else was very keen to buy it and the sale finally went to sealed bids.' She glanced at Pearl and Dolly as she explained: 'Having lived in Italy for so long, I couldn't help but give it a bit of an Italian touch.'

'I think it's wonderful that you did,' said Dolly. 'I love the shutters on the front windows.'

'Yeah,' agreed Layla. 'Maybe we could have some of those on our place, Stevie? *Très continental*.'

'Maybe,' he replied sparingly, leaving Layla to explain further to everyone: 'Stevie and I have bought a place in Tunbridge Wells but it's taking forever to finish.'

He looked at her and said in mitigation: 'It *is* a complete renovation.'

'Of course!' she gushed, as though it could hardly be anything else. 'You simply *have* to put your own stamp on a new home, don't you think?' Her broad smile quickly faded with her next comment. 'I just hate all the turmoil involved, but well . . . you can't just disappear and leave the builders to it, can you? So we've been taking a few trips away — a kind of pre-honeymoon, if you like. And then this *Cooking with Nico* week came up which was perfect timing for us, eh, Stevie?' She snuggled up to her fiancé once more. 'You *so* deserve a rest after all that supervising you've been doing, honey.'

Pearl noted a hint of tension as he replied, 'Project managing,' trying to maintain some gravitas as Layla nuzzled his neck.

'And is that your line of business?' asked Dolly.

Before Steven could respond, Layla answered for him. 'We're in property development, Dolly. We have a company together now. Don't we, honey?' Once again she had left little for her fiancé to add, so he merely gave a casual nod and murmured: 'That's right, darling.'

A silence fell, broken by Simona enquiring, 'Would anyone like some more wine?'

Anemone put a hand across her glass but Layla piped up: 'I'll stick to Pimm's, if there's another one going. Very more-ish, isn't it? *And very British*. Just like you, honey.' She patted Steven's hand and a flock of starlings flew overhead, a welcome distraction, it seemed, as everyone looked up at the blue sky above them as though thankful for the fine weather.

Anemone turned to Pearl and Dolly. 'So, you both live in Whitstable?'

'Home of the oyster!' said Marshall.

'I'm afraid I don't tolerate them very well — or shrimp or prawn,' said Anemone. She looked apologetically across at Simona. 'Not exactly an easy house-guest, am I?'

'Nonsense,' said Simona. 'We have a list of all your intolerances so there's really no problem at all.'

Anemone turned to the others to explain. 'I've struggled for years with my allergies but I'm pleased to say I'm at least on top of my hay fever with some wonderful new medication. A while ago I wouldn't even have been able to sit outside at this time of year — especially around rapeseed.'

Layla grimaced at the thought. 'Stuck indoors all summer — and without so much as a Pacific prawn?' She gave a shrug. 'Still, I can't say I'm too keen on oysters.'

'Me neither,' agreed Dolly.

Marshall sipped his wine before commenting: 'A little ironic, seeing as Pearl here has a seafood restaurant.'

Layla suddenly exclaimed as she pointed at Pearl. 'Oh, I see! You're angling after a few tips from Nico, are you? Something to make the slippery little suckers more palatable?'

Pearl was just about to defend her seafood menu, which offered a comprehensive selection of both raw and cooked oysters served in a variety of ways, but Dolly got in first. 'Actually I've brought Pearl here as a birthday treat. Though I must admit I'm a big Nico fan.'

'Aren't we all?' smiled Layla.

'Oh yes,' said Anemone dreamily.

'He's a real star,' nodded Simona.

'And an acclaimed chef,' added Marshall.

'Of course!' Dolly agreed. 'Didn't you love his first TV series — *The Heart of Italy?*'

'The one shot in Tuscany?' asked Layla.

'That's right,' Marshall said. 'They actually used La Valle for a location.'

At this, Layla looked blank so Steven leaned in to her and whispered. 'La Valle was Simona's home in Tuscany.'

'Ohmigod!' Layla gasped as she turned to Simona. 'That was *your* place?'

'Yes,' Simona answered modestly.

'Perfect location,' said Steven.

'Beautiful olive groves,' murmured Anemone.

'A veritable palazzo,' Marshall affirmed.

'Too right,' said Layla. 'All that style — and sunshine too?'

Simona failed to reply but looked deep in thought as though she had been transported back to her former home.

'And what made you return?' asked Pearl, curious. 'To England, I mean.'

Simona snapped out of her reverie and glanced at Marshall for a moment as though for some assistance. He caught her look and duly replied for her. 'We all need to move on,' he said simply.

The comment seemed to act as a punctuation mark to the particular topic of conversation but Pearl noted Simona appeared preoccupied as the other guests chattered on. The loud tone of Layla's voice continued to dominate the conversation. 'Of course my favourite Nico show was *Pasta with Passion*, remember that one?'

'Set in the South,' said Dolly.

'Sicily!' Layla exclaimed.

'Sorrento,' Dolly corrected. 'I can still see him serving that *spaghetti alla pescatore* on the quayside at Marina Grande. In denim shorts.' A collective sigh from Dolly, Layla and Anemone went round the table, followed by a silence which Marshall filled — along with Simona's glass.

'Well, we're all very pleased that he's made himself available to us this week.'

'Too right,' said Layla.

'And he *is* the perfect choice of chef to have

here at the Villa Pellegrini,' commented Steven, adding to Pearl, 'Present company excepted, of course.'

'Yes,' said Dolly. 'Pearl's a very talented cook but she follows her nose rather than recipes. I don't know how she does it, but she can even boil a perfect egg without a timer.'

'How on earth d'you do *that?*' Layla was distinctly impressed.

Pearl gave a shrug. 'I honestly don't know.'

'Instinct,' Dolly announced. 'She also knows when the tide's in without needing to consult a tide table.'

'How very interesting,' said Anemone. 'Perhaps you have the Gift.'

'Gift?' asked Pearl.

'Anemone has it,' said Simona. 'It's a kind of . . . spiritual foresight?'

Anemone smiled for a moment, resting her gaze on Pearl as though she might just have found a kindred spirit, but Pearl quickly deflected the remark. 'Oh no, it's really nothing special like that.'

'I wouldn't be too dismissive,' Anemone replied, speaking with confidence for the first time. 'These seemingly small and insignificant signs are often part of a greater perception — a heightened sense that we all once possessed — but which many of us have now lost, because we no longer need it.'

'You mean some kind of psychic ability?' asked Layla.

'I mean a special awareness of our surroundings — or people,' Anemone continued. 'It's been said there's a certain morphic resonance at work in the way that some animals and insects organise themselves, like ants in a colony or bees in a hive, and I do believe we are sometimes drawn together in such a way — by giving out an unconscious signal through which we may sometimes be able to find old friends, or family, in the most unexpected places.' She paused, musing to herself for a moment. 'You know, I once bumped into an old friend during the *Palio* horse race in Siena. The chances of that were incredibly slim — that we'd be there at the same time and at such an event. But how much slimmer were the chances that we should have found one another among tens of thousands of people?'

Layla pointed a manicured finger at Anemone. 'Funny you should say that.' Turning to Steven, she said, 'Tell them how we met, honey.'

Having finally been given some encouragement to speak, Steven merely offered a laconic response. 'At an airport.'

'No!' Layla protested. 'Not just *any* airport, honey. Dubai International — one of *the* busiest airports in the whole world.'

Steven looked suitably corrected as Layla took up the story. 'We got talking in the airport lounge. Stevie gave me a hand when the heel broke on my Blahniks — and blow me down if we didn't find out we were actually on the same flight. Not only that — we were booked into adjoining seats. How's *that* for coincidence?'

'Synchronicity,' Anemone decided.

'More like Fate,' argued Layla. She smiled at

Steven beside her. 'You and I meeting like that when we did? By the time we came off that flight . . . '

'We were in love,' he said softly.

'There,' said Anemone. 'I rest my case. There are patterns in all things, even in the murmuration of starlings in the sky. Nothing is chance.'

At this, Layla clenched Steven's hand tightly and planted a kiss on his temple. He gazed into her eyes and it occurred to Pearl that as they were the only couple in the party, everyone else seemed to be looking on at them much like guests at a wedding. Addressing Simona, she asked: 'Robert mentioned there would be seven guests this week?'

'That's right,' said Simona. 'But I'm afraid the other two have been delayed.'

Marshall sipped his drink. 'You've heard from them?'

'From Frank, yes,' she said. 'His Eurostar train was late, but I haven't been able to get through to Georgie, and she really should be here from London by now.' She looked unsettled. As Robert approached from the direction of the road, she asked anxiously: 'The new sign?'

'It's up,' he replied before moving into the house.

'That's good,' she said, relieved. 'It would be very easy to miss the turning in the dark but hopefully they'll both be here long before that.' Setting down her glass, Simona smiled warmly at her guests. 'In the meantime, please do feel free to spend the rest of the afternoon enjoying this lovely weather. There's a nice walk along the river on what was once the old Pilgrims Way, or if you'd rather stay here at the house there are plenty of books and loungers on the lawn — and the hot tub, of course.'

'And I hear you keep bees?' asked Pearl.

'Yes,' said Simona proudly. 'Though I'm not the bee-keeper. Robert's kept them all his life so he's something of an expert. Just beyond our herb garden is a field we keep as a meadow for local wildlife. The hives are there and Robert and Maria live close by in a thatched cottage down by the river.'

'What an absolutely magical place to be,' sighed Dolly. 'For the bees — and for us all.' Sipping her drink and leaning back in her chair, she looked at Pearl who, for all of her earlier reservations, had to agree.

★　★　★

Once lunch was over, Dolly and Pearl crossed the Great Stour over an old iron bridge that was set with timber planks. Halfway across, they paused to watch the flow of the clear river on its journey eastwards. The banks were edged with sycamore, ash and field maple together with stunning displays of purple loosestrife glowing vibrantly in the sun, but Dolly appeared to be listening to something. 'You hear that rushing water?' she said.

'A weir?' asked Pearl.

Her mother explained. 'The riverbed was lowered in the 1800s and the point where the old leat, the artificial mill channel, re-joins the river is known around here as Tumbling Bay. Kids used to swim there until a local boy almost drowned. Now there are Deep Water signs to warn of the danger.' She glanced back across at the house, shrouded by the magnificent weeping willow, and moved on along the bridge as she commented: 'Interesting bunch of people, don't you think?'

'Yes,' Pearl agreed, following her mother, but she said nothing more and Dolly now noted her daughter's thoughtful look.

'You're thinking that the Bright-Sparkes are an odd coupling?' she guessed. 'Layla clearly does the talking for both of them — not that it seems to bother that good-looking fiancé of hers.'

'They're in love,' said Pearl. 'And just because they're so different doesn't mean to say they're odd. They seem to rather complement one another.' In that moment, Pearl was thinking less about the Bright-Sparkes and more about her own relationship with McGuire as she recognised that opposites so often attract.

'That's not what I meant,' said Dolly, breaking into Pearl's thoughts. 'Another man would surely assert himself but she treats him like a lapdog. All that billing and cooing?'

'It's called affection.'

'Well, does she have to display so much of it in public?'

They had just reached the other side of the bridge and found themselves on a path which led in, one direction, to the village of Chartham, and in the other, towards Canterbury. Heading away from the latter they approached a crafted log bench on which they sat down for a moment.

'Amazing, isn't it,' said Dolly, 'to think of all the tens of thousands of pilgrims who must have walked this route into Canterbury over the centuries. And there are still plenty who walk a pilgrimage from the city all the way to Rome, you know. Twelve hundred miles. You can get a special passport from the cathedral which they'll even stamp for you.'

Pearl sensed that her mother was stalling for time in an effort to avoid any uncomfortable questions.

'So why *did* you keep *our* 'pilgrimage' here a secret?' she asked.

Dolly looked at her daughter. 'I told you, I wanted it to be a surprise.' But she lasted only a moment longer before she gave up and admitted, 'All right. I knew you wouldn't come if I told you what it entailed, but I thought the break would do us good — you especially — and that you might actually stop moping about the Flat Foot.'

Pearl flinched. 'I haven't seen McGuire in over a month,' she said defensively.

'Exactly,' said Dolly. 'And that's *why* you've been moping.'

Pearl was well aware that Dolly had never approved of her relationship with McGuire. Aside from the fact that any man would have to be special to gain a blessing where her beloved daughter was concerned, Dolly disliked the idea of authority figures in general and had become disappointed with the police in particular when, some thirty years ago, she had failed to persuade them to come on side and join in a protest against cruise missiles at the Greenham Common Women's Peace Camp in Berkshire. She pressed her point to Pearl.

'It's painful for me to see, because I don't think you realise what a catch you are. You're a beautiful woman.' Pearl looked back at her mother, softening with the compliment, until Dolly suddenly added, 'And forty's no age at all these days.'

'Thanks for reminding me,' said Pearl, stung. As she got to her feet, Dolly tried to explain.

'No, look, what I'm trying to say is, if you hadn't been so busy with the restaurant for so long you would probably have met Mr Right before now. But these days, I'm not sure you'd recognise him even if he was standing right in front of you.'

'You think I'm a bad judge of men?'

'I think you're a good judge of people.'

'You're dodging my question.'

Dolly made another effort. 'You've always been fussy when it comes to men — and that's no bad thing — but the Flat Foot seems to have turned your head and it might just be wise to remember that there are plenty of other fish in the sea, *and* in the river — but the last thing I want to do is argue. In fact, *all* I really want to do is to spend some quality time with my daughter, away from the restaurant, away from Whitstable — just you and me.'

'And Nico Caruso?' Pearl said pointedly.

Dolly gave a small shrug. 'Well, I must say that *was* an added attraction. But I haven't actually seen Marshall in all these years so when he told me that Simona was willing to offer a special rate . . . '

'How special?'

Dolly considered Pearl's question before deciding to come clean, 'Totally gratis, as a matter of fact.'

Before Pearl could speak, she went on, 'I think she feels we might be able to spread the word for her.'

'So we're here to help Simona?'

'She could certainly do with some help,' said Dolly frankly. 'She's just extricated herself from a very bad marriage — to a drunk and a wastrel who's gone through half her money.'

Pearl took this in. 'And that's why she left Italy.'

'Apparently so,' Dolly nodded. 'But now she's back and she can hopefully make a new start — with Marshall's help. I don't know what she would have done without him. And that's her view, not mine. He was a loyal and trusted friend of Peter Cartwright, her father.'

'The man in the painting in the hall?'

'How did you know?'

'Because he looks so much like her,' said Pearl. 'And Marshall mentioned a funeral?'

'That's right,' said Dolly. 'It was the last time I saw Marshall, though we've tried to keep in touch over the years. Simona was just a child when her parents died — as were you. Peter adored her, and his wife, Lucy.' She became thoughtful, as if in that moment she was being drawn back to the past. 'He was the kindest, most sensitive man. Perhaps too sensitive,' she added ruefully.

'What do you mean?'

'He was an engineer and often away due to his work. Lucy became lonely and unhappy. She felt neglected and asked for a divorce, but Peter couldn't cope with the idea of losing her.' Her mood darkened. 'They argued one night. He shot her and then turned the gun on himself.' Falling silent, Dolly stared down at the river. 'It was terrible. Especially for Simona, who had to grow up without either of her parents. And you're right, of course, she does look like her father. I was quite taken aback when we met earlier.'

'And Marshall?'

'He's a retired schoolmaster and magistrate. A man of duty. He lives over in West Kent but I gather he's due to have a much-needed operation on his knee soon, and once he's convalesced he's planning to downsize so he can move nearer to Simona. He's always taken his role as her godfather very seriously. He helped financially with her education and has always tried to do his best by her.'

'But he couldn't stop her marrying a wastrel?'

'No,' said Dolly softly. 'Though he's clearly doing all he can to help her get over him.'

She then continued in a brighter tone, 'Look, we only have a short time here, the two of us, but I'm sure we can enjoy it — *if* you allow yourself to?' Her gaze fell on the sunlight playing on the surface of the river before them. 'Is it really going to be so difficult in a place like this?'

On returning to the house a while later, mother and daughter found Anemone dozing in a lounger beneath the willow, a book resting on her chest: *Psychology of the Unconscious* by Carl Jung. The Bright-Sparkes were in the hot tub, with flutes of champagne, and offered up an invitation for Pearl and Dolly to join them — which was declined. Instead, Dolly was keen to catch up on old times with Marshall while Pearl headed upstairs to her room, unable to resist making a call to The Whitstable Pearl to establish how the lunch service had gone without her. On learning that there had been no problems, no complaints and no dramas, she slipped off her shoes and lay down on the bed, staring idly up at the canopy above her. The four-poster was much larger than her own bed at home and she spread out her limbs, like a starfish, trying to fill the space, then she checked her mobile again just to make sure she hadn't missed any messages. Finding that she hadn't, she scrolled idly through her contact list until she came to McGuire's name. There were two numbers stored for him — one a mobile and another that would reach him at Canterbury CID, but no landline at his home. His apartment also overlooked the Stour, not in the blissful setting of Chartham, but in the heart of the city, where McGuire always needed to be.

Though the Villa Pellegrini was less than an hour away from the centre of Canterbury its tranquil setting offered such a striking contrast, it might have been situated in another country entirely. But the period of time since McGuire's last call to Pearl seemed the greater distance to her right now and she began to reflect on what Dolly had been trying to convey to her earlier. While Pearl had resisted the idea that she could possibly have been 'moping', it was nevertheless true that McGuire's absence in her life had become some kind of haunting presence, which she now considered might easily be remedied by simply calling him. The phone was already in her hand and the touch of a button would quickly reconnect them.

For a fleeting moment, Pearl allowed herself to imagine sitting across a restaurant table from McGuire as he refused yet another offer of a native oyster — a rejection which Pearl always took personally because she, like the oyster, was also a Whitstable 'native'. There was nothing preventing her from calling him now except for her pride, but pride was important to Pearl, so she took a deep breath and resisted temptation, closing her eyes and clearing her mind to simply focus on the heady fragrance of jasmine still drifting in through the open window . . .

★   ★   ★

An hour later, her mobile rang. Fumbling around for it she found the phone lying beside her on the bed and registered that it was Dolly calling.

'Where are you?' her mother was asking.

'In my room,' Pearl said drowsily. 'I must have fallen asleep.'

'Good,' said Dolly. 'You're relaxing already. But the new guests are here, and we're having a sun-downer before supper. So do come and join us.'

Pearl gathered her thoughts, gazing around her elegant room as a gentle breeze wafted in from the river outside. 'OK,' she said. 'I'll get changed and be right down.'

4

After a quick shower Pearl went through the few items of clothing she'd brought and decided against wearing the scarlet dress. Instead, she chose a vintage 1950s outfit she had picked up at an antiques fair in Canterbury: a white halter-necked sun top and matching Capri pants which she wore, not with heels, but a pair of casual pumps. Heading out of her room she paused to admire the artwork on the walls of the upper landing. For the most part it consisted of bucolic Italian prints set in antique gold frames — but one painting in particular caught her attention: the subject being a young woman who looked to be in her late twenties, with shoulder-length hair the colour of burnished copper. Her pale skin was flawless and her green eyes stared out from a face that was attractive rather than pretty, though a lively spirit that had been captured so well by the artist had a beauty all of its own. The name plate on the painting's frame showed the subject to be Lucy Cartwright. While it appeared to Pearl that Simona had inherited none of her mother's colouring or features, both women had yet shared the same misfortune in making bad marriages for themselves — in Lucy's case, one that was to rob her of a future and the chance to play a role in her daughter's life. Now, Lucy Cartwright continued to exist only in a work of art on the upper landing of the Villa Pellegrini, forever facing in the opposite direction from the man who had murdered her.

Once downstairs Pearl encountered a woman in the grand hallway who turned at the sound of Pearl's footsteps.

'Hello there,' she said in a soft Irish accent. 'I'm Maria, the housekeeper.'

Pearl introduced herself, noting that Robert's pretty wife was in her early thirties, short in stature and with a wholesome appearance. The strings of the apron she wore over a lilac floral patterned dress were pulled tight around a narrow waist and the pale blue glass beads around her throat perfectly matched the colour of her smiling eyes.

'You can go straight through the kitchen,' she explained, before noting that Pearl was hesitating at the choice of three sets of doors before her. 'Here, let me show you,' Maria added helpfully. 'Simona's office is on the right, then to the left is the pantry and the freezer room, and beyond that are these double doors that lead into the kitchen and straight out on the terrace through the French doors.' She entered the kitchen with Pearl, who lingered for a moment, taking in not only the large and stylish space before her but the delicious aromas wafting from the large oven.

'Chicken and garlic?' she asked.

'Spot on!' said Maria, adding, 'And plenty of rosemary from the herb garden. It's just a simple *cacciatore*, so I'm afraid it won't be up to Mr Caruso's standard, but I do hope you all enjoy it.'

'If it's as delicious as your lunch earlier, I'm sure we will,' said Pearl. Looking around, she noted that the kitchen was fully equipped with two large range cookers, several microwaves and a variety of copper pots and pans hanging on hooks from the ceiling. A floating island offered plenty of preparation space as well as room for dining. Some fine pieces of crockery sat behind the glass of an old dresser which had been painted a delicate ivory shade to match the colour scheme of the walls.

Maria read Pearl's thoughts. 'It's a wonderful kitchen,' she said. 'Not quite as large as the one in Tuscany but far better equipped. There's a wood-fired oven right outside on the terrace and a huge freezer room off the walk-in pantry — everything we could ever need for Mr Caruso's course.'

'I'm sure,' said Pearl. 'I wish I had space in my restaurant for even half of what you have here.'

'You have a restaurant?' asked Maria with interest. Pearl nodded and Maria looked pleased to be meeting a kindred spirit. 'Then let me show you around.'

Pearl was suitably impressed as Maria led the way through a door which opened up into a spacious pantry. 'This is almost as large as my bedroom!'

'It's a fair size all right,' Maria agreed. 'And perfect for us here. Simona consulted with me carefully about everything we might need.' The shelves surrounding them were stacked with myriad jars of exotic items such as slivered pistachios, pomegranate molasses and rose-infused olive oil.

'So you and Robert were with Simona in Italy?' Pearl asked.

Maria nodded. 'For almost eight years. We were out in Tuscany on a working break when we heard that a housekeeper and gardener were needed permanently at La Valle. It was a dream come true when we got the jobs.' Then her expression clouded for a moment as if with regret before she rallied and said, 'Here, take a look at this.' She opened another door and pushed aside two heavy plastic curtains. The cold air hit as soon as Pearl stepped past them to find herself in a large freezer room. Plastic bags filled with meat, fish and prepared vegetables lined the stainless-steel shelves while some large joints of pork hung from the ceiling.

Maria sighed. 'How I could have done with this in Tuscany,' she said. 'It was often forty degrees in the summer and the freezer we had there was far too small for our needs.' She turned and led Pearl out again. 'But, all in all, this place is heaven-sent and, in many ways, it's nice to be back in England.'

Once in the kitchen she went to a fridge and took out a bottle of Prosecco, opening it in expert fashion and pouring a flute which she handed to Pearl, saying, 'I'll be out in a second with some refills.' As Pearl moved towards the open French windows she saw that the lowering sun was casting a rosy glow on the western side of the property as though signalling that the long-neglected manor was being brought back to life; there was the sound of unfamiliar voices — the addition of new guests on the terrace.

51

Dolly looked up at the sight of Pearl. 'Ah, there you are. Come and meet Frank and Simona's friend — ' She broke off, mortified. 'I'm so sorry, I've forgotten your name.'

'Georgina Strang,' said the guest.

A tall and graceful woman with striking dark looks, Georgina was standing apart and not seated with the others. Perfectly groomed, her make-up seemed to have been expertly applied to emphasise her almond-shaped eyes and full mouth. There was something of Queen Cleopatra about her flawless olive skin stretched tight over high cheekbones and her poker-straight auburn hair, which was cut at a sharp angle to her jawline, as though to show off her slender neck. Her long fingernails were manicured and painted with dark red polish and she wore a light, emerald-coloured silk shift dress which matched loose trousers over flat gold sandals. It was an outfit that might have swamped another woman but it hung elegantly on Georgina's slim, broad-shouldered frame as it would upon a designer's mannequin. She wasn't a natural beauty but Pearl was sure that Georgina Strang's style was both attractive to men and a challenge to some women.

Dolly smiled. 'This is my daughter, Pearl.'

Frank Ellis got up from his seat and raised the folding Panama hat he wore as a polite acknowledgement. He was of medium height and in his mid-forties with straight dark hair brushed back at the sides and a short black beard. Dressed in a white linen suit and a collarless shirt lying open at the neck, he looked as though he might have stepped out of the early part of the last century, his style echoing that of a bohemian set like the Bloomsbury Group. He shook Pearl's hand, after which they both stood and admired the walled garden above which they were situated. The terrace was the perfect vantage point from which to appreciate the borders of herbs lining a central path which led to an open archway in a tall box hedge at its furthest perimeter.

'All Robert's work,' said Simona. 'There's lavender, sage, rosemary — everything we could possibly want in the way of culinary herbs. And honey, of course, from our bees. Perhaps you'd like to try some tomorrow with breakfast?'

'I would indeed,' Anemone said eagerly. 'I developed quite a taste for it when I discovered how local honey can help with hay fever.'

'I'm glad you won't find the rapeseed too much of a problem,' said Simona. 'It's a shame the pollen affects so many people, but the sight of a good crop is very beautiful at this time of year and Robert says the bees will actually pass over the nearby orchards just to get to it. Isn't that right, Maria?' Simona's housekeeper had just appeared from the kitchen and was re-filling glasses.

'For sure,' she replied cheerfully. 'He reckons it's like diving into a great yellow swimming pool for them.' She set out some trays of olives for the guests before disappearing back inside.

'You had some travel problems?' Pearl asked the new arrivals.

As if feeling the need to explain their status,

Georgina quickly clarified. 'We're here separately. I drove down from Chelsea where I keep a flat, but the motorway was a total mess.'

Frank now explained. 'There were delays at Ashford International station too,' adding, 'I live in southern France.'

'Oh, which part?' asked Layla as she waved a colourful fan before her face.

'Bourgogne,' he replied. When Layla looked at a loss, he clarified: 'Burgundy.'

Marshall smiled. 'A fitting base for a wine expert.'

'Oh, I wouldn't describe myself as an expert,' said Frank humbly. He gave Pearl a shy smile. 'I worked in the wine trade for many years and I still do the odd blog, but these days I'm mainly a travel writer.'

'Frank came to stay at La Valle when he was touring the area,' Simona explained.

'Your old home in Tuscany,' noted Pearl.

Simona nodded. 'And Georgie here is a good friend. She has a wonderful fashion company in Milan.'

'Enough of that,' said Georgina, waving her hand dismissively. 'We're all here this week because of one person. Not Nico but you, my darling Simona.'

At this, their hostess gave an embarrassed smile but Anemone agreed, 'Absolutely! *And* a love of good food,' she added, sipping her Prosecco.

Pearl recognised that Anemone was right. They were a disparate set of people in age, outlook and social standing, but it was undeniable that they were connected by the theme of the break — food. With that thought, Pearl reached for a plump green olive and savoured it in the warmth of the setting sun.

'Dinner will be served in an hour,' promised Simona, 'whether Nico makes it here in time or not.' She checked her watch, looking slightly fretful. 'He'll be coming from London so I do hope the traffic has cleared.'

Pearl glanced across at Georgina, who was now leaning idly against one of the French doors, the stem of a champagne flute resting between the fingers of one hand while with the other she held what Pearl first thought was a cigarette in a holder until she realised it was a vaping device. Georgina raised it to her lips and after drawing deeply on it she exhaled a long trail of blue vapour into the air. Taking a sip of her drink, she then lifted her face to the lowering sun, looking to Pearl in that moment every inch a model striking a classic pose for a fashion shoot.

Marshall spoke to Frank beside him. 'I'd be interested to hear what you think of a certain Chianti I have. Shall we try it over supper?'

'I'll look forward to it,' said Frank.

'I've never been too good with red wine,' Anemone said ruefully.

'You're allergic to wine too?' said Layla, appalled.

'Only red,' Anemone told her. 'It usually leads to a migraine.'

'Probably due to histamine,' said Frank. 'Some reds have up to two hundred per cent more histamine than white. But there again, you could be reacting to tannins — that's the dry-tasting flavonoid that's found in grape seeds and skins.' He gave a benevolent grin. 'Reds also have far more tannins than white.'

'You're so well informed, Frank.' Simona was impressed.

Clearly encouraged by the compliment, he went on: 'Tempranillo and some of the Italian grapes are lighter on tannins, as are some of the reds from near my home in Burgundy, but Barolo, Barbaresco and Bordeaux are particularly tannic — and the Syrah, of course,' he said, before adding: 'Shiraz.' He nodded to himself, satisfied he had offered up as much information as possible on the subject, then he sipped his drink.

'Well, you learn something every day,' said Layla, turning to her fiancé. 'Did you know that, honey?'

''Fraid not,' said Steven languidly. 'But then of the lighter French wines I do prefer the Courvoisier.' He tossed an olive into the air and caught it in his mouth.

A moment's silence fell before Layla nudged him. 'Oh . . . you!' The guests broke into laughter.

'Very good!' said Frank, enthusiastically over-compensating for the fact that Steven was clearly making fun of him.

Layla snuggled closer to Steven but Pearl noted that as he sipped his drink his eyes remained on Georgina. Simona suddenly tipped her head to one side as though having heard something at a distance.

'What is it?' asked Marshall.

'A car engine, I think.' She set down her glass. 'Will you all excuse me?' She moved off quickly towards the side of the house as the sound of a car approaching now became evident to everyone. A loud blast of opera accompanied it, a soundtrack that was cut off abruptly with the car's engine. A few moments later a door was heard to slam and an expectant hush fell before footsteps were heard, followed by the four words: '*Buona sera a tutti!*'

Standing on the terrace, appearing taller and slimmer than Pearl remembered of his TV persona, was the chef — Nico Caruso. He was dressed casually in faded jeans and a pale pink shirt that was unbuttoned at the neck, the sleeves of a deeper pink sweater tied loosely around his neck. His hair was much longer than the slick style he sported in the Villa Pellegrini brochure and a slight growth of beard around his sharp jawline contributed to an altogether more relaxed style. His skin bore the glow of a natural tan while his eyes were the colour of dark caramel. In spite of the fact that he was in his early forties, there was clearly a boyish charm about him as he stood before the guests, his arms thrown wide, a pair of expensive sunglasses in one hand and a satchel in the other. Simona appeared beside him and judged the perfect moment for a proper introduction as a reverential silence seemed to fall among the guests.

'Meet Nico, everyone.' Her announcement

proved totally unnecessary since everyone knew precisely who he was.

Marshall tried to get to his feet but on seeing him struggling with his cane, Nico stepped quickly forward, protesting, 'No, no, my friend. Please stay.' He shook Marshall's hand and went on to introduce himself to every other guest, beginning with Anemone, who couldn't help but make hamster-like squeaks of pleasure as he kissed her proffered hand. Layla and Steven were next, followed by Frank and then, finally, Dolly and Pearl. Holding Pearl's gaze, he murmured, '*Buona sera*, Perla.' But it was at that moment that Simona suddenly realised one of her guests had disappeared.

'Does anyone know where — '

'I'm here.' Georgina's voice sounded before she appeared from the French doors. Nico spun round, pausing at the sight of her, and for an instant he appeared speechless but Georgina gave a slow smile, seemingly satisfied with this reaction. 'Has it been so long you've forgotten me?' she said.

Nico managed a half smile and cocked his head to one side, as though unsure if a joke was being played on him. It was clear he was experiencing some mild confusion, which Simona moved quickly to dispel.

'Of course not,' she said. 'Georgie was staying with us at the time you made the TV programme. Remember, Nico?'

'But of course!' he exclaimed.

Georgina held out her hand to him. 'Good to see you again . . . Signor Caruso.'

58

His eyes, now fixed upon hers, seemed to regain their sparkle. 'Call me Nico,' he replied, kissing her hand as everyone else looked on. Simona seemed relieved.

'We'll be eating soon,' she reminded her guests.

Nico turned brightly to her. 'Yes. And for tonight's supper I have something *very* special.'

It was Simona's turn to be confused. 'But Maria has cooked . . . '

Nico interrupted her with a wave of his hand. 'Another time,' he said, 'because tonight I have brought . . . ' he paused for effect before announcing' . . . black gold!'

Reaching into his satchel, he produced a clear plastic bag. All eyes were on its contents — a selection of small black fruits with diamond-shaped projections on their outer skin. Opening the bag, Nico raised it to his face and inhaled deeply before offering it to Frank, who did the same, his eyes remaining closed as he exhaled a long sigh.

'Delicious,' he finally whispered, as though having just tasted a fine wine. 'Such a rich earthy aroma, with undertones of wild mushroom, garlic and . . . perhaps some hazelnut?'

Frank looked at Nico, who smiled devilishly before replying: 'The aroma that Epicureans likened to the tousled sheets of a brothel bed!'

Layla screwed up her face. 'Ohmigod! What on earth is it?'

'*Tuber aestivum*,' Frank told her. 'A species of subterranean edible fungus, otherwise known as the Italian Black Summer truffle.'

Nico patted Frank heartily on the back, almost sending him forward with the impact, as he confirmed, 'That's right, my friend. *All* the way from Amalfi.' Turning to Simona, Nico now slipped his arm tightly around her shoulder, reminding her, 'I said I would bring you a *sorpresa* tonight and I have kept my word.'

Simona looked suitably charmed as she met his gaze. '*Scorzone*,' she whispered. 'How very kind of you, Nico.' Looking back at her guests, she was clearly thrilled. 'We're in for the most wonderful treat.'

'Oh yes,' said Nico, lowering his voice with conviction. '*That* I can promise you all.'

5

Dinner was served in the formal dining room, by candlelight, and with the French doors opened once more on to the lawn. Simona sat at one end of the table with Nico at the other, as if confirming to the guests that the second official host was finally in place. The meal comprised a fine egg-rich *tagliolini* smothered in a truffle-infused sauce dressed with Parmesan and further shavings of *scorzone*, so fine as to be the consistency of snowflakes.

In spite of the fine food and the elegant surroundings, the evening was a casual affair with a tone set by Nico who, having settled into his room, arrived back downstairs in a loose white cotton shirt and jeans, his hair wet from having taken a quick shower. Over dinner, he was attentive to the guests, his dark eyes flitting around the table, ensuring no one was left out of a lively conversation. Dolly and Anemone were captivated by his amusing anecdotes which were littered with the names of the many celebrities, models and politicians who had once favoured his restaurants. Layla was also entranced, though mindful of her fiancé whose hand she clutched at the table. Georgina kept an altogether more dignified stance, chatting to Simona and Marshall, while Pearl, for the most part, simply observed the proceedings while savouring the meal Nico had prepared.

Frank wasn't to get to taste Marshall's Chianti as Nico insisted on pairing the course with an old Burgundy, while offering a lecture on the nature of the Summer Black truffle, issuing a warning as to how its volatile compounds could be compromised by overcooking. After a few glasses of wine Pearl noted the twinkle in his eye as he said, 'Of course, *scorzone* are also an aphrodisiac.'

'Yes, that's right,' said Frank. 'I think I remember reading somewhere that they were always off the menu for monks for that reason.'

Steven looked across at Pearl. 'Aphrodisiac, eh? The same as Pearl's oysters.'

Nico looked up at this, musing for a moment before he asked: 'And how would you rate my truffle versus your oyster, Perla?'

Before she could respond, he laughed to himself, giving permission for the other guests to do the same, then he picked up his glass and leaned back in his seat. He had insisted on calling her 'Perla' all evening. Now she felt his eyes on her, prompting her for an answer, but she took her time and sipped her wine, still contemplating the buttery pasta that had combined so perfectly with the black earthy truffles and Parmesan.

'The *scorzone* were truly delicious,' she said simply, refusing to rise to any competitiveness regarding their individual cooking skills.

Nico took another sip of his wine before settling on an idea. He pointed to her. 'Then tomorrow I will give you my recipe and you can add it to your restaurant menu — *tagliolini al tartufo scorzone Caruso!*' He smiled broadly and Pearl was about to respond on the issue of recipes when Dolly's eyes flashed a warning.

'How kind of you,' she said quickly on Pearl's behalf.

Nico waved a hand in the air. 'It's nothing. This restaurant of yours, this . . . '

'Whitstable Pearl,' Dolly said helpfully.

'Where is it?' Nico was tearing into some rosemary *focaccia* which he used to scoop the last of some truffled cream sauce from his plate before he eyed Pearl.

'Only an hour from here,' she replied.

'A little village?'

'A small town,' she corrected him.

He looked up at this and acknowledged the distinction. 'And you have a good chef?'

Pearl met his gaze. 'My customers think so.'

He considered this and gave a casual nod. 'Good. Every restaurant lives or dies on the skill of its chef.' He took a bite of his bread. 'What's his name?'

Dolly set down her napkin, about to explain. 'Actually . . . ' she began.

But it was Pearl who spoke next. '*I* do the cooking,' she said proudly.

Nico looked up with some surprise, 'You are the cook?'

'I am the *chef*,' she replied with emphasis.

Nico frowned, then relaxed a little as if suspecting she was playing a trick on him. 'So who is cooking at your restaurant tonight?'

Dolly chimed in once more. 'Dean is very good.'

'Dean,' he repeated. 'So you have two chefs.' He said it in such a way as to pour scorn on the idea, which forced Pearl to defend herself. 'The menu is all mine and I've adjusted my dishes over time so that they can be prepared or assembled when I'm not there. I serve some signature dishes . . .'

'Such as?' he pounced.

Pearl began to feel she was under interrogation but continued on regardless: 'Squid in a light chilli tempura batter, fried scallop dotted with breadcrumb, marinated sashimi of tuna, mackerel and wild salmon, and — '

'Sashimi?' sneered Nico. '*Raw* fish?'

'Marinated,' she repeated. 'I always aim to serve uncomplicated dishes that are created with the very best ingredients.'

'Like oysters.' Nico was clearly unimpressed.

'Yes,' Pearl replied stoutly. 'Pacific rock oysters and Whitstable natives. And throughout the annual festival, we serve Oyster Fritters, Oysters Rockefeller, Asian — with rice wine, vinegar and ginger — or presented very simply with lemon and Mignonette sauce. Good food should be allowed to sing out on its own rather than be drowned out by an overcomplicated symphony of ingredients, don't you think?'

Having said her piece, she now saw that all eyes were upon her. Anemone's jaw had dropped open, but rather than becoming embarrassed at these reactions, Pearl began, instead, to feel emboldened. Picking up her wine glass, she concluded, 'That's what we're known for at The Whitstable Pearl.'

Feeling her mouth had dried from tension, she took a sip of wine. Nico watched her carefully then suddenly threw up his hands.

'*Brava!*' he said. 'With that spirit, I'm sure your little restaurant will grow in time.'

Pearl didn't know if she was more infuriated by the patronising statement or the wink he gave her straight afterwards, but as she took a deep breath, ready to set him straight on the fact that The Whitstable Pearl had no great ambitions to 'grow' but instead was more than satisfied with a reputation that had been gained from catering for a small but very appreciative clientele, Nico suddenly clapped his palms and leaped to his feet.

'Enough talk,' he decided. Wrapping his arms around Dolly and Anemone's shoulders, he announced, 'Because now, it's time for dessert. In a moment I shall return with the finest *ricotta granita* you have ever tasted!'

With that, he raced off to the kitchen, leaving Anemone staring after him, sighing deeply before she uttered to Dolly, 'Oh, what a force of nature he is.'

'Isn't he just?' Dolly agreed, but as she looked at Pearl, she saw that her daughter's mouth was set tightly like a knitted buttonhole.

⋆   ⋆   ⋆

A few hours later, while climbing the stairs with Dolly to the upper landing, Pearl glanced back down towards the open doors to the dining room as laughter signalled the end of yet another of

65

Nico's anecdotes. The guests were relaxed, after a dessert that had fully lived up to his description, and they were now enjoying some coffee, along with a *grappa* that Nico insisted everyone should try — an Italian oak-aged pomace brandy.

Dolly reacted to the expression on Pearl's face as she whispered, 'Well done for keeping your temper. I know you're seething, but well . . . you wouldn't expect a chef of Nico's standing to appreciate what we do at The Whitstable Pearl.' And when Pearl bridled at this, Dolly quickly qualified: 'What *you* do, I mean.'

Pearl opened the door to the *Fiammetta* suite and entered to toss her handbag on to the bed. 'I honestly don't know what you all see in him!' she exploded. 'The man's a dinosaur, an egotist! A self-important chauvinist!'

'He's a chef,' said Dolly simply. 'He's temperamental.'

'He's arrogance personified,' Pearl decided. 'There was absolutely no reason for him to mothball Maria's dish this evening. His pasta could easily have been served as a starter, followed by her *cacciatore*. She'd prepared it especially for this evening and I'm sure it would have been delicious but, no, the famous Nico Caruso would never share a menu with a housekeeper, would he? He insisted on grabbing the limelight for himself, and you *all* allowed him to do so — including Simona.' She paused for breath. 'He doesn't even consider that *I* could be a chef too. I'm just a woman who cooks!' Opening the door to her balcony she stepped outside and allowed the night air to cool her temper. Dolly joined her there.

'He's Italian — it's a different culture.' She then added mischievously, 'But you're clearly a bit of competition for him. Two chefs under one roof? That's like having two women in the same kitchen.'

Pearl sighed, admitting flatly, 'I honestly don't think I can put up with Nico Caruso for a whole week.'

At this, Dolly moved closer. 'Oh yes you can, my love. You can do anything you set your mind to. You always could.' Her daughter felt her anger beginning to thaw with the compliment. 'Besides, there are more guests here now,' Dolly continued. 'Frank seems a nice fellow and then there's Georgina, the vaping vamp?' She giggled at this, then laid a hand on her daughter's arm. 'It's very important we creep out of the safety of our own worlds from time to time, Pearl, experience some new people and deal with some challenging views. Besides, I'm now rather curious to see how you deal with Signor Caruso. I sense wonderful chemistry here, and whatever he has planned for us tomorrow, I'm sure you'll be more than a match for him.'

She picked up something from Pearl's bedside table and tossed it to her, saying, 'Sleep well.' Then added mischievously: '*Perla*.'

With that, Dolly headed off to her own room, leaving Pearl to stare down and see the brochure she had just caught. Opening it, she reviewed the first day of an itinerary: '*Arrive at the Villa Pellegrini for a light lunch and a glass of*

67

Prosecco. *Make new friends over a delicious evening meal before we begin our culinary journey with Nico . . .* ' On the next page, the second day of the itinerary was entitled: '*The Journey Begins!*' It continued: '*Nico reveals the art of making perfect pasta.*' A full-page photo showed the chef grinning proudly with a large sheet of pasta stretched in his hands. Pearl was able to look at it for only a few seconds before she slapped the brochure shut and tossed it on to the dressing table. As a distraction, she picked up her mobile and found a text from Charlie. It read: *Everything's fine here. Hope you're having a GR8 time! Love U.* A photo accompanied it, showing her son with some of the staff at The Whitstable Pearl, thumbs raised to indicate the day had gone off well without her.

Pearl set down her phone and moved into the bathroom, reflecting on what Dolly had just said about embracing new experiences. She respected her mother's point of view, but nevertheless she also enjoyed the world she had moulded for herself in Whitstable and the company of those who now populated it. There seemed little point in putting up with uncomfortable experiences for the sake of it.

She brushed her teeth and took off her make-up. Looking at her reflection in the mirror, she saw she had caught the sun, a sprinkling of freckles across her nose and some white strap-marks left from her halter-neck top. Heading back into the bedroom, she switched off the light rather than closing the curtains and had just put on her nightdress when she noticed that

68

the balcony doors were still open. For a moment, she thought of the river close by, and the prospect of midges, but the night air was still warm and she decided against closing the doors and instead opened them a little wider. As she did so, a soft breeze entered the room with the sound of voices from the grounds below.

Moving closer to the threshold of the balcony, Pearl could hear two people chatting near the tall cypress trees by the parking area. One voice was recognisable as Nico's. A woman was talking to him in a softer tone, but as they were both speaking Italian it was impossible to make out who she was, or what she might be saying. A silence followed, leaving Pearl with the impression that the conversation was finally over until Nico's voice sounded once more, in an urgent tone as he clearly asked the question: '*Perché ora?*'

A few moments later, a door was heard to close. Leaning across the balustrade, Pearl could see no one in the grounds below and heard nothing more but the gentle flow of the river at the foot of the lawn. Back in the bedroom, she picked up her phone and searched for an Italian translation. Two words appeared on the screen to match those she had just heard. In English they read: '*Why now?*'

6

The next morning, Saturday, rattled past at a brisk pace in contrast to the leisurely tempo of the previous day. After breakfast on the sunny terrace, Nico arrived to divide the guests into small groups before explaining that the recipes he had decided upon for the day would consist of a light lunch and supper that they would all enjoy later. But first, they were to experience a lesson in the importance of tradition in Italian cuisine — or *cucina italiana*, as he constantly referred to it. Having also insisted on calling Pearl by the Italian equivalent, *Perla*, he now seemed to have given almost everyone else an Italian nickname too, apart from Layla, whose name seemed sufficiently Italian not to require a translation. Steven had become Stefano, Frank became Franco and Georgina was abbreviated to Gina. The pronunciation of the poetic Anemone was transformed into something sounding more like Annie Moanie while Dolly lost all nominal identity other than the grand title of *Madreperla*.

In the spacious kitchen the guests took up their positions at various workstations and although Pearl issued a preference for making pasta, she found herself on pizza dough with Anemone. Georgina and Dolly were allocated salad and dessert duties while Frank was paired with Steven on the preparation of a variety of vegetable dishes — including *melanzane alla parmigiana* — one of Pearl's favourites. It remained a mystery to her as to why Nico had chosen to put the men together rather than trying to spread them out among the women, as any good hostess would have done at a dinner party, but the chef's boyish charm seemed to vanish as he adopted a professional manner, informing them that eating and cooking are two things that are taken extremely seriously in Italian culture. He went on to issue a series of self-evident technical warnings — that oil should never be allowed to reach smoking point, and a chiller room should never be entered without notifying another member of the course. Pearl found her attention wandering. She gazed towards the French doors wishing she was out in the sunshine, wandering through the meadow beyond the herb garden, but the morning session carried on.

Nico was boasting about the high quality of Italian cuisine, its use of seasonal ingredients and the diversity of dishes that can be found in the different regions across the whole of the country — and in keeping with every season — from a light *insalata caprese* consisting of creamy mozzarella cheese, tomato and fragrant basil, to the hearty Tuscan bean, bread and vegetable soup known as *ribollita*. He also stressed the versatility of Italian cookery and the fact that, while it was possible to labour for a week on the preparation of a dish of *baccalà*, or salted cod, it was also possible to create a quick and delicious pasta supper with as little as three or four simple ingredients. Having done so well to promote his own national cuisine, he then brought everyone down to earth by introducing the term *all'Inglese*, explaining, somewhat disparagingly, how this was used by Italians to describe food cooked in the most utterly flavourless way — such as plain boiled rice or vegetables.

Pearl baulked at this, reminding everyone that a roast beef dinner was just one traditional English meal to be proud of, along with the many other dishes and influences which had been absorbed into British cuisine and had enriched it. She gave as an example the breakfast option kedgeree, which had evolved from the Indian rice and lentil dish *Khichri*. To this, Nico merely offered a wry smile as though in due consideration of her nerve for speaking up, before he dismissed her assertion with the withering statement: 'Assimilation is not cuisine.'

He returned to lecturing the guests, and Pearl was left to take out her frustration on her pizza dough as Anemone commented on the vigour with which she pulled, punched and stretched it. 'You certainly have tamed that,' she said, impressed.

'Haven't I just!' puffed Pearl, wishing she could do the same to Nico Caruso.

Anemone laboured on the preparation for the pizza toppings, which Nico stressed must strictly follow the rules of a culinary governing body known as the *Associazione Verace Pizza Napoletana*. The latter gave the strictest regulations in the making of an authentic Neapolitan pizza, with ingredients such as San Marzano tomatoes grown in the shadow of

Mount Vesuvius, and dough that has never seen a rolling pin and is only ever hand-stretched. Finally, he gave his approval as Pearl moulded her own dough-making efforts into a perfectly round ball before she reached for a knife and sliced a neat cross in the top of it. Dropping it into a large bowl, she expected it to rise perfectly for the occasion — along with the increasing irritation she felt towards the pedantic Italian chef.

The sun was still shining when they finally stepped out of the kitchen and headed for the table on the terrace, which had been laid by Maria with a red and white gingham tablecloth and a small vase of colourful sweet peas. Georgina ferried her own contribution of an attractive Sicilian salad while Steven and Frank brought across the *melanzane* and wine.

Nico took control like a bossy dad at a barbecue, introducing the pizzas to the beehive-shaped wood-fired oven with a great sense of drama as he declared that the cooking must be for no longer than ninety seconds in a temperature of at least 485 degrees Centigrade. He also decreed that the mozzarella should be introduced to the pizza only halfway through cooking, so that the base should not become too watery. Beads of sweat poured from his brow as he took great pains to indicate that when cooked, the perfect Neapolitan pizza must be crisp on the bottom, but slightly chewy on top, with the edges of the crust forming a ridge known as a *cornizone*, which must always be tinged black, with the cheese blistered to form peaks and troughs on the pizza's surface. Such effort on his part ensured that it was he, and not Pearl and Anemone, who received the ultimate credit but, as if that wasn't enough, he then went on to issue instructions on how to eat the pizza, insisting that it should never be shared in slices but eaten instead with a knife and fork or folded into the shape of a *libretto* — or little book.

Nevertheless, the delicious meal compensated for Nico's interminable lecture and even Pearl's glass was raised as he proposed a toast. 'To pilgrims and good food!'

The wine was welcome after the morning's hard work and once Nico had replaced his glass on the table he sighed to himself. 'To make a true Neapolitan pizza is to undertake a true labour of love.' He offered a charming smile to Pearl but on catching sight of her furrowed brow, he asked: 'Something wrong, Perla?'

At that moment, she was still considering the taste of her *marinara*. 'I think perhaps some bitter *friarielli* wouldn't have gone amiss.'

Nico gasped. 'Some *what?*'

'*Friarielli*,' she repeated. 'That wonderful green vegetable, like a delicate broccoli, that's sometimes included in pizza — *even* in Naples.' Adding: 'And I must admit I always enjoy the anchovy in a spongy Sicilian *sfincione*.'

She knew she had committed sacrilege with this statement, but it also served to embolden Layla who gave a small shrug and now offered an opinion of her own. 'And I do love a nice slice of Roman pizza,' she said. 'Delicious with pro-sciutto, artichokes and . . . '

'*Basta!*' snapped Nico. Feeling an obvious

74

need to quell a mood of rebellion, he indicated his plate. 'This is *perfezione!*' As if to confirm this, he then took a large bite of pizza.

Pearl considered him for a moment before asking: 'So, you don't think it's possible that a respect for tradition can be balanced with some . . . innovation?'

Instantly Nico stopped chewing and assessed the reactions of the others. No one dared offer an opinion. He swallowed. 'Innovation?' he echoed with disdain.

'Yes,' said Pearl. 'There has to be room for variety in cookery or we'll never move forward and discover anything new. Your own dish last night, the *tagliolini?* It included a hint of *pancetta?*'

He studied her for a moment then smiled and pointed at her with his knife. 'You noticed. *That* is what made it *alla Caruso.*'

'Exactly,' Pearl agreed. 'You put your own stamp on it.'

But before she could say more, he interrupted her. 'And *that,*' he stated firmly, 'is the privilege of the chef. He alone must make the final decision.'

Pearl set down her glass. ' "He"?' she repeated. 'You're actually making the assumption that all good chefs are men?'

Nico glanced around the table to note that the women were all looking on, eagerly awaiting his response, while the men seemed decidedly uncomfortable. 'I am a great champion of women,' he asserted diplomatically, and Simona agreed.

'I can vouch for that,' she said.

Her smile gave Nico all the encouragement he required. 'And it is natural for me to say 'he' because *all* the great chefs throughout history have been men.'

An awkward silence fell as the guests considered his statement.

Frank ventured, 'It's true there's only one woman who holds three Michelin stars.'

'And she's only the fourth to be awarded it — unfortunately,' Anemone added.

'Perhaps it is a question of temperament,' Nico said.

'Or opportunity,' broached Pearl.

'Yes,' said Georgina. 'I'm sure there are lots of these male chefs who have needed support from women.'

'What do you mean?' asked Marshall.

'I 'mean' that they probably wouldn't have achieved half of what they did without wives at home to facilitate their careers,' Georgina explained.

'Nico's single, aren't you?' asked Layla, confused.

'Yes,' he replied. 'Though, like a monk, I am married to my work.' He picked up his glass of wine. 'Only men have the technique, discipline and passion that makes cooking consistently an art.' He finished his drink and looked totally unrepentant.

'Oh my goodness!' Anemone was clearly shocked by the boldness of this statement but Nico merely laughed.

'You think I would dare say this in front of such a tigress as Perla?' He fixed her with a look and smiled but Pearl remained impassive.

'He's just repeating something said by the French chef, Fernand Point,' she informed everyone.

'The father of Nouvelle Cuisine?' said Frank.

'Exactly,' said Nico. 'Anyone can be a cook — but a chef? The clue is in the name! The *chef de cuisine*. This is not just a cook, but the head of the kitchen. A great responsibility for which you need a capacity for hard work, a steady nerve, respect from your staff — and, above all, a commitment to the highest standards of cuisine. Isn't that right, Perla?'

He waited for her reply but it was Dolly who gave it. 'Precisely,' she said. 'My daughter has all of that — *and* more.' She smiled tipsily, before raising her glass to Pearl.

★   ★   ★

After a dessert of raspberry sorbet, the guests were free to relax for the afternoon before early-evening drinks and supper. Most preferred to remain around the lunch table as they chatted in the glorious sunshine but Pearl excused herself to make some calls, feeling the need to distance herself from Nico, of whom she had had more than her fill.

She headed away from the Villa Pellegrini and on towards the herb garden, where the heavy scent of lavender hung on the warm air. Taking up a large area, the herb garden created a balance between the ordered grounds and the uncultivated land which lay beyond the tall box hedge. Like a half-open door, the archway offered only a glimpse of what lay beyond . . . Tempted, Pearl passed through it and found herself in the meadow which was, as Simona had said, given totally over to wildlife. It appeared almost like a dreamscape in the afternoon sun, with the lazy drone of bees filling the air as they settled on plants such as wild meadow clary, the stamens of which always helpfully curled down to drop pollen onto the backs of worker bees as they probed for nectar.

Three hives and a wooden storage chest were situated near to a large pond upon which water striders skimmed effortlessly across the surface. The lid of the storage chest was closed, its hasp secured over a staple, but the padlock was missing. Curious, Pearl opened it, to find it contained white overalls, like the ones worn by Robert on their arrival, together with a set of heavy-duty gauntlets, a beekeeper's veil and a metal device, comprised of a nozzle with a set of bellows, which Pearl recognised as a 'smoker' — used to calm bees during hive inspections.

Closing the lid, she turned her face towards the warm breeze that blew in from the direction of the rapeseed fields, grateful in that moment that she suffered no allergy and could enjoy the sight of the golden crop glowing beneath a sulphurous sun. She couldn't be sure if it was the wine she had drunk or the soft humming of the bees that was making her feel so sleepy, but for a second she considered how good it would feel to lie down in the long grass among the many scarlet poppies and simply take a nap. She began to whisper the opening words of a favourite ode by Keats: '"My heart aches and a drowsy numbness pains My sense, as though of hemlock I had drunk . . . "' But before the next words had come to her, she became aware of someone standing close behind her. On turning, she saw it was Nico.

'I scared you?' he asked straight away.

Pearl caught her breath, her heart beating fast as she realised that he had come up on her without her knowing.

'I'm sorry,' he said. 'Today, over lunch, I upset you then too.' He ran a hand through his hair as he tried to frame his thoughts. 'Perla, you are like me, you feel things passionately, but you don't need me to tell you who you are. You have a restaurant of your own. You've succeeded.' He paused for a moment. 'You are a chef.'

'In *spite* of being a woman?'

'Perhaps *because* you are a woman. This is, after all, the twenty-first century.'

He quickly explained: 'Sometimes I have to take part in . . . a little theatre.' He gestured with his hands to show the opening of a pair of stage curtains. 'It's expected of Nico Caruso.'

'You mean you don't actually believe any of what you said today?'

'I believe in what I do.'

'Which is?'

He shrugged. 'I cook. I use food to create. But Gina was right — many men have achieved great things because a woman has been there to support them.' He then added: 'Just like Signora Rossini.'

'Who?' asked Pearl, confused.

'You like opera?' he asked.

'What has opera got to do with this?'

'Gioachino Rossini,' said Nico. 'He was the greatest Italian composer of his time and wrote almost forty operas by the time he was thirty-eight. He once said, 'Give me a laundry list and I'll set it to music', but he also said . . . ' he reached into his pocket for a leather-bound notebook, which he opened. Clearing his throat, he read the following from it: ''Eating, loving, singing and digesting are, in truth, the four acts of the comic opera known as life, and they pass like bubbles of a bottle of champagne. Whoever lets them break without having enjoyed them is a complete fool.'' He closed his notebook, slipped it back into his pocket and smiled. 'You see, Rossini was a great composer but he was a gourmet too. You have heard of *tournedos Rossini*? Of course you have. But many great chefs dedicated their dishes to him so we have chicken *alla Rossini*, fillet of sole *alla Rossini* and even poached eggs *alla Rossini*. Yes, he was a great man, but without a good wife he might have been nothing. So, maybe a man alone is . . . a bit like an unfinished opera?'

He looked at her now with doleful eyes and Pearl felt all the tension of the day released as she suddenly burst out laughing.

'What's so funny?' asked Nico, completely taken aback by her reaction.

'You,' she smiled. 'How could you possibly say something so . . . '

'So *what?*'

'So cheesy!'

He looked at her, aghast at the suggestion. '*Cheesy . . . ?*'

'Yes. Unsubtle. Obvious. And . . . cheesy.'

He looked wounded. 'You think this of me?' He took a step away from her and shook his head as though trying to make sense of this, and after gathering his defences, he then turned back to her and said: 'OK, so go ahead, laugh at me. You are in a position to do so, Perla. You have a restaurant, don't you?'

'Yes.'

'A nice home?'

'Yes.'

'A loving family?'

'Yes.'

'And so you stand here before me and you insult me this way, and I . . . ' he laid a hand on his chest . . . 'I can do nothing. Because all I have is a reputation built on the past. I made a mistake, Perla. I paid the price. And if it wasn't for Simona I would not even be here. All this belongs to her. She is — ' He broke off again, this time his attention caught by bees returning to the hive. 'She is the queen,' he said. 'But I — I am just a worker. Nature teaches us our place, don't you think?' He drew slowly closer to Pearl. 'But then, maybe *you* are a queen too.'

In that moment, Pearl knew something magical was taking place. Unsure if it was the hot sun or a trick of the light being cast across the meadow, the blood-red poppies that had hovered in the breeze seemed suddenly stilled, while butterflies appeared frozen in the air like an image in an Impressionist painting. The smell of lavender intensified from the herb garden and the drone of the bees on the warm air seemed to grow louder . . . Compelling. Hypnotic. And then Nico broke the moment.

'Come, Perla.'

Snapped back to reality, Pearl saw that he was holding out his hand to her — a gesture of reconciliation, a truce he was offering. In the light of all that had been said, it seemed churlish not to accept. Reaching out, she took his hand, surprised by its warmth and the strength of his grip as they walked on together back towards the house.

★ ★ ★

When they met up later, Dolly demanded with bated breath, 'So what happened, then?'

'Nothing,' said Pearl casually. 'We walked back through the herb garden and found Simona waiting on the terrace. She had something to discuss with Nico. And I needed to call the restaurant.' She braced herself for Dolly's response but her mother was uncharacteristically silent.

'What are you thinking?' Pearl asked suspiciously.

'Nothing,' Dolly said brightly, though her look was one of affected innocence. 'Most men aren't used to being challenged, you know. But some happen to like it. From everything you've told me, I think Nico's rather smitten with you.'

'I hardly think so,' scoffed Pearl.

'Then why did he bother to come looking for you today? He clearly felt the need to make his peace with you.'

'Perhaps it wouldn't do to be at war with a guest here,' suggested Pearl.

'Don't underestimate your own powers,' said Dolly. 'Most people fawn over Nico Caruso but, like I say, some men enjoy a challenge.' She gave a knowing smile then moved to the door, where she paused as she suddenly remembered something. 'Oh, and by the way, Simona's suggested that Robert could give a little talk tomorrow for anyone who'd like to learn more about bees. It'll be in the afternoon, before supper. I said I thought you'd be interested.'

'Thanks,' said Pearl, and she meant it. 'I would be.'

Once Dolly had left the room, Pearl went to her window and looked out. She saw that Layla and Steven were in swimsuits as they lay sunbathing on loungers on the lawn. Georgina sat at a slight distance, wearing a wide-brimmed sun hat and a light sequinned shift that shielded her body from the sun as she thumbed the pages of a glossy magazine. Frank and Anemone were chatting animatedly together on a bench near the water's edge. After a few moments, Pearl saw Dolly joining Marshall, who seemed to be waiting for her on the lawn. She took his right arm and looked back up towards the window just as Pearl stepped away from it. Dolly strolled on with Marshall while Pearl watched them cross the lawn.

Picking up the Villa Pellegrini brochure, she

opened it at the page of Nico's photo. The wide grin and gelled hair bore little resemblance to the man she had been speaking to this afternoon, and as she put the brochure back, she began to wonder who the real Nico Caruso might be.

7

The following morning sped past, taken up with a lesson from Nico in how to prepare a Tuscan eggless pasta called *pici* — followed by some delicious wine pairings. Nico was still very much in professional mode, though his mood was generally lighter — possibly helped by the music he chose to play throughout the session — a selection of lively pieces from the Rossini opera, *The Barber of Seville*. To Pearl it still seemed a cliché — the opera-loving Italian chef — but Nico explained to the group that he was proud of having the same surname as the great Italian tenor, Enrico Caruso, who had also been born in Naples.

As he glanced across to Pearl throughout the lesson, his smile seemed sincere and the way in which he paid attention to the other guests was increasingly endearing. He flirted with Dolly and encouraged Anemone, and it became apparent to Pearl that he had teamed the only two men on the course together so that they might enjoy a sense of camaraderie in view of them being outnumbered by the women. It also seemed apparent that, like Pearl herself, Nico was a 'people person', though he appeared to be keeping a noticeable distance from one guest on the course — Georgina — for what reason, Pearl could not fathom.

The sun still shone brightly through the

French doors but the air had become increasingly heavy throughout the morning so, after a light lunch that was eaten in the shade, Pearl headed to her room for a cool shower. Changing into a swimsuit and a pair of faded jeans, she was planning to spend some time relaxing in the grounds, but just as she was about to leave her room she found that a note had been pushed under the door. Picking it up, she read the following, unsigned message: *Meet me at the jetty as soon as possible.*

The sultry torpor of the afternoon had clearly kept the other guests inside for once and as Pearl ran downstairs to the cool, tiled hallway, she saw that Dolly and Marshall were seated in the lounge playing Scrabble with Anemone and Frank, while Simona could be heard talking in Italian to Georgina and Maria in the kitchen. Strolling across the lawn, she found that the loungers and hot tub were deserted, and the Range Rover belonging to the Bright-Sparkes was absent from the car park, suggesting that they had gone off exploring for the afternoon. Nico's vintage red Fiat Spider, complete with Italian numberplates, was parked close to Georgina's stylish Alfa Romeo.

As she reached the river, the weeping willow tree partly concealed the jetty from view and Pearl hesitated for a moment before lifting its trailing branches to discover who it might be that had summoned her. Leaning back in the skiff, eyes closed, arms laced behind his head as he relaxed in the sun, was Nico, wearing cut-off jeans and an unbuttoned white shirt that exposed his tanned chest. Stepping forward, Pearl allowed the willow's branches to fall behind her like a curtain, the sound of which alerted him to her presence. Instantly, he sprang up into a seated position and gave her a winning smile, his arms stretched out to her. 'You came!'

'It was *you* who left the note?'

'Who else?'

'Well, why on earth didn't you sign it?' she asked with suspicion.

'Would you have come if I had?' He smiled at her then tugged on the boat's painter so that the skiff was pulled tight alongside the jetty. Then he held out his free hand. 'Come on, Perla. It's too hot to stay around the house.'

She frowned. 'But . . . where are we going?'

'You'll find out. Come on — *andiamo!*'

A picnic basket lay behind Nico's seat, instantly arousing Pearl's curiosity as to what could be inside. The chef continued to wave his free hand impatiently. 'Come on. What're you waiting for?'

And, finally, Pearl made her decision. Slipping off her shoes, she tossed them into the skiff before taking Nico's hand and joining him aboard. Rooting for something beneath the basket, he now produced a white parasol, which he opened and handed to her, urging her to take it. Pearl did so and settled back in her seat as Nico untied the painter, picked up an oar and pushed the skiff away from the jetty before taking up the second oar and rowing away.

Out on the river, the air was refreshingly cool with only the sound of birdsong to accompany them on the voyage. The clear waters that had once been a natural home to plentiful numbers of white-clawed crayfish now supported bream, barbel and brown trout, reminding Pearl that the inherent qualities of any river were forever in flux with water levels rising and falling, boundaries shifting with the erosion of banks and the effects of the changing seasons. A family of mute swans glided by in the river margins where reed mace and yellow flag iris had taken root in the shallows. Dragonflies drifted past on the warm air and Pearl watched their progress before her gaze met with Nico's as he pulled heavily on the oars to gain control against the current.

'What are you thinking?' he asked.

She smiled. 'That you make for an odd gondolier.'

He looked up at the blue sky above them. 'On a day like this there are worse places to be than out on the water.' Leaning his head back, he closed his eyes for a moment as he soaked up the sun.

'You speak English so well,' said Pearl. 'Where did you learn?'

'At school and out in the world,' said Nico. He smiled. 'I like to do everything as well as I can.'

He returned to pulling hard on the oars while Pearl trailed a hand in the cool water as she watched the serpentine drift of emerald-green water crowfoot beneath the surface, brought back suddenly to the memory of how she had once come upon the body of a dead fisherman surfacing beneath her in the estuary waters of Whitstable — a haunting image that would never leave her. This was the catalyst that had first brought her into contact — and conflict — with McGuire, but she had stood her ground throughout the summer-long investigation until the truth had been discovered — not by McGuire but by Pearl herself. The case now seemed an age ago and the Villa Pellegrini a million miles away from Whitstable's shores at this moment in time.

'This place is special,' said Nico, his voice snapping Pearl back into the present.

'The river or the villa?' she asked.

'Both.' He nodded to the pathway running alongside the river on the opposite bank to the jetty. 'This is your Pilgrims Way?'

'Part of it. It was an old route for pilgrims into Canterbury. Walkers and cyclists call it the Great Stour Way but people have been using the old route for centuries.'

'And still the pilgrims come?'

'Yes, but these days by many other routes too.'

'And perhaps for other reasons,' he said thoughtfully. He glanced around before making a quick decision. 'Here is good.' Rowing in closer to the bank, he secured the painter to an old mooring post, telling her, 'What I brought for you won't wait.' He smiled.

'I'm intrigued,' she said truthfully.

Turning his attention to the picnic basket, Nico opened its lid and brought out an iced platter set with six Pacific rock oysters on the half shell. Placing a quartered lemon beside them, he made a grand gesture of presenting the plate to Pearl. 'There,' he said. 'Oysters fit for a pearl.'

She looked up at him, astonished. 'Where did you get these?'

'I had them delivered — especially for you. Go on, try.'

Pearl picked up a shell and put it to her mouth. Tipping her head back, the soft cold flesh of the oyster brushed her lips as it entered her mouth with a salty tang, before she gave a quick bite and swallowed. Nico observed her as he opened a bottle of wine and poured her a glass. 'Here,' he said. 'Did you know that there are actually fossilised oyster shells in the soil of the Chablis region?'

'I'm afraid not,' she admitted. 'But I do now.'

'What do you think of those oysters?' he asked.

'Good,' she nodded. 'But not quite as good as mine.'

He took one for himself now and swallowed it whole. Clearly satisfied with the taste, he indicated the empty shell. 'Then one day, Perla, I will have to try yours.' As he took another oyster and devoured it with relish, Pearl found herself thinking again of McGuire, wishing that she could find more in common with the detective than crime — and that one day he might find time in his busy schedule to enjoy good food as Nico clearly did.

He looked across at Pearl and studied her for a moment. 'Last night, I was talking to Simona,' he began. 'She tells me you have a detective agency — as well as a restaurant?'

'That's right. It's something I always wanted to do,' she told him, 'and now I actually have the time to do it. It's a local agency. I know my town and many of the people in it, and — '

'And you like to solve mysteries?'

'Yes.' For a second she thought of explaining how, having succeeded in the roles of restaurateur and single mum, she now felt compelled to revisit old dreams to see if she could find new purpose by re-treading a path she had always felt instinctively to be hers. Twenty years ago she had passed up her only possible chance of making it to McGuire's rank in the force, but nevertheless she felt she matched him in ability. Among all the parochial jobs that came the way of Nolan's Detective Agency — finding lost pets and errant spouses — there would always be one special case that posed a real conundrum to match her perseverance and natural instinct to leave no mystery unsolved.

'How long have you known Simona?' she asked unexpectedly.

Nico paused to consider this before saying casually: 'Maybe three years.'

'Since the making of the programme at La Valle?'

He nodded. 'It was her home in Tuscany.' Pouring a glass of wine for himself, he took a sip.

'With her husband?' Pearl went on. 'At that time she was married, wasn't she?'

'Sure,' he replied.

'But not any more.'

Sipping his wine, Nico failed to reply but merely commented, 'You are being a detective now.'

'I'm not prying,' said Pearl. 'I know Simona had to return here after her marriage broke down.'

'It's no secret.' Nico shrugged. 'Jake Rhys

91

treated her badly. He has demons.'

'Demons?'

Nico looked at her. 'We all have demons but most of us keep them under control. Jake was a fool to lose her. Simona is a good woman.' He stared down at the glass in his hand. 'Maybe too good,' he added darkly.

Pearl frowned. 'What do you mean?'

'Just that. She deserves better. And one day, maybe she'll find it.' At this, he tossed the empty oyster shells and ice into the river and turned his attention again to the picnic basket, producing a new dish — a slice of chocolate cake, its thick creamy icing glistening in the sunlight.

'Here,' he said. 'You must try this before it melts.'

'You made it?'

'But of course. This morning before class. It's a *torta Caprese*. Something really special.'

'But we've already had lunch, and oysters, and now . . . '

'Perla, come on,' he teased. 'You know if you really enjoy good food there will always be room for a taste of heaven. This is made without flour — only a little for dusting. And in my recipe I use finely chopped almonds and a special liqueur, *Strega*, which has seventy herbal ingredients, including . . . no.' He broke off. '*You* tell me what you taste. *Mangiamo!*'

Nico leaned forward, looking on expectantly as Pearl finally bit into a small piece of the cake but he was forced to wait for her reaction because for a moment she was speechless. The cake was a heavenly mix of chocolate and coniferous notes from the liqueur. 'Mint . . . and fennel?' she guessed.

'*Di preciso!*' smiled Nico.

'It's divine,' she sighed.

'At last,' he said, finally satisfied, 'at last I have Perla's approval.'

And with that, his glass met her own.

★   ★   ★

It was gone 5 p.m. when they docked back at the jetty. Pearl closed her parasol and picked up her shoes from the deck as she waited for Nico to tie up the boat. Stepping from it, he offered his hand to her from the jetty and she took it to find herself pulled up and towards him, her body pressed close to his. In that moment, she caught the mischievous look in his dark eyes. His face moved slowly towards hers and she failed to look away, trapped in his gaze until a voice suddenly sounded. 'There you are!'

Turning quickly, Pearl saw Anemone on the bank.

'Everyone wondered where you'd got to.' She looked between Pearl and Nico, then at the skiff. 'Been for a little trip on the river?'

'That's right,' Nico replied. He hauled the picnic basket up onto the jetty.

'How very nice,' Anemone commented before turning her attention to Pearl. 'Your mother sent me to find you, Pearl.'

'Is anything wrong?'

'No, quite the contrary. Robert's about to do his talk. Bees?'

'Of course. How could I possibly forget?'

'How indeed,' said Anemone, looking meaningfully at Nico.

'Go on,' he smiled. 'I will see you ladies later but right now I have to get this back to the kitchen.' He indicated the picnic basket.

Pearl had just started off back to the house with Anemone when she hesitated. 'Are you sure it's safe for you to be around bees?'

'My allergies, you mean?' asked Anemone. 'I'll be fine. You see, I have this.' She produced something from her pocket and explained, 'Looks a bit like an ordinary pen, doesn't it? But it's actually an EpiPen and will administer a shot of adrenaline should I ever get stung, but I'm very confident I'll be safe. Simona said Robert's been doing this for a very long time, so he must know what he's doing.' With that, she gave Pearl a winning smile.

★   ★   ★

The sky was becoming a little overcast by the time Robert was halfway through his talk. Frank had joined Pearl and Anemone for it but Dolly had sent her apologies, as had Georgina, who claimed that she needed a nap. The Bright-Sparkes were still not back from their drive. Although Pearl, until now, had found Robert to be a man of few words, he was voluble on the subject of bees. Very little was required in order to begin keeping them, he said, apart from a home in the form of a hive and access for them to a variety of plants which would flower from early spring onwards. Some basic knowledge was essential, however, and to that end he proceeded to empty the locker chest while carefully emphasising the need for protective clothing. A beekeeper's overalls were always white, he went on, or, at least, light in colour to provide a contrast to the dark colouring of bees' natural predators — such as wild bears. He also explained that while he always used a hat and protective veil, he often worked without gloves, which he found to be cumbersome when handling the frames. He then produced the 'smoker' and handed it around so that everyone was afforded a good view of this device. Smoke could be generated from a variety of fuel sources, he informed them, but his own favourites were pine needles and rotten wood, though the flowering plant, sumac, from which the spice was derived, was also a good option, being low on odour.

The purpose of the smoke, he pointed out, was to calm the bees before an inspection. It provoked a dual response in the bees: causing them to feed in the expectation of having to evacuate the hive due to fire, while also masking the pheromones that are released by guard bees when facing physical threat.

'Pheromones?' queried Frank.

'Yes, it's a hormone which acts as a chemical messenger to affect and control the bees' behaviour.'

'In the hive, you mean?' asked Pearl.

'In the whole colony,' Robert said. 'The pheromones given out by the queen are so powerful they can even prevent any female worker bees from laying eggs.'

'How fascinating!' said Anemone.

Robert took back the smoker from Pearl. 'Smoke promotes the feeding response in the bees,' he said, 'but there's also less chance of a keeper being stung because the swelling of the bee's stomach with honey makes it more difficult for it to use its sting reflex.'

'And presumably you've been stung many times?' Frank asked.

'I have,' Robert confessed. 'One does tend to build up an immunity, but I've known some keepers who began to suffer such bad reactions to venom, they had to give up beekeeping altogether. The face and neck are always the most vulnerable areas,' he added. 'Especially since bees can be attracted to your breath.'

'Hence the importance of the veil?' asked Pearl.

'Exactly.'

'And a hive can have only one queen, is that right?' asked Anemone.

'Yes,' Robert continued. 'She's the mother of all the female workers and male drones in the colony, and in a lifetime of three years or more, she'll lay half a million eggs — at this time of year up to three thousand a day, which is more than half her body weight. However, if she doesn't manage to leave the hive to mate, she'll stay infertile.'

'What happens then?' asked Frank.

'The workers will have to kill her off, or else the whole hive is doomed.'

There was a short silence before Pearl said, 'So, the hive is totally dependent on the success of its queen?'

Robert nodded. 'Even the nature of the hive. An aggressive queen will make for an aggressive hive — and you can't have that.'

'So . . . what do you do about it?' asked Anemone, fascinated.

'Exchange her for one that's more docile,' Robert replied. 'It's easy enough. You can start by . . . ' Just then, a few large spots of rain began to fall upon the hive.

'Oh dear,' said Anemone, looking up at the black clouds gathering. 'That's the first rain we've had for days. I do hope it's just a passing shower.'

Robert dropped his veil and gloves into the locker. 'Best get back to the house,' he advised, adding, 'We can always continue this another time.'

★   ★   ★

That evening Simona opened the French doors in order to allow in some fresh air from the grounds. The earlier spots of rain had amounted to nothing more than a brief cloudburst but the night air continued to be heavy, with candles having created rather too much heat for comfort in the dining room. Maria now lit verbena lanterns to deter mosquitos but Anemone was armed with a repellent spray, which she offered to anyone who wanted to try it. Layla professed never to be bothered by flying bugs but Dolly gratefully accepted.

'So where did you get to today on your drive?' she asked Layla and Steven.

'Not too far,' he replied.

'We found a quaint little chapel,' Layla said, 'and were hoping to take a look inside, but it seems to be used only for storage these days.'

'That'll be the old church of St Nicholas,' said Marshall, 'on what was once Milton Manor.'

'While we were there,' Layla continued, 'we met a man walking his dog, who told us a perfectly grisly story about some place nearby called the Hanging Banks.'

Steven took up the tale. 'Apparently the bodies of thieves were left there to deter sheep rustlers,' he said.

But Marshall dismissed this. 'I'm not sure the Hanging Banks were anywhere near here,' he said. 'That's if they ever existed at all.'

Layla went on: 'Well, this guy seemed to know his local history all right. He also told us about a monk who died trying to save some people at a fire at another old manor?'

'Not this one,' said Simona.

'Are you sure?' asked Layla. 'I mean, have you really looked into the history of this place?'

Before Simona could respond, Marshall did so for her. 'There's no evidence of a fire ever having taken place here and Simona hasn't yet seen any ghostly monks flying around.'

'Nor is she likely to,' Frank said firmly.

'You don't believe in ghosts?' asked Layla.

'Does anyone?' said Frank. Pearl caught the brief smile he gave to Simona, as though trying to put her at ease.

'What do you think, Nico?' asked Georgina. Wearing a slinky black dress with a low neckline, she was toying with the silver chain at her throat.

Nico looked across at her and paused before saying in measured tones, 'Ghosts come in many guises, Gina.'

She held his look for a moment but then the mood was broken when Anemone suddenly piped up brightly:

'Indeed, you're right.' She held up her index finger. 'I happen to be reading about the psychologist, Jung, at the moment. Apparently his mother, Emilie, was a depressive who spent a lot of time confined to her bedroom, where she was visited by all sorts of spirits during the night.'

'Clearly Mrs Jung was a troubled woman,' Marshall said flatly.

'I think that may be true,' said Anemone. 'But there are accounts from Jung himself of having witnessed a strange figure drifting out of his mother's room one night — a head detached from its body, just floating in the air.'

'Sounds like Jung needed to see a shrink himself,' said Steven, but Anemone ignored him as she looked up at the sky from the French doors.

'What is it?' asked Pearl.

Anemone replied slowly, 'I don't know, but . . . there's a strange energy this evening. Can you feel it?'

'There's a full moon,' said Dolly.

'And it's stormy,' Pearl noted.

'All this talk of ghosts probably isn't helping,'

said Layla. 'Can we change the subject?'

'You brought it up,' said Steven.

'I know, but maybe we can talk about something else now?'

'Like the weather?' suggested Georgina languidly.

Anemone continued to look troubled. 'The rain we had earlier should have cleared it, but it's still there.'

'What is?' asked Steven.

'The energy,' she said. 'It feels so negative.' She rose to her feet. 'Clapping out the corners of this room might help — that's where it often gets trapped.' As the others looked on, Anemone moved to each corner and proceeded to clap her hands loudly up and down the space.

'Here,' said Nico, 'why don't you have another one of these.' He had just poured a glass of *grappa*, which he held out to Anemone. She took it from him then sat down close beside Pearl.

Frank stared into his own glass, as if for some inspiration, then offered a new subject for discussion. 'You know, I once heard about an interesting project to test if walls have ears.'

'What *are* you talking about?' said Georgina testily.

'If you think about it, it's a perfectly reasonable proposition,' he continued, 'because I believe most walls are mainly made up of silica and iron particles — the same as recording tape.' He then qualified his statement. 'At least, I do know the magnetic side of most tapes is made of an oxide of iron.'

'So walls can absorb sound?' asked Marshall.

'And voices,' Frank told him. 'Apparently, the scientists involved were able to amplify what had been taken up into the walls of some ancient buildings and they heard quite a cacophony — just from the brickwork.' He looked around him. 'Think about it. Imagine what walls as old as these might have to say . . . '

'Have you ever conducted a séance?'

Georgina had broken into Frank's speech to ask the question of Anemone, but before she had a chance to reply, Steven refilled his glass and said: 'I think we can amuse ourselves without having to resort to that.'

'If there are such things as spirits they don't all have to be bad,' Simona said peaceably.

Dolly nodded. 'Yes, you're right. They might even be able to tell us something of use.'

'Or something we'd rather not know,' murmured Nico.

'Are you scared to find out?' Georgina asked, noting his mood and challenging him.

'Of course not,' he snapped.

At that moment a streak of lightning filled the sky.

'My goodness!' said Anemone, flinching. A loud clap of thunder sounded.

'The storm's close by,' noted Nico.

Maria appeared at the door. 'Shall I ask Robert to take in the loungers?'

Simona nodded. 'Yes, please, Maria.'

The housekeeper left, but as the door closed behind her, a sudden gust of cold air blew in from the French doors and the candles guttered and died. The room was plunged into darkness but more lightning flashed, followed even more quickly by thunder.

'Could somebody please put on the light?' asked Simona.

Pearl reached out towards the table lamp beside her. Fumbling for the switch, she soon found it but the room remained in darkness. 'It's not working,' she said.

'The main lights are out too,' said Nico from the door.

'Must be the breaker switch,' Marshall decided.

'Yes,' Steven agreed. 'Newly rewired systems can be sensitive.'

'Has anyone got some matches?' asked Frank.

'On the table,' said Simona. 'Near the candelabra.'

A match was struck several times. Finally it produced a flame with which Nico lit several candles. All eyes were upon him, but as he set the candelabra closer to the guests, Simona suddenly gasped.

Everyone followed her gaze to the French doors, where a figure was now framed. The man was ghostly pale, his jet-black hair and clothing soaked with the rain that was now falling heavily outside. Wearing pale blue jeans, a white T-shirt and a crumpled black linen jacket, he carried nothing in his hands and merely stood for a few moments more in the rain like a ghostly apparition. No one spoke but the man finally staggered forward, and once he had crossed the threshold, his eyes immediately locked with Simona's as though she was the only person in the room. Only then did he turn and squint in the candlelight to survey the other guests. Looking back at Simona, it was now with a mock expression of injured pride.

'So,' he began, in a voice that was both low and slurred. 'You didn't choose to invite me to the party?' He waited for a response but when none came, he reached out and seized the bottle of *grappa* from the table, using it to point at Simona. 'Don't worry, darling. You're a brilliant hostess, Simona, but I can entertain myself.' Taking a deep swig from the bottle, Simona's former husband wiped his mouth roughly with the back of his hand.

'How did you get here?' asked Marshall, struggling to his feet. Jake Rhys ignored him and took another swig.

'Clearly he didn't drive,' Georgina said drily.

'That's right,' said Jake. He failed to look at her but continued to address Simona. '*Clearly* I'm incapable — but not so incapable I couldn't find you, my sweet. You see, in spite of everything, I'm still here.' He raised his hand slowly and reached out to touch her face but she pulled away.

'I think maybe you should leave,' said Nico.

'Is that right?' asked Jake. 'Surely you wouldn't turn a man out of his own home, Nico.'

'This isn't your home. It's Simona's,' Frank said reasonably.

Jake now turned to him with a patronising smile. 'Oh dear. Poor old Frank! Still holding a torch for my wife, are you? Such devotion deserves rewarding. Have you not rewarded

103

Frank yet, my darling?'

'Please go,' Simona said simply.

'Have some respect and listen to her for once,' Marshall ordered. 'You have no right to be here.'

'Trespassing, am I?' Jake turned unsteadily to face him. 'If I am, hadn't you better call the police and have me arrested?'

Georgina spoke up. 'Dear Jake, I'm sorry to say you're becoming rather a bore.' She rose to her feet, but as she tried to move past him to reach the door, he blocked her.

'And maybe there was a time when you found me less boring?' he taunted. In the next instant Georgina had slapped his face but Jake lashed out and the wine glass she was holding was knocked from her hand. It smashed against the floorboards.

Anemone let out a scream and Maria quickly entered but Jake put up his hand. 'It's all right, Maria,' he said. 'No one's dead. But you'd better get this glass cleared up in case one of my wife's guests hurts themselves.'

'Please go,' begged Simona, increasingly upset, as she hung her head in shame.

But Jake only moved closer to her, gently pushing a strand of her blonde hair from her face as he explained: 'You've not been listening, have you? I'm going nowhere, my love. You may have come here to escape me, Simona, but you can't ever escape your past. Wherever you go, I'll be there — to haunt you.' He spun round unsteadily on his feet, pointing a finger at all he surveyed. 'And come to think of it, this isn't a bad place to haunt. In fact, I'm finding it more attractive by the minute.' His eyes finally settled on Layla. ' . . . As I'm finding your new lady here, Stevie.' He stepped across to Steven and Layla, swaying on his feet as he studied them both. 'Aren't you going to introduce me?'

He had started to offer his hand to Layla but it was knocked away by her fiancé, who followed this with a quick and brutal jab. Lake, however, blocked it before landing a clenched fist on Steven's jaw. As Steven fell hard on the floor, Layla bent quickly to minister to her fiancé. 'Oh my God! Stevie, are you all right?'

'He's fine,' said Jake lazily, rubbing his knuckles. 'Like a cat, he has nine lives. And he still has a few left, don't you, my old friend?' He paused now, looking back towards Simona. 'Strange, but these days he seems to prefer keeping company with my wife than with me.'

'Thankfully, she's not your wife any more,' said Marshall.

Jake turned to confront him but Simona put herself between the two men. 'For the last time, please go.'

Jake threw up his arms. 'But the party's just starting, my love!' he exclaimed. Draining the last of the *grappa*, he turned the bottle upside down. 'Except it looks like we could do with some more . . . ' He had just turned with the empty bottle raised in his hand when Marshall leaned forward and struck him hard on the back of the neck with his walking cane. Jake staggered forward and appeared to hesitate for a moment before his eyes spun and he finally slumped to the floor.

Nobody moved, but at that moment Robert suddenly appeared at the French doors with Maria, and Pearl quickly stepped forward, bending down to feel for a carotid pulse in Jake's neck.

'Has he killed him?' asked Georgina, completely unfazed.

'Of course not,' said Marshall. 'I was just trying to shut him up.'

'Well, you did that all right,' Dolly told him.

Pearl knelt down and put her cheek close to Jake's mouth. He was still breathing but the stench of alcohol from his breath was almost overpowering.

'He's dead drunk,' she announced.

'So . . . what do we do now?' asked Simona helplessly.

Pearl got to her feet. 'I'd say there's not much chance of him coming round before morning but he'll need somewhere to sleep it off safely.'

'Not here,' said Marshall determinedly. 'I'll call the police.' He reached out towards the phone.

'*No!*' Simona cried. 'No, I don't want them involved. It's bad enough Jake's found his way here at all, I couldn't bear having to deal with the police . . . ' She looked imploringly at Marshall, who finally capitulated.

'Very well,' he said reluctantly. 'Tomorrow he'll be sober and we'll try to talk some sense into him. Do you think we can get him into Simona's study? There's a sofa there.' The question was aimed at Robert, Nico and Frank, who each came across to help.

Simona turned to Maria to ask, 'Could you please bring some bedding?'

Maria nodded and made for the door, but Marshall called out roughly, 'A blanket will do. He's no guest and deserves no comfort here.'

Maria disappeared while Nico, Frank and Robert prepared to lift Jake's drunken frame — no easy task since he was a dead weight. Frank and Robert took his arms and trunk, while Nico lifted his feet. Jake gave a drunken groan as, together, they swung his body from the room. Marshall followed after them while Simona finally summoned sufficient courage to address her remaining guests.

'I'm so terribly sorry this has happened,' she said in a trembling voice before hurrying out of the room.

As the door closed after her, Pearl heard Anemone murmur to herself: 'Sometimes this gift is a curse.'

★ ★ ★

That night Pearl slept fitfully as the low crack of thunder was heard straight above the house. At one point, she woke to the sound of her balcony doors banging against their frame. Getting out of bed, she closed them and looked up at the sky to see clouds travelling fast across a full moon. A dark silhouette loped across the lawn — not a wolf, but a large dog fox. It came right up to the terrace then appeared to look up at her, its amber eyes glowing in the darkness before it suddenly made off in the direction of the river.

Although Pearl had closed her balcony door, a chill ran through her, and as she climbed back into the four-poster bed she found herself struggling to keep warm.

The weather had finally broken — along with the magical spell of the Villa Pellegrini.

8

'What do you mean, he's gone?'

Heading down from her room the next morning, Pearl paused on the stairs as soon as she saw Simona with Maria in the hall below. Dolly was down there too, standing close to Marshall, all waiting for the housekeeper's reply.

Maria pointed to the open door of Simona's office. 'When I came down this morning there was no sign of him,' she explained.

At that moment, Robert entered the house from the rear garden. 'I've checked the grounds,' he told them. 'And the meadow.'

'And?' asked Marshall.

Robert shook his head.

'Well,' said Dolly comfortingly, 'at least he *has* gone.'

'But he could come back,' Simona said fearfully.

'If he does, we must call the police.' Marshall's voice was firm. Simona looked troubled by this but as her gaze wandered to the painting of her father at the top of the stairs, she noticed she was being observed.

'I'm sorry,' said Pearl, hurrying down to join them.

'No, I'm the one who should apologise,' Simona told her. 'The whole evening was ruined. A nightmare for us all.'

'But it's over,' said Dolly. 'Maria's just

explained — Jake's gone.'

Simona's expression lifted as though, for the first time, she dared to believe this. 'Yes,' she said. 'He's gone.'

'But do we know how he got here last night?' Pearl asked. 'Or how he left?'

Robert glanced back at the door. 'There are some car tracks on the path, but for the most part they've been washed away by the rain.'

Dolly frowned. 'Well, he certainly couldn't have driven here last night — not in that condition.'

'Then perhaps he took a cab,' Pearl said.

'Perhaps,' Simona agreed.

'But the main thing is, he's gone,' said Marshall forcefully. 'And if we're lucky — gone for good.'

Breakfast in the dining room that morning was a subdued affair. Steven was sporting a black bruise on his jaw and though Layla did her best to minister to him, he was in a foul mood and rejected her attentions. 'I'm going for a walk,' he said finally, after finishing his coffee.

'If you wait, I'll come with you,' said Layla, who was halfway through her breakfast.

'No,' he insisted. 'I need some fresh air right now.' He threw down his napkin on to the table and marched out of the room while Layla stared glumly down at her cereal.

'That brute of a man last night has got a lot to answer for.'

'You can say that again,' muttered Georgina, her gaze drawn to the rain-smeared windows which seemed to reflect everyone's mood.

'Poor Simona, she deserves so much better,' said Anemone.

Pearl noticed that Frank looked up at this but he said nothing, allowing Dolly to comment, 'When it comes to men, some women are just bad pickers.'

★ ★ ★

Straight after breakfast Pearl headed off outside. The sky was finally clearing, though the air still had a chill to it. The lawn was sodden as she made her way towards the jetty then back across the grounds to the tall cypress trees. She rounded them to reach the parking area where Dolly's Morris Minor still sat incongruously alongside the Range Rover belonging to the Bright-Sparkes, while Georgina's Alfa Romeo was sandwiched between Nico's Fiat Spider and the two cars Pearl had seen on arrival: the staid Volvo belonging to Marshall and what she now recognised must be Simona's silver Mercedes. None of the cars were splattered with mud, and their tyres still rested in puddles created by the night's heavy rain.

Moving on to the path, she saw that Robert was right: there were tyre tracks on the road but they indicated to Pearl only that a vehicle had been driven to the house where it had made what appeared to be a three-point turn. She was considering this when Steven appeared on the road.

'Feeling better?' she asked.

'Much,' he said tersely, marching on towards the house.

111

When Nico came down at 10.30 a.m., he was wearing a kaftan over some loose white trousers, and Greek sandals on his suntanned feet. Pearl thought he looked less like a chef and more like a yoga teacher, but then it occurred to her that he might be trying to create a more relaxed atmosphere for the guests after the tension of the previous night.

Instead of sticking to the plan, which involved a complex menu that included a Venetian risotto with asparagus, saffron, chicken breast and *Grana Padano*, he announced that he thought they might spend the morning exploring the ways in which the look of a dish can add to its overall appeal. To that end, he had brought with him a laptop on which he displayed various dishes from his old restaurant, Mangiamo, as he explained the importance of 'plating' a dish in order to create something which satisfied not just the appetite but the eye. He talked of the need to contrast colours and textures, and revealed how the use of an odd, rather than an even, number of food items on a plate nearly always resulted in a more attractive display. He gave instruction on how to use a few brightly coloured herbs to enliven a bland landscape of pale food items and how to physically create a tower of flavours while constantly asking the question: 'To garnish or not to garnish?' Only two thirds of the plate should ever be filled with food, he advised them, and the rest left empty so that the negative space offered a contrast to the food and made its appearance more dramatic.

He then set the group a task of transforming a favourite meal into something that was a true feast for *all* the senses.

As if to soothe frayed nerves Nico also began playing some more Rossini, not the frantic pieces from *The Barber of Seville*, but this time something altogether slower and less familiar. Pearl found the music helped her to concentrate during the preparation of her lunch dish: sea bass fillets resting on a bed of green samphire with roasted capers and vine tomatoes. It wasn't a difficult meal to prepare but having taken careful notice of Nico's advice she worked harder on its presentation, adding some fine-cut parsnip chips and a smear of green *wasabi* horseradish sauce. As the Rossini played on, featuring a captivating solo for the harp, she felt the sudden warmth of Nico's hand on her back and accepted it as a gesture of reassurance.

'It's looking good,' he decreed and, rather than feeling patronised by the remark, Pearl found herself returning his smile, pleased with the approbation. The opera continued in the background — a recitative followed by the introduction of the orchestra. 'What is this piece?' she asked.

'*Assisa a' piè d'un salice*,' he replied. 'It means, literally, seated at the foot of a willow.' He listened for a few moments before looking towards the grounds beyond the kitchen window, as though contemplating the willow which wept upon the jetty. 'It's Desdemona's aria from the opera *Otello*,' he went on. 'Rossini wrote it for the prima donna, Isabella Colbran. They were in

113

love and she sang in ten of his operas. Some say the love is there in every line of the scores he wrote for her.'

'Signora Rossini?' asked Pearl.

'*Precisamente.*'

He smiled gently and Pearl allowed the music to wash over her, wishing to forget the memory of Simona's humiliation at the hands of her former husband and for the beautiful house to be cleansed of the 'negative energy' that Anemone had described the night before — and which still seemed to be all-pervading.

'Listen,' murmered Nico. 'Offstage here you can hear the song of the gondolier.' He looked into her eyes, aware that the boat ride they had taken together on the river must still be fresh in Pearl's memory — and it was.

The other guests were all fully engaged in their own endeavours: Georgina, Dolly, Anemone and Layla were each preparing their own dishes while Frank and Steven were quietly discussing their next choice of ingredient. The prima donna's voice rose and the sound of a solo flute emerged from the orchestra to produce a single high note which caused Pearl's heart to soar with it. She closed her eyes for just a second, lost in the moment, before she realised that the same note was now blending with another, more discordant, tone.

It was Nico who moved first. Recognising that the long and plaintive scream was coming from the direction of the pantry, he raced there, followed by Pearl, only to find the room empty — a trail of blood upon the floor. Following the

114

trail, they found the door to the freezer room was open. Maria was standing beside it, trembling, and only half revealed by the single plastic curtain which still hung at the threshold. Nico pulled it fully back and saw, with Pearl, what it was the housekeeper had discovered.

Jake Rhys was propped in a seated position on the floor, his back resting against a stainless-steel shelf, his head turned slightly to one side as though he might have been listening intently to the music that still played, were it not for the fact that his position fully exposed a gaping head wound around which his black hair was matted with dark blood that resembled the consistency of thick jam. His hand tightly clutched the second plastic curtain to his chest and his lower jaw gaped open as though he was in mid-speech, though what it was he might be trying to say would go forever unsaid, along with the message he attempted to convey in his lifeless black eyes.

Somewhere in the background, an aria came to an end, applause sounding for the faultless performance of a prima donna as a bloodied wooden mallet in Maria's hand fell to the floor with a dull thud.

★　★　★

Inspector Mike McGuire was in a meeting at Canterbury police station when he noticed the text from Pearl on his phone. Succinct, it read simply: 'Call me'. Unfortunately, he was unable to oblige as Superintendent Maurice Welch was only halfway through a diatribe concerning the results of a recent review of CID procedures. McGuire had already found his mind wandering throughout the discourse, as so often happened when Welch was in full flow, and the view from the window behind the Superintendent seemed more interesting at this point in time, showing a broad section of the Canterbury skyline with its ancient city walls and the new shopping centre rising above them in the background. In spite of the encroachment of new retail buildings, the historic city was still dominated by the cathedral spires — the attraction for most modern-day pilgrims.

As Welch droned on, commenting on important changes regarding the submission of paperwork, McGuire took another glance at Pearl's text, feeling increasingly frustrated, not only because Welch's lecture made it impossible for the call to be made but also because McGuire was well aware he should have called her weeks ago. Having failed to make their sailing date, he had also failed to arrange a suitable alternative, and while it was true that his time had been taken up with tracking down a gang responsible for several raids on jewellery stores, and the subsequent preparation of evidence for the CPS, he knew he could, and should, have made contact with her. But what had occupied his mind at the time was the grudging sense of having to constantly fight two battles: one to hunt down criminals and another to persuade the CPS to prosecute. Any failure regarding the latter he took personally.

So the days had drifted by and, with them, the

intention to call Pearl had been buried beneath a weight of mounting chores and responsibilities.

McGuire also had a stack of leave to take, the thought of which loomed before him like an oasis in the desert of his working days — days that were increasingly spent in the acrid confines of the station, in stuffy interview rooms and cramped offices where he found himself too often fuelled only by strong coffee, cheap takeaways and the overwhelming need to put a case to rest. Ultimately that was only finally achieved with a guilty verdict from a city magistrate or Crown Court jury, but the process in between was arduous and sometimes futile, though it still had to be pursued. Such a schedule left little time for dates with Pearl, but a proper explanation to her might not have gone amiss. McGuire snapped shut the notepad before him. While it may have given his superior the impression that he had been keeping careful track of the new procedures to be observed by officers, he had, in fact, been using it only to doodle a cartoon of Welch — a tiny body with a large head dominated by a mouth that never seemed to be silenced.

Filing out of the room and into the hallway, McGuire's phone rang. Half-expecting it to be Pearl he answered it — quickly bracing himself to invent a list of excuses — only to discover the call was work-related, as usual. He swiftly took in the essential details: the discovery of a dead body in the freezer room of a property in Chartham; an ambulance and medical team having been dispatched to confirm that life was extinct while

117

a local team of detectives were already at work at the house, securing the scene of crime for Forensics. Statements were being taken from a number of guests as well as the owner of the property — Simona Cartwright. The officers had also noted that the presence of a celebrity might attract some media attention, which in turn could prove problematic for an investigation.

'What celebrity?' asked McGuire. On receiving the name, he looked it up on his phone. A number of links appeared and a selection of images which ranged from a smiling, suntanned Nico Caruso beneath the news headline: *Chef Nico to open Fourth Restaurant* — to a brooding figure escaping from the judgement of a bankruptcy court hearing with a story entitled: *Caruso's Mangiamo Empire Collapses*.

Reflecting on this, McGuire decided, with mounting frustration, that his call to Pearl Nolan would, yet again, have to wait.

PART TWO

PART TWO

9

As the first people on the scene to discover the body, Pearl, Nico and Maria had also been the first witnesses to be interviewed by the SOCOS, or Scenes of Crime Officers, from the local police station. Before any statements were taken, the guests had been separated to prevent any discussion of their impressions of events which might, in turn, influence any of the accounts of other witnesses. The crime scene and the body had been photographed and videoed and the whole crime area sealed off by an inflatable tent to protect any possible clues and forensic evidence. Pearl knew from her police training that this early period of an investigation was crucial, not only for recording witnesses' recollections when they were still fresh in the mind, but also because the perpetrator of a crime may have had little time to plot an alibi or make a getaway.

It was made clear to everyone that the voluntary statements they gave now were as witnesses, not suspects — though Pearl knew full well that this status could easily, and very quickly, change. Maria had needed some treatment for shock, administered first by Pearl in the form of a blanket and a cup of weak sweet tea before the paramedics had arrived at the villa, following the initial call to the emergency services. Anyone coming upon the scene, as Pearl

121

and Nico had done that morning, could well have jumped to the conclusion that the bloody mallet in Maria's hand was testament to her having committed the crime, but the housekeeper had subsequendy explained to everyone, including the police officers, that having found the mallet on the floor of the pantry that morning, she had followed the trail of blood to the freezer room, where she had discovered Jake's body only seconds before Nico and Pearl had been summoned by her scream.

The Villa Pellegrini was duly transformed from idyllic holiday retreat to a temporary police incident room while the voluntary statements were taken and a full examination was made by the forensics team.

Only then was Pearl allowed to talk to Nico, while Maria was released to go home to her cottage.

'Why do you keep looking at your phone?' Nico asked Pearl as he sat with her at a table near the river where the parasol that had once shaded Simona from the sun on the day of Pearl's arrival now protected them from any further downpour of rain.

'No reason,' she lied. In fact, she had been checking for a text or voicemail message from McGuire but, disappointed to find neither, she now heaved a sigh as she glanced towards the river, just in time to see a young swallow diving low to drink on the wing before soaring up again into the sky. Life was going on — except for Jake Rhys.

'Last night,' she said, 'you left Jake on the sofa

in Simona's office?'

Nico nodded. 'We carried him there but it wasn't an easy job, even for Steven, Frank, Robert and me.'

'And Marshall?'

Nico shrugged. 'He followed us in with Simona. We were careful to prop Jake on his side then Maria brought a blanket and put it over him.'

'And he didn't wake at all while you were there?'

Nico shook his head. 'You saw the condition he was in last night. The last of the *grappa* did for him.'

'*And* Marshall's cane,' said Pearl thoughtfully.

'He struck out with it, yes,' Nico agreed. 'But not with the force needed to kill someone. There was not a mark on Jake when we laid him on the sofa, he was still alive. You know that.'

'Yes,' said Pearl. 'But judging from that head injury, at some point he was struck again and dragged into the freezer room where presumably he died.'

'He could have died before that — and his body was moved there,' said Nico.

'You saw what I saw, Nico. Jake's hand was clinging to one of the plastic curtains. It had been pulled from the doorway and so he must still have been alive when he did that.'

Nico looked away in an effort to make sense of what she had just told him.

'But who would leave him there to die?'

Pearl remained silent.

Nico read her mind. 'No,' he insisted. 'It's true that Jake had . . . '

'Demons?' she asked quickly. 'You said that to me when we were out on the river.'

'Yes,' he agreed. 'Jake was like a scorpion — deadly but also self-destructive.' He waited for a moment before adding finally, 'His dreams went bad on him.'

'What do you mean?' asked Pearl. 'What do you know about him?'

'Not much.' He shrugged. 'Just that when he met Simona he was writing a film script. A producer was interested, offered him a contract and some money to finish it, but he took too long and the result wasn't good. Jake preferred to believe it was the producer who was wrong. He carried on writing but he never finished what he started. All the while Simona supported him but then she needed support too so she began to rent out La Valle. That's how she met Frank and Anemone.'

'And Georgina?'

'She was at La Valle too when we filmed the TV series. But the three of them weren't together. Steven was an old friend of Jake's, while Gina is a new friend of Simona's.' He fell silent.

'And you don't like her much, do you?'

Nico looked at Pearl as he answered: 'She's a beautiful woman. She's smart, stylish . . . ' He broke off and threw up his hands. 'Soulless.' He held Pearl's gaze. 'I've met many women like this. They are like jewels — they make some men happy just by being on display. But in truth they are ghosts — the life has been sucked from them. They parade nice clothes but there is little else to them. A shard of ice where a heart should be.' As if recognising that he might have said too much, he laid his hand on hers. 'I need to go and see how Simona is.'

'Of course,' Pearl said softly, still reflecting on what he had just told her. 'I'll be in soon.'

As Nico got to his feet and returned to the villa, Pearl felt an urge to call him back but the sound of a vehicle approaching prevented her from doing so. Unable to see beyond the cypress trees, she got up just in time to hear the slam of a car door, followed by footsteps crunching on gravel before a figure appeared on the path.

McGuire stopped in his tracks, unsure if his eyes were playing tricks on him as he saw Pearl, then he strode quickly across the lawn. Once he was standing before her, he felt a range of conflicting emotions as she looked up at him, waiting for him to speak. She was beautiful, her dark suntanned skin contrasting with her pale moonstone-grey eyes, and in that moment he wanted only to lean forward and hold her close before he reminded himself that he had just arrived at a crime scene. Instead he asked in a hushed and urgent tone, 'What're you doing here?'

Any hope of a tender reunion with McGuire disappeared with his question. Immediately Pearl was put on the defensive. 'Perhaps if you'd responded to my message you'd have found out?' she said tartly.

McGuire's thoughts instantly returned to the stuffy police conference room in which Welch had been droning on as Pearl's text had come through, but before he could explain, she added: 'If you must know, I'm here on holiday.'

'Busman's holiday?' he asked knowingly.

'I called you as soon as the body was found,' she said. 'Is there something wrong with your phone?'

It was McGuire's turn to feel defensive. 'No.'

'Well, you could have fooled me,' she said, giving him an accusing look.

McGuire knew she was referring to the weeks that had drifted by without a call from him. It was time to make his peace and he took a step forward, hoping to sit down at the table with her to explain and apologise for his absence in her life when a voice suddenly called from the patio. 'Guv?'

Turning, McGuire saw a dour-faced uniformed sergeant at the French doors to the living room, trying to gain his superior's attention. Conflicted, McGuire called across: 'I'll be right there.' Then he looked back at Pearl. Before he could offer another word, however, she quickly took in the situation, well aware that a relationship between a CID officer and a local private detective, who now happened to be a general suspect in a murder investigation, could prove problematic for McGuire.

'OK,' she began before reporting to him in a business-like manner: 'I've been staying here with six other guests, including my mother, as well as the owner of the property, her godfather and two members of staff.' Reaching into her bag, she took from it the *Cooking with Nico* brochure and handed it to him. 'Not forgetting

Nico, of course.' When McGuire opened it at a page showing the smiling photo of the chef, she added, 'It's a pretty good likeness. Except that he's rather better-looking in real life.'

McGuire looked up at this, then away to the sergeant who was still waiting for him at the door. He closed the brochure, feeling increasingly torn. 'We'll talk again soon,' he said efficiently.

As he walked off towards the sergeant, Pearl called out: 'I'll look forward to that,' pausing for just a moment before adding, '*Inspector.*' McGuire glanced back at her and saw her arch look — then he entered the house.

★ ★ ★

Twenty minutes later, in Simona's study, Marshall declared: 'It's a tragedy but I'm sure the police will get to the bottom of it.' He got to his feet, leaning for a moment on his walking cane before he limped across the entire length of a beautiful Afghan rug to reach the window. In contrast, his god-daughter sat perfectly immobile, her gaze transfixed on the empty sofa. Neither Pearl nor Dolly, beside her, needed to guess Simona's thoughts, which clearly dwelt on the man who had lain there upon the same sofa the previous night when he was still alive. But today the body of her former husband had been transferred from a kitchen freezer room to a chilled drawer in a police morgue where it awaited an autopsy because, as yet, no one had any explanation as to how Jake's death had come about.

127

'The police want to interview Steven and Layla right now,' Simona said in a weak voice.

Marshall turned back to face her. 'That means they'll soon have statements from us all.'

'And then what?' Simona asked, lost.

Pearl saw that she was looking to Marshall in the same way she had done so often in the last few days — for advice, support or confirmation. This time, however, he seemed unable to respond so Pearl took over for him.

'An investigation structure will be put in place,' she explained. 'Autopsy results will establish the time and cause of death and it's highly likely the SIO will re-interview all the witnesses.'

'SIO?' asked Simona.

'Senior Investigating Officer. He's just arrived,' Pearl said. 'DCI McGuire.'

Dolly sighed. 'The Flat Foot.'

'You know him?' asked Marshall.

Pearl nodded and the older man considered this thoughtfully before saying to Dolly, 'I wonder if you would take Simona for some air while I have a word with Pearl?'

His old friend looked about to argue before agreeing. 'Of course,' she said, smiling kindly at Simona.

Marshall waited until the two women had left the study before asking Pearl: 'Can this officer be trusted?'

'Trusted?' Pearl was clearly puzzled by his choice of words.

'Is he competent?' Marshall said impatiently.

'He's very experienced,' Pearl replied. 'From London.'

'Transferred?'

'At his own request.'

'I see, the big fish in a small pond.' Marshall then added: 'I ask because, for obvious reasons, we need this investigation to be conducted with as little press attention as possible. We have Nico here, and Simona has put everything into this venture. Something like this . . . well, it could kill it for her. And she's been through enough. You saw that for yourself last night.'

'Yes, I did,' agreed Pearl.

Marshall frowned. 'She was just beginning to look forward again — to a future, to a life. And then *he* had to turn up again.'

'You didn't expect him to?'

'Of course not. He received an excellent settlement from the divorce and, due to his abusive conduct with Simona in Italy, there had been a restraining order on him for some time. Simona gave him no notice of where she was going next and the last we had heard of Jake, he had settled in Puglia.'

'In Southern Italy?'

'That's right.'

'Then,' said Pearl, thinking on this, 'he suddenly turns up here, out of the blue. Why? It doesn't make any sense.'

Marshall shrugged. 'Your guess is as good as mine. But he's done so for the very last time. I can't say I'm going to mourn his loss but I *am* concerned for Simona. You see, I have an operation scheduled soon. I'm hoping it will help my mobility, not to mention the pain, so I don't want to cancel it. But if I have to, I will.' He paused. 'Look, Pearl, I've been thinking. It's entirely possible that Jake had enemies who tracked him here last night.'

'So you . . . do believe this was premeditated murder?'

'Don't you?' asked Marshall. 'I spent fifteen years as a magistrate and I know the importance of evidence. As far as I can see, the facts here do not point to an accidental death and I want whoever is responsible to be caught and brought to justice. So . . . if you can bring any influence to bear with that Detective Chief Inspector, I'd be grateful. For Simona's sake.' He gave Pearl a look that seemed a mixture of defiance and quiet desperation.

★　★　★

After leaving Marshall, Pearl walked through the archway of the herb garden and into the meadow beyond. In spite of the showers that were still falling at a distance, the clouds above the villa were lifting and the pale sunlight that shone through was creating the faint glow of a rainbow, visible above the field of rapeseed. The landscape was worthy of a fairy tale but Pearl was distracted from it by the sound of a dog barking. Just then, a young black Spaniel raced through the long grass to dance around, panting before her, tail wagging. At a distance, Robert called to the dog — 'Toby!' — before hurrying over, a lead in his hand.

'I'm sorry,' he said quickly. 'He's friendly enough, just a little nervous when anyone approaches the cottage.'

Pearl bent to stroke the dog. 'I understand.' She looked at Robert. 'How is Maria?'

'Resting,' he said. 'The doctor's been and given her something. It was a terrible shock.'

'Of course,' said Pearl. 'And for us all.'

Robert frowned. 'The trouble is, she feels responsible.'

'Why?'

'Because having the freezer room at the villa was all her idea.' He heaved a sigh. 'It had a brand new safety system,' he continued, puzzled, 'so I can't for the life of me understand why it didn't work.'

'What do you mean?'

'There's a safety release handle,' he explained. 'It should open the door from the inside if anyone's ever trapped inside, but if it fails for any reason, there's also an alarm. That should have sounded in case of emergency.'

Pearl took this in. 'But it didn't.'

'No,' said Robert, looking troubled. 'That's what has upset Maria the most, the thought that Mr Rhys couldn't possibly escape — and he must have tried.'

'The curtain in his hand?'

Robert nodded silently then looked away to see the dog idly chasing a white butterfly among scarlet poppies. For a few moments, neither Pearl nor Robert said a word until she asked tentatively, 'Robert, I wonder if you have a book on beekeeping that you could possibly lend me?'

He looked a little taken aback at this change of subject before replying, 'Of course, I'd be glad to.' Then he whistled to Toby, calling, 'Come on, boy!' The Spaniel bounded obediently across, and as he put the animal back on the lead, Robert told Pearl, 'If you don't mind, I'd better get back to Maria.'

She nodded and Robert headed off with his dog, down towards the river and the direction of his cottage, while Pearl turned back to the Villa Pellegrini.

★ ★ ★

It was late afternoon before every witness statement had been taken. Exhibits had been logged and the forensic team had finally left, having taken with them the inflatable white tent within which they had photographed the crime scene and Jake's body. They had conducted numerous tests for such possible clues as prints — including hand, palm, finger-and footprints — as well as treadmarks left by shoes. There had also been the usual hunt for fibres, like hairs — the most common materials to be transferred between murderer and victim — but, unfortunately, the crime scene at the Villa Pellegrini had been 'contaminated' by those who had first come upon it: Maria, quickly followed by Nico, and then Pearl herself.

Pearl knew the importance of preserving a crime scene for investigating officers so that they might account in court for the authenticity of any forensic evidence, but she also knew that merely walking in and out of a crime scene resulted in evidence. The ability to photograph or even to 'livestream' film a crime scene decreased the need for the physical presence of numerous officers, but in spite of all that, the arrival that morning of three people, including herself, in the pantry and freezer room had led to problems for the investigating team in terms of elimination. For this reason, forensic teams always wore protective overalls made of Tyvek, a lightweight synthetic material which limited contamination even by a hair dropping on the scene. Gloves were important too because of the possible transference of a suspect's DNA from one item to another, so it remained crucial for an officer to change gloves whenever touching a fresh item. All protective clothing and overalls had to be carefully saved and documented until such time as it was certain they were no longer required. It was clear to every investigating officer that forensic evidence could make or break a successful prosecution — so it was crucial that it had to be treated with the utmost care.

Only when the forensic teams had finally left the Villa Pellegrini was the pantry made fully accessible again, but McGuire had alerted everyone staying at the house to remain in place until further notice. He planned to return in the morning when, hopefully, he would have a better idea of events leading up to the death of Jacob Rhys. Until then, he had twelve witness statements to go through, although the one question that continued to burn for him above all others was the one he now posed to Pearl as she walked with him to his car.

'Why is it that whenever there's a murder, you're never far away?'

Pearl let the question hang for a moment before she replied, 'I told you, I'm — '

'I know,' said McGuire, breaking in. 'You're on holiday.' He glanced around — at the sumptuous grounds, the imposing villa and the river running close by — then he looked back again at Pearl. 'Why here?'

'Why not?' she asked, deciding not to tell him that it had been her mother's idea. 'It's a beautiful house in the most stunning setting.'

'And you get the chance to spend time with a celebrity chef?' He said the words with such disdain that Pearl was left in no doubt that he was uncomfortable with the idea. He now posed another question for her. 'What exactly were you doing just before the body was found?'

'Listening to opera,' she replied simply.

'Opera?'

'If you read my statement carefully, you'll — '

McGuire broke in again. 'I'm asking you, Pearl,' he said tetchily. 'Since when have you been a fan of opera?'

'Since Nico introduced me to Rossini.' She met McGuire's gaze with a challenging look. 'He was telling me about Rossini the other afternoon, when we were out on the river.'

McGuire's gaze drifted to the Stour. 'And what were you doing on the river?'

'He invited me for a picnic.'

'Picnic?' echoed McGuire.

'Yes. He got some oysters delivered and also made a cake, specially — *a torta Caprese*. That's

134

a flourless chocolate cake with . . . '

'I'm sure it was delicious.'

'It was.'

For a moment, neither said a word until McGuire's frustration spilled over into an apology. 'All right, Pearl,' he said. 'I should have called you before now, but I didn't. The truth is, I've been busy.' He waited for her reaction but when it came, it wasn't quite the one he had expected.

'I understand,' she said sparely, taking the wind from his sails. 'I've been busy too.'

McGuire frowned. He knew it was time for a difficult conversation and one made all the more challenging by the circumstances. Still, he was willing to try, but before he could say another word, someone else spoke.

'Perla!'

Turning, they saw Nico standing by the open French doors, gesturing back inside towards the dining room. 'Your mother wants to know if you'd like a drink?'

Pearl called back to him. 'Yes, please.'

To this, Nico nodded and vanished back inside.

'*Perla?*' repeated McGuire.

She said nothing more but started walking away, back towards the house. McGuire remained rooted to the spot for a few moments, before he glanced around the idyllic gardens once more — this time finally recognising that he might have allowed himself to be out of Pearl's life for far too long.

10

'It's rather ironic that what was meant to be a break away from that restaurant and agency of yours should have put a murder in our midst,' said Dolly, glancing across at her daughter who was standing near the balcony in her room, texting Charlie at the restaurant.

Pearl knew that what her mother really meant was that this break had been intended as an opportunity for Pearl to get over McGuire; the real irony lay in the fact that it had actually thrown the two together once more.

Since Pearl and Dolly would have to remain at the Villa Pellegrini during McGuire's ongoing investigations, they were now somewhat at the detective's mercy, but Dolly had never taken kindly to being told what to do — particularly by the police. In fact, twenty years ago, she had actually welcomed Pearl's resignation from the force, having been more comfortable with the idea of her daughter as a single mum — than a Flat Foot. For Pearl, however, McGuire's arrival back in her life had sparked conflicting emotions. Seeing him today had set her pulse racing, though whether from animal attraction or anger she couldn't be sure. Being at the Villa Pellegrini was acting as a confusing catalyst for her, causing her to question things that had previously seemed certainties. The first was that McGuire was the only man in a very long time to make her feel sufficiently dissatisfied with her single and independent status to consider allowing someone back into her heart. For almost two decades, since the break-up with Charlie's father, Carl, Pearl had dedicated herself to her restaurant and to her son, but now neither seemed to need her for their survival. Both were flourishing without her, so the resulting vacuum had been filled with Nolan's Detective Agency — and McGuire, when he wasn't consumed with his work. What was becoming clear to her now, however, was that she didn't much relish the idea of filling a vacuum in the police detective's life — as and when he deemed fit, and all on his terms.

The second thing these brief few days had also clarified for Pearl was that a natural dislike for Nico Caruso, the television personality, had apparently softened into affection — and perhaps some attraction — for the man himself. This was no less confusing to her for, in every way, Nico seemed the antithesis of McGuire, being hot-headed, passionate and romantic (she had now decided to cross 'cheesy' from the list).

Dolly's intention to distract Pearl from 'moping' about McGuire had succeeded. But two stones had now been tossed into the previously calm waters of Pearl's life. One was Nico Caruso, and the other was the death of Jake Rhys — though, as yet, she could not know if the two were in any way connected.

'So I assume we're all under suspicion as far as the Flat Foot's concerned,' Dolly said now.

Pearl shrugged. 'Until McGuire has some

evidence to the contrary we'll all be considered general suspects,' she confirmed, adding, 'Nico, Maria and I are technically witnesses, since we discovered the body at roughly the same time.'

'And what did Marshall have to say?' Dolly wanted to know.

'He offered up the possibility that Jake might have been killed by someone who came to the house last night.'

'And what do *you* think?' Dolly asked.

'It's hard to see how they would have got here though I found tyre tracks on the path this morning.'

'The killer's?' asked Dolly, with a fair degree of melodrama.

'I don't know,' Pearl admitted honestly. 'Jake arrived here but, as you said yourself, he wasn't in any condition to drive. Even if he had driven, the car would still have been here this morning since he failed to leave last night.'

'So he was driven here?'

'Yes,' said Pearl. 'I think that's the most likely option though we can't be sure — yet.'

Dolly mused on this. 'It's also possible he arrived by boat — or the killer did.'

'Good thinking,' her daughter said. 'It occurred to me too that it might be possible to get here on a small craft from another point nearby, but it was raining heavily last night and I saw no footprints this morning on the wet lawn leading up from the jetty to suggest that anyone might have arrived that way.'

'So . . . you're saying you believe the killer is one of us?'

'We can discount two of the guests,' said Pearl. 'You and me.'

'That leaves five.' Dolly began counting them on her fingers. 'Layla, Steven, Georgina, Frank and Anemone.'

'And Nico,' said Pearl.

Dolly stared at her. 'You can't possibly think that Nico could have . . . '

'And Marshall and Simona.' Pearl continued inexorably.

Dolly's mouth remained agape but Pearl explained: 'It's still true that most murders are committed by spouses, family members or others who knew the victim very well.'

'And I suppose your Flat Foot will be thinking along those lines *and* jumping to the wrong conclusion as usual?' Dolly said vehemently. 'There is no way Marshall could have committed murder. Apart from being physically incapable of dragging an unconscious man into that freezer room to die, he simply has too much respect for the law. And Simona is too gentle a person to be capable of even harming a fly. She put up with Jake for far too long as it was, so why on earth would she murder him now they are finally divorced?'

'I can't answer that,' said Pearl. 'But I do know there are at least ten people who had the opportunity of murdering Jake last night.'

'Ten?' asked Dolly, confused.

'As you mentioned,' said Pearl. 'Excluding you and me, there are five guests . . . '

'Yes, yes,' said Dolly impatiently. 'Plus Nico, Marshall and Simona — but who else?'

139

A light knock sounded suddenly on the door and after Pearl called for the person to enter, the door duly opened and Robert appeared. 'Ms Cartwright asked me to let you know that supper will be served in half an hour.'

'Thank you. We'll be down right away,' said Pearl.

Robert stepped forward now, exposing something he was carrying in his left hand. 'I brought the book you asked to borrow.' He handed her a weighty tome entitled *A World of Bees*, then gave both women a polite smile and left.

Once the door had closed after him, Dolly said softly, almost to herself, 'Robert and Maria.'

'Exactly,' agreed Pearl. 'Robert and Maria.'

★　★　★

McGuire was sitting on the sofa in his living room at his Best Lane apartment in Canterbury. It was early evening and behind him the open window looked out on to the river as it snaked its way through the city. In front of him, on a large coffee table, sat his supper, which he had picked up on his way home. He often enjoyed a fiorentina pizza on returning from the station, but for some reason this evening he was finding the idea of Italian food rather unappealing. The dough had become soggy in its takeaway box and the egg looked particularly unappetising on its spinach base. Closing the lid on the pizza, he gave his attention instead to the paperwork spread out across the rest of the table and on the sofa beside him.

The paperwork consisted of the statements that had been taken today by the local investigating officers at the crime scene. They had done a good and thorough job and McGuire was now going through every statement, making notes for himself while trying to form a timeline of events and searching for any discrepancies or ambiguities, anything in fact which might fail to substantiate, or corroborate any of the witnesses' versions of events. So far he had found none. What seemed clear was that the deceased was last seen alive at around 23:50 hours by his former wife, Simona Cartwright, the house-keeper, Maria Bingley, and her husband, Robert, who along with Frank Ellis, Steven Sparkes, Marshall Taylor and Nico Caruso had left Jake Rhys on the sofa in Simona Cartwright's study.

Shortly after that time, all the house guests, including Georgina, Layla, Anemone, Pearl and her mother, Dolly, had retired to bed with no one hearing anything suspicious until the next morning when the scream from Maria had alerted Pearl and Nico to her discovery of the body in the freezer room.

McGuire's pen hovered over his notepad as he considered the two names — Pearl and Nico — noting how they looked on the page together and the sound the words made in his head. *Pearl and Nico.* He didn't like it at all, but neither did he like the images that had crept into his mind during the drive home following his conversation with Pearl. Like a set piece in a play he imagined the discovery of the body that morning, the dull thud of the bloodied mallet falling from Maria's hand to the floor, echoing the same thud of disappointment McGuire now felt at the thought of Pearl having possibly turned to Caruso in that moment to bury her face in his broad Italian shoulder as some Rossini opera continued to play on in the background.

McGuire was no fan of opera himself. It seemed an arcane, over-theatrical, elitist art form — voices strained to hit notes outside a normal range, there was nothing normal about it at all to the police detective. In fact, he much preferred to listen to country rock, something which provided a suitable soundtrack while he was driving: Chris Rea, Shania Twain and at times, the Eagles, allowing him to imagine he was heading somewhere important out on a big American highway rather than stuck in a queue of traffic that was usually going nowhere fast on the A2. He had had no idea that Pearl might possibly like opera. Perhaps she didn't. Perhaps she was only pretending to Caruso that she liked it since he was an opera buff. What was it that she had told McGuire? That Caruso had introduced her to it? He wondered grimly what else Caruso might have introduced her to in the time she had spent with him at the Villa Pellegrini. The man was meant to be giving lessons in cookery — but what did a successful restaurateur like Pearl need with cookery lessons? And why had she taken her mother along with her?

Suddenly it occurred to McGuire what must have happened: the trip had been Dolly's idea since Caruso was just the sort of man Pearl's eccentric mother would find attractive — some-one with the dark good looks of the Spanish flamenco teacher she had been infatuated with two summers ago. Perhaps she had found a way to persuade Pearl to go along with her — suggesting that her daughter needed a break . . . a break with the past, a break with McGuire . . . Yes, that was it.

Leaning back on the sofa, he pushed the window behind him wide open. Straight across the river stood the Italian pizzeria and its pretty alfresco dining area above which climbed a well-established vine. At this time of year, its terracotta pots were filled with flowering geranium — red and white — just like at the Villa Pellegrini. Couples sat at the tables enjoying glasses of red wine in the warm evening sun, chatting and laughing together or simply gazing into one another's eyes. For a moment McGuire imagined himself sitting at such a table with Pearl, but the image slowly morphed into one of Pearl and Nico Caruso as he recalled her telling him about the picnic they had enjoyed on the river. A jetty stood on the opposite bank from McGuire's apartment, ferrying tourists all day long on boat trips from the pizzeria to visit the fourteenth-century Dominican priories, finally ending up in a peaceful garden area that had been the site of the old Abbot's Mill in the city. Never once had he taken such a trip with Pearl and yet Caruso had found time to take her out on the river at the Villa Pellegrini, and had even managed a picnic.

Food. That was something else Pearl and

Caruso had in common, McGuire thought. Not just regular food but fine food and its preparation. They had eaten oysters together — another thing McGuire had failed to do with Pearl, even though oysters were the focus of her restaurant menu. He had always used the excuse of a seafood allergy to avoid them, which now seemed rather lame set against the idea of Pearl eating oysters, with Caruso, on the river, in the summer sun. The Italian chef had even baked some special Italian cake for the occasion. McGuire had never attempted to make anything remotely resembling a pudding or a cake in his entire life.

With this thought, he ran his hand quickly through his blond hair and remembered that he needed a haircut. He looked again at the statements spread out in front of him, then checked his watch, deciding he might give them more attention when he returned from the unisex hair salon in St Peters Street, which didn't close for another hour. Getting up from the sofa he grabbed the pizza box and shoved it into his kitchen bin, trying to remember the name of the opera Pearl had mentioned in her statement, saying that she and Caruso had been listening to it just before they heard the housekeeper's scream. It was an opera named after some Shakespearean character. One of the tragedies. *Othello* — that was it — the story of a man consumed with jealousy about the woman he loved.

★ ★ ★

Supper that evening over at the Villa Pellegrini consisted of the chicken *cacciatore* Maria had prepared for the guests on the night of their arrival, re-heated for the occasion. Looking pale and drawn, she had served it herself, but few of the guests found themselves with much appetite and the dish was soon cleared away. Everyone was doing their best to avoid upsetting Simona with a discussion of Jake's death but it wasn't long before Steven filled his wine glass and commented, 'It's quite a large elephant.'

'Elephant?' echoed Layla beside him.

He turned to his fiancée. 'The one in the room we are all trying so hard to ignore?'

Despite Simona's downcast expression, he carried on: 'It's clear we're all under suspicion as far as the police are concerned or we would have been allowed to return home.'

'So does that mean we're going to have to stay here until the police get to the bottom of this?' Layla frowned sulkily.

Georgina took a deep inhalation of her vaping device. 'Until they find the murderer, I expect.'

Frank suddenly asked: 'But surely there's a chance it could have been a tragic accident?'

'Being locked in a freezer, perhaps,' said Dolly, 'but how do you explain the bloodied mallet?' All eyes moved to Pearl. 'The police will have to consider the autopsy results,' was all she said.

'And how long will they take to come through?' asked Simona.

'It depends,' said Pearl cautiously.

'In other words, it could take some consider-able time,' Steven commented.

'So, we could be here for days?' Layla exclaimed, before turning to Simona to add: 'I'm sorry. This place is really beautiful, but . . . '

'A murder does tend to spoil the atmosphere somewhat,' said Georgina.

'That's quite enough,' warned Marshall decisively.

'No. It's OK.' Simona countered. 'I understand how upsetting this must be for you all.'

'And especially for you,' Frank insisted. 'Jake was your husband, after all.

'Yes,' nodded Simona. 'But our relationship was over. We were newly divorced and I've been coming to terms with that.'

'Thank goodness,' Georgina sighed.

Frank shot her a challenging look. 'All the same,' he continued to Simona, 'if there's anything we can do to help . . . '

'The best way to do that,' said Marshall, 'would be to find out what happened here last night. And I'd say we're very fortunate to have Pearl here among us; a detective who is actually acquainted with the Senior Investigating Officer.'

'The handsome blond guy?' asked Georgina.

'I saw him arrive,' said Anemone.

'So did I,' Layla chimed in, showing a sudden interest. 'He looked far too sexy to be a policeman.'

Steven looked at her sharply but she gave an innocent shrug. 'I'm Australian, honey.'

'This was the man I saw you talking to earlier?' Nico asked Pearl.

She nodded. 'Detective Chief Inspector McGuire.'

'The Flat Foot,' said Dolly again, unimpressed, as she refilled her glass.

'He's very capable,' said Pearl.

'But?' asked Steven.

Pearl hesitated. 'No 'buts',' she said finally, restraining herself from voicing any of the reservations she harboured about McGuire's reliance on procedure.

'So . . . ' Layla said in businesslike fashion. 'What can we expect?'

'More questions,' said Georgina.

'Yes,' said Pearl. 'I'm sure he'll be back tomorrow after he's been through all our statements.'

'But what can we possibly tell him that we haven't already told the other officers?' Frank sounded at a loss.

'That's right,' agreed Simona. 'None of us saw or heard anything during the night, which is when this must have happened.'

'We left him in the study,' said Nico.

'Just before midnight?' asked Frank.

Steven shrugged. 'For what it's worth, it had just gone eleven forty-five,' he said. 'I noticed the time on the clock as we left.'

'We must all have been in bed shortly after midnight,' said Anemone.

Frank noticed Simona's fixed expression. 'What is it?'

She admitted, troubled. 'I . . . thought of locking the study door last night.'

'Locking him *in*, you mean?' asked Dolly.

Simona nodded guiltily.

'But you didn't?' said Marshall. 'That wouldn't have been a good idea in his condition.'

'I know. I thought if he woke and found that he couldn't get out, he would just cause another terrible scene, or even call the police, but perhaps it would have been better if I *had* locked him in, because at least he might still be alive.'

As her voice cracked with emotion, Frank leaned in and comforted her. 'You can't blame yourself for any of this,' he said kindly. 'Jake wasn't meant to be here.'

'Yes,' said Anemone. 'He was the uninvited guest.'

'That didn't warrant such a cruel death,' said Dolly.

'No one's saying it did,' Marshall corrected her.

'But it's true, isn't it?' said Pearl. 'If he had stayed away, he might very well be alive.'

The truth of her statement settled for a moment in the silence that followed until Georgina spoke up. 'Strange, don't you think?' she drawled. 'That it was only last night we were talking about a séance?'

Nico went round with the wine, filling everyone's glass. '*You* were talking about a séance,' he said pointedly.

Georgina came back at him: 'I mentioned it because Anemone had been talking about 'negative energy'.'

'That's right,' agreed Simona.

'It was the storm,' said Dolly.

'But what if it was something else?' asked Layla. 'Something more?'

'What are you talking about?' asked Marshall.

Layla looked to Anemone. 'What if Anemone

148

really did sense that something was about to happen?'

'*Una premonizione*,' said Nico.

'Is that possible?' Simona asked. But Anemone did not respond.

'We could hold a séance right now and find out what happened?' Georgina went on.

'Ask the spirits, you mean?' said Simona.

'Ask *Jake's* spirit,' Georgina replied boldly.

For a moment nothing could be heard but the ticking of a carriage clock until Marshall declared, 'I've never heard anything so distasteful in all my life.'

'I agree,' said Frank, looking solicitously at Simona to check her reaction.

Nico rose to his feet. 'I need some air.' He moved to the French doors and stepped out into the grounds, and Georgina saw that everyone else in the room was staring accusingly at her.

Giving a nonchalant shrug and a wicked smile, she pouted, 'It was just an idea.'

★　★　★

Pearl found Nico sitting on the bench near the jetty. The moon was rising above the trees on the opposite bank while the river ran fast and dark below. She sat down beside him and stared across at blond reeds quivering in the cool breeze. After a moment or two she asked, 'You and Georgina slept together, didn't you?'

Nico said nothing so Pearl continued. 'I heard you talking together on the night we arrived. You were in these grounds by the trees beneath my balcony talking to a woman who spoke Italian fluently. For a while, I thought it could have been Simona, or Maria, who also speaks Italian — as does Anemone. But now I know it was Georgina.'

He finally looked at her. 'How?'

'Your tone,' she replied. '*Perché ora*'? Why now? You were admonishing her for having come here.'

Nico took a deep breath before declaring, 'You are a good detective, Perla.' He pulled a tendril from the willow tree and tossed it into the river, watching as it disappeared in the current. 'Yes,' he said. 'I was looking forward to this week, to be here, away from Italy, away from worries. Just away,' he repeated. 'And Simona said there were to be six guests — but at the last moment, Gina decided to come. Like a black cloud, she blotted out the sun for me.'

'Because of an affair you had?'

'Hardly an affair,' he said dismissively. 'I made the mistake of getting caught in her web. But I wasn't the only one.'

'What do you mean?'

Nico got to his feet. 'She pretends to be something she's not. A friend to Simona. And Simona now talks of Gina helping her with this business. But Gina helps no one but herself . . . and always helps herself to everything.' He turned now to look at Pearl as he added: 'Including Simona's husband.'

'You're saying that she and Jake . . . '

'Yes,' said Nico, softly but decisively. 'Something I learned when I was staying at La Valle.'

'But Simona doesn't know?'

'Of course not. If she did, she would never have invited her here.'

Pearl tried to assimilate this. 'You and Georgina . . . '

'A stupid mistake,' he confessed. 'I was charmed by her. She said she wanted to help me. You see, I had financial problems. The bankruptcy . . . '

'But she didn't help?'

'No,' he said finally. 'I told you, she helps no one. It was just Gina playing her power games, that's all. And I only have myself to blame for trusting her.' He looked down as though ashamed.

Pearl moved closer and touched his hand. 'Thank you for your honesty,' she said.

He reached out and framed her face with the palm of his other hand. 'And thank you, Perla,' he whispered. In the next moment, she felt his lips gently brush her cheek before he stood up and headed back to the house, leaving her to stare thoughtfully down into the river below.

★ ★ ★

Later on, Pearl was on the upper landing, searching in her bag for the key to her suite when a voice said, 'Ah, I see you are *Fiammetta*.' It was Anemone. She rounded the top of the stairs and approached Pearl to point to the sign on her door. 'Such a novel idea of Simona's, don't you think? I'm *Lauretta*, and I noticed Simona's room is *Pampinea* — very apt, since

151

she's the one who persuaded everyone to up sticks for the countryside.' She indicated the direction of the room on the other side of the hall but Pearl barely responded, still thinking about Nico.

'Characters in *The Decameron*,' said Anemone, recognising the need to explain further.

'Yes,' said Pearl distractedly. 'But I'm afraid I've never read it.'

'Oh, but you must,' Anemone told her. 'Especially since our own Geoffrey Chaucer may have been inspired by it. He was known to have travelled to Italy so he's bound to have read Boccaccio. *The Decameron* is set much earlier than the *Canterbury Tales*, of course, and it's all about the *Brigata*, ten people fleeing the city of Florence for the safety of the countryside. Each character takes a turn as king or queen of the day, while they entertain one another by telling stories. It covers a period of ten days, hence the title — meaning *Ten Days' Work*. I think I spotted a copy in my room if you'd like to borrow it?'

'Thanks,' said Pearl. 'But tomorrow will be fine. I'm rather tired.'

'Yes, of course,' said Anemone. 'The last twenty-four hours have been exhausting. And whatever Jake might have done in his short life, as your mother pointed out, he didn't deserve such a cruel death.'

The two women reflected on this for a moment before Pearl asked, 'The characters in the book . . . you said that they were fleeing somewhere 'for the safety of the countryside'?'

'That's right,' said Anemone. 'Escaping Florence. Seeking refuge.'

'From what?' asked Pearl.

Anemone looked surprised for a moment. 'Didn't I mention that?' she said. 'It was 1348, the year of the Black Death.' She paused for a moment before adding: 'They were all fleeing the plague.' She moved off to her room and gave a little wave before calling, 'Sleep well,' leaving Pearl with food for thought.

11

Pearl's telephone conversation with Charlie on Tuesday morning was strained — for one thing because her son was naturally concerned that a mysterious death had marred what was meant to be a well-earned break in the countryside, but also because he knew there was a risk that his mother might well become embroiled in the ensuing investigation.

'Why can't you come home?' he asked. 'You're not under house arrest or anything, are you?'

'No,' she said. 'But for now it helps the police if we all remain here in one place at the villa. It also helps to contain the news, so please don't mention any of this until the police issue a media statement.'

'McGuire, you mean,' said Charlie. 'He's in charge of this?'

'That's right.'

Charlie was quiet for a moment as if computing this news.

'Good,' he finally replied.

'You approve?'

'Of course,' said Charlie brightly. 'He knows you.' Then: 'Let him deal with this and don't get involved, Mum.'

'Who said I would?'

'I know you too well. Please just listen to what he says, stay out of trouble and look after Gran.'

Pearl smiled at her son's list of instructions.

'As long as you promise to let me know if there are any problems at the restaurant. You will tell me, won't you?'

'I promise,' said Charlie.

When she finally set down the phone, Pearl reflected for a few moments on the call. The fact that McGuire had won Charlie's trust some time ago was not only reassuring for her, it made a welcome change from Dolly's snide comments about the detective. Charlie had a wide circle of friends in Canterbury but as McGuire lived there too, Pearl always felt glad that there was someone nearby he could turn to in a crisis — and what better contact could a young man have at such a time than a member of the local CID?

Having split up with Charlie's father before her son was born, Pearl was aware that, one day, Charlie's curiosity might be piqued sufficiently to ask for more information about his dad — perhaps even with a view to tracking him down, though that was one investigation which, for now, Pearl would rather remain closed.

Over the years, she had dated various men and been set up on blind dates by friends but had never felt anything to match the white hot heat of that summer romance with Carl, a romance that was perhaps too preciously preserved in her memory for real life ever to eclipse it, although her feelings for McGuire were real enough. There was chemistry between them but, having experienced the same with Charlie's father — moments of passion snatched together in Whitstable all the while knowing that Carl was about to move on — Pearl now wondered whether this was a pattern she was allowing herself to fall into. McGuire was a man who was clearly keeping himself at an emotional distance so perhaps this made the times they had come together feel all the more intense? If so, Pearl was now becoming aware of it and that there was a parallel to be made in respect of food: starving oneself before a stunning feast.

She knew she had needed no man while bringing up Charlie, because her son was the man in her life. She had become totally absorbed in his upbringing because she loved him so much, and though her love for him was undiminished, having turned forty she felt as if she was entering a new era, the second act of a play in which she was the main character — but unsure of her role.

The problem was perhaps as Dolly had indicated: Pearl was too accustomed to being in control — and so was McGuire. Something had to give, even if it was simply agreeing to meet one another halfway. Pearl had allowed the detective to enter her world but she still knew almost nothing about McGuire and his past — or the reasons why he had left London for Canterbury. Though frustrating, this lack of knowledge served only to intrigue her more, because one thing Pearl could never resist was an unsolved mystery.

With that thought, she was about to get ready to join the others downstairs when a text came in on her phone. Immediately, she sensed a problem at The Whitstable Pearl but saw, instead, that the message was from McGuire, asking if she would meet him in Chartham. She quickly texted her response. The day was already looking up.

★ ★ ★

McGuire wasn't acquainted with Chartham; most crimes on his patch were confined to the city and kept him busy enough without sorties out to quiet country villages. But he had driven through Chartham the day before and noticed the quaint little pub lying about 300 metres south of the river. He would have stopped for a quick drink right there and then, had he not been consumed with the urgency to head home and study the witness statements. He had also been in a bad mood — not something from which McGuire usually suffered, since he believed that for the most part negative thoughts and emotions could be kept at bay by keeping busy.

For the past two years since his move to Kent, he felt he had largely conquered the 'bad times' — the immediate period after Donna's death when he had come, too often, to rely on gambling and Bourbon to displace his feelings about losing his fiancée to a senseless accident. Two drugged-up kids had mown her down one rainy night on the streets of Peckham. He had never allowed grief or anger to overwhelm him, but neither had he 'worked through' Donna's loss — as so many people talked about these days. Instead, he had sought something else to

157

distract him and had turned to the one constant in his life. His work.

The move to Canterbury had been a temporary one — and made permanent only after he had met Pearl. Finding themselves working together on the same murder case in Whitstable, she had challenged his authority and almost sent him on a collision course with his superior, Welch, although it was fortunate that McGuire's superintendent set more store on the results of his detectives than the manner in which they were achieved.

For now, McGuire sensed he was safe at Canterbury, though he was well aware things could change — especially since he wore the conspicuous badge of an outsider. It was a badge he didn't mind wearing, because at times it was also something behind which he could hide. While no one knew too much about where he had come from and why he had chosen to stay, he could continue to operate with relative freedom. His relationship with Pearl hadn't threatened that freedom too much, because two of the things he liked most about her were her independent free spirit and the fact that her life seemed full: of friends, family and a career involving The Whitstable Pearl restaurant.

The detective agency was tricky for McGuire because there were always strict protocols to be observed in the manner in which police officers were allowed to operate with private investigators and informants. Pearl was now a general suspect in a murder investigation, having been one of the first witnesses on the scene, so McGuire knew he would have to tread carefully and avoid compromising his position. Nevertheless, having come to admire the way she used her particular skills at crime solving — with a mixture of intuition and an understanding of people in general — he knew that any information she could offer him at this time would be more than worthwhile.

It might have been easy for McGuire to dismiss Pearl's conclusions merely as gut feelings and lucky hunches if she hadn't come up with them so often and just when they were required. She had inspired a sense of competition in him but also pride because, above all else, he knew that she was special and he knew he had a place in her life, if not her heart. He had yet to discover whose image she held in the silver locket she so often wore at her throat. Charlie was in there for sure and he sensed there was room for one more, but now he also sensed that this space might be usurped by another — an Italian celebrity chef by the name of Nico Caruso. And all because McGuire had neglected her.

He checked his watch. She was nine minutes late, having agreed to meet him at the Artichoke at midday but in the meantime, the pub had provided an interesting distraction, being a fifteenth-century timber-framed building with oak beams, lots of exposed brickwork and a dining table consisting of a glass-topped well. Its friendly landlord had cheerfully explained how the pub's cellar had once been used as overspill space for the storage of corpses from an old asylum, then he left that thought with McGuire and moved off to serve some more customers.

McGuire had just picked up his glass of lager and lime when he noticed that a group of locals were throwing the odd glance his way, no doubt wondering what he was doing in this quiet village pub all alone. He sipped his drink but before he had set his glass back down on the table, Pearl entered. Looking first towards the bar, she smiled at the locals and the landlord, which seemed to instantly lighten the mood at the bar as well as arousing some further curiosity. Moving straight to McGuire she said quickly, 'Sorry I'm late. I just walked along the river path — the old Pilgrims Way. It's so beautiful out there today. I just saw a kingfisher.'

McGuire was trying to concentrate on what she was telling him but his attention was totally distracted by the fact that she looked more beautiful than ever, not in a glamorous sense, for she seldom had time for make-up, but to McGuire she always seemed to glow with a natural energy that he found as captivating as the colour of her moonstone eyes. Another reason to appreciate her beauty at this time was because he was now aware that she had been out on the same river with another man.

'There's a garden outside,' she said. 'And the sun is shining.'

'OK,' said McGuire, taking the hint. He picked up his glass and followed her outside.

They decamped to an attractive beer garden that was decorated with flowering baskets of lobelia and petunia. A small number of tables, shaded with colourful parasols, overlooked the rear of the pub and the charming old cottage which sat beside it. Pearl took off her jacket and slipped it on to the back of her chair before sitting down to face McGuire. She wore a low-necked lilac blouse and the silver locket glinted in the sunlight against her suntanned chest.

'Why did you suggest we meet here?' she asked. 'You could have come to the house.'

McGuire was well prepared for the question. 'I wanted to talk to you alone,' he said. 'And without any interruptions.'

She noted his businesslike manner and met it with the following question: 'Any forensics results?'

He gave a nod, adding, 'And the autopsy.'

'That's quick.' She was right. It was unusual for an autopsy to have been concluded so soon, but sometimes things went McGuire's way. 'And?' she asked.

'No fingerprints.'

'Apart from Maria's on the mallet?'

He nodded. 'The scene of crime was contaminated but Forensics turned up nothing to incriminate any of the guests. It was a clean job. Perhaps too clean.'

'But it *was* murder?' she said.

'It certainly wasn't an accident — and I can think of easier ways to commit suicide than locking yourself in a tightly sealed freezer.'

'So . . . the blow on the head was presumably to render him unconscious?'

'While the freezer room finished him off,' said McGuire.

161

'But not before he came to?' She frowned. 'His eyes were open and he was clutching one of the plastic curtains.'

'And it may even have saved him — if he'd only been found in time.'

Pearl looked perplexed. 'What do you mean?'

McGuire picked up a menu from the table and handed it to her. 'Would you like something to eat?'

She scanned the menu, noting it contained a whole section on Allergy Information — listing a comprehensive record for each of the dishes produced — allergens which ranged from dairy products to sulphur dioxide, shellfish, sesame and soya. Instantly, this reminded her of Anemone's allergies as well as McGuire's own antipathy towards oysters. 'You see here?' she began. 'Crustaceans are listed separately from molluscs in this list of food allergens.' She showed him the menu.

'So?'

'So, as I've told you before, your 'seafood allergy' may only run to shellfish like prawns and shrimp.'

'And not to oysters.'

'Exactly.' She became thoughtful for a moment. 'One of the guests at the house is allergic to a whole range of foods, including oysters, as well as pollen.'

'And one day I'll take the time to find out about oysters,' said McGuire. 'But not today, all right?'

A waitress appeared at their table to take their orders and explained that the catch of the day was pan-fried fillet of trout.

'I'll take it,' said Pearl, turning to McGuire. 'How about you?'

McGuire opted for a Ploughman's Lunch.

'Not very adventurous,' Pearl noted.

'Comes with carved ham,' he argued, ordering another small lager and lime for himself and a glass of white wine for Pearl.

She waited for the waitress to move off before asking, 'So, what else did Forensics come up with?'

McGuire took a notepad from his pocket and began to flick through it. 'From what I understand, the temperature of that freezer room ranges from nought to ten degrees Fahrenheit, and the walls, ceiling and door are all at least six inches thick.'

'And presumably made with some kind of insulating foam?' she asked.

'That's right. Urethane — covered in sheets of galvanised steel, as is the floor. There was some dim lighting provided by a single fixture and, as you saw, two plastic curtains hung in the doorway, but it's basically a sealed metal box.'

'In which Jake Rhys froze to death.'

'Drinking alcohol lowers core body temperature,' McGuire explained just as their drinks arrived, 'so he would have been more susceptible to hypothermia. Trapped inside, at that temperature, he would have quickly become tired and confused, with a loss of feeling or movement — and frostbite. Hypothermia can cause cardiac arrest but it seems Jake had the right idea by trying to use the plastic curtain to insulate

163

himself from the cold. If he'd only been able to do this quickly enough, he might even have kept his body temperature close to normal. But remember, there was also a problem with air supply. The freezer is around twenty by ten by eight feet in size and, like I say, completely sealed — but nevertheless there would still have been around sixteen hundred cubic feet of air to breathe. The problem is, as you'll no doubt remember from your biology lessons, breathing consumes oxygen and releases carbon dioxide. Once that concentration of carbon dioxide had risen to above five per cent, it would have been cards for our Mr Rhys.'

'You mean it was the *carbon dioxide* that killed him?'

McGuire nodded. 'The alcohol he'd drunk and the crack on the head no doubt contributed to his confusion, and with oxygen a precious commodity in an environment like that, if he'd managed to stay calm, his chances of survival would have been greater. But he didn't make it.'

Pearl frowned. 'So, whoever is responsible for leaving him in the freezer room . . .'

' . . . is responsible for his death,' said McGuire finally.

Pearl added thoughtfully, 'And they were careful not to leave any clues for Forensics. Like you say, it was a clean job, which infers premeditated murder.'

'Correct.' McGuire's tone was grim. 'Whoever killed Jake Rhys took time and plenty of preparation to cover his or her tracks.'

'And it definitely was the mallet that caused

the blow to the head?' Pearl sipped her wine.

'That's right. Jake's blood was on it as well as a DNA match to his hair.' McGuire took a mouthful of his drink. 'Why d'you ask?'

Pearl said slowly, 'Simona Cartwright's god-father walks with the aid of a cane. It's a rather magnificent specimen, with a heavy metal figure of an owl for a handle. He used it on Jake last night in the dining room.'

'Yes,' said McGuire. 'I've read the witness statements but when it comes to Jake's murder, the owl is innocent.'

'And have you established how Jake got to the villa that evening?'

'Yes. He was driven there by a Canterbury mini-cab service. The driver said he wasn't too happy about ferrying a drunk so far out of town but it appears Jake made it worth his while.'

'Drunken largesse,' commented Pearl, as she took this in.

McGuire continued, 'Death took place between one a.m. and three a.m. when everyone claims to have been asleep. But you were there, Pearl,' he stressed, '*at* the house *with* the guests that night. So what can you tell me?'

'Very little, I suspect,' she said, 'beyond what you have in those statements. Jake's arrival that night ruined the evening.' She stopped as the waitress emerged from the kitchen with their orders and set their food on the table. When she moved off, McGuire turned to Pearl.

'Sorry I couldn't run to a *tarta* Capri.'

'*Torta Caprese*,' she corrected. 'And don't knock it. It was delicious.'

McGuire buttered the crusty French bread of his Ploughman's Lunch. 'Are you actually learning anything from him?' he asked.

'Nico?'

'He's the one giving the lessons, isn't he? Cooking, opera . . . ' Pearl looked up from her meal and McGuire said outright. 'Did you know that his business folded under a mountain of debt?'

'It's no secret he was made bankrupt,' Pearl said casually.

McGuire continued: 'But it's clearly a step down for him, having to do something like this.'

'Something like what?' she asked tartly.

'Giving cookery lessons.'

'It's a *Cooking with Nico* week,' she clarified.

'But it seems there's a lot more to it than that, is there?'

'Well,' she said, 'I'd say I've learned quite a lot, yes.'

McGuire swallowed a piece of ham. 'Really?'

'Really,' she replied. 'But then what has any of that to do with your case?'

'Background,' he said. 'Caruso remains a general suspect.'

'As do I?'

'For the time being.'

'And why would I have murdered Jake Rhys?' asked Pearl. 'Why would Nico?'

'You tell me,' said McGuire. 'You seem to know more about him than I do.'

She took his point. 'OK. He's a friend of Simona Cartwright. She's the owner of the Villa Pellegrini and Nico agreed to take on the first of what promised to be a series of *Cooking with Nico* weeks — although a brutal murder like this could be the kiss of death for the whole venture. Simona's godfather, Marshall Taylor, keeps a very protective eye on her. He's disabled, can only walk with the aid of that owl cane at the moment and I've been told he's expecting an operation soon — but perhaps you can check on that? Frank Ellis is a food and wine buff. He's based in Burgundy in the south of France and is clearly smitten with Simona. He, along with Anemone Broadbent, had stayed previously at La Valle — together with Simona's friend, Georgina Strang.'

'La Valle — that's Simona Cartwright's home in Tuscany,' said McGuire.

'Former home — sold after her divorce, and with a fair amount of profit having gone to Jake, who had been living in Puglia, I believe, until he arrived here two nights ago. Steven Sparkes was an old friend of his, though I'd guess they were no longer on the best of terms judging by the fight they had that evening. Maybe Steven sensed that Jake was a liability and decided to side with Simona — it happens sometimes with a partnership break-up, doesn't it? But Steven's now engaged to Layla Bright, an Australian businesswoman who clearly adores him — and the feeling seems to be mutual, unless he simply enjoys being adored . . . ' Pearl savoured a delicious mouthful of trout before going on. 'Maria, the housekeeper, and her husband, Robert, worked for Simona for eight years in Italy but now live in a cottage by the river near the Villa Pellegrini. As I mentioned, Robert keeps bees.'

McGuire considered her. 'And you've learned all this in just the last few days?'

'Five, to be precise,' said Pearl. 'Just from last Friday. Oh, and it appears Georgina had a secret affair with Jake. At least, it's still a secret to her friend, Simona.'

'Who told you that?' asked McGuire. But before she could respond, the penny dropped. 'Don't tell me, Nico.'

'They had a brief fling too,' said Pearl. 'But Georgina failed to help him out of debt so there's no love lost there.'

McGuire put down his knife and fork; with all this talk of Nico he was beginning to lose his appetite. 'Why did Caruso take you out for that picnic on the river?'

'Why do you ask?'

'I'm curious.'

'But it has nothing to do with the case.'

'I'm still curious.'

'All right.' She too set down her knife and fork. 'Nico and I did not get off to the best of starts. If you must know, I found him rather patronising — especially about women in the restaurant business.'

'And now?'

She noted McGuire's expectant look but decided not to answer and instead posed a question of her own. 'Tell me, what were you so busy doing you couldn't possibly find time to call me?'

McGuire took a deep breath before replying: 'Working.'

168

'And you were too busy *working* to even pick up the phone? Or to send a card?'

McGuire broke in. 'Pearl . . . '

But she carried on, regardless. 'Some flowers? Or even a simple text?'

'I was . . . ' He started, but ran out of steam.

'What?' she asked challengingly.

'Waiting for some space so I could ask you out to dinner,' he said. 'Spend some proper time with you instead of . . . ' He looked at her again.

'Instead of what?'

'Offering lame excuses,' he finally admitted. 'But then . . . time went on and . . . ' He looked increasingly torn. 'I should have called.'

'Yes,' she said. 'You should have.'

He held her look. 'So, how do you find Caruso now?'

She left a pause for devastating effect. 'Absolutely charming.'

McGuire set down his glass at this but Pearl explained, 'He's a great chef, attractive, attentive and his *scorzone* are to die for.'

'His what?' asked McGuire, agape.

'Summer black truffles,' she said with a cheeky smile.

McGuire remained unamused. 'Look, Pearl, I . . . ' For a moment he felt the sudden need to reach across the table and take her hand but just as he was about to do so, his phone sounded. Answering it, he listened to the caller for a time as Pearl finished her lunch.

Then he ended the call and told her. 'Welch. He wants an update. New procedures.' He shoved his plate away in frustration.

'What — right now?'

'Yes, right now.' He heaved a heavy sigh. 'I'm really sorry, Pearl. Let me give you a lift back.'

'It's fine,' she said, covering her disappointment. 'I think I prefer to walk.'

They finished their drinks and McGuire left payment for the bill. Pearl watched him as he did so, noting he looked considerably smarter than he had done yesterday, wearing a crisp white shirt and some citrus aftershave. She commented, 'I see you managed to fit in a haircut last night?'

Embarrassed, McGuire's hand moved to his newly trimmed hair. She smiled. 'I guess you'll be in touch?'

'You can depend on it,' he replied.

The waitress came over to take McGuire's payment and clear the table. Pearl gazed across as McGuire got into his car and his eyes met Pearl's before he started up the engine and drove off. After he had done so, she remained rooted to the spot as though staring at an after-image, reflecting that while crime so often brought them together, it was also responsible for driving a wedge between them.

★   ★   ★

On leaving the beer garden, Pearl felt she had succeeded in maintaining a sense of dignity at the meeting but she now regretted that she had been unable to show more warmth towards McGuire because, in spite of her injured pride, it was still true that her heart beat a little faster every time she saw him. 'Treat 'em mean, keep 'em keen' may have been Dolly's general maxim when it came to the opposite sex, but Pearl herself seemed to be proving the truism of 'absence makes the heart grow fonder'. It appeared to her that if ever there was a lesson to be learned from a woman needlessly enduring abuse from a man, it had surely been demonstrated that fateful evening when Jake Rhys had arrived at the Villa Pellegrini to shame his wife. Could it really be that kind, gentle, beautiful Simon, had finally snapped and lashed out? And even if she had done so, was she really capable of having left him to such a cruel death, abandoning him in the cold darkness, after deliberately cutting off his only means of escape?

Pearl was about to cross the road and head back along the river past the old mill when she recognised a familiar figure on the opposite side of the street. Robert was alone and walking purposefully on ahead, beyond the village church of St Mary's, when he suddenly stopped at a convenience store. Pearl decided to follow him. As he entered the store, she peered through the shop's window, noting there was little on offer for customers beyond a few basic groceries and a selection of chilled sandwiches. Robert was at the counter talking to the sales assistant, his back turned to the store window, on which were pinned some postcards advertising gardening services, house clearance and some home tuition in maths for local children. It occurred to Pearl that Chartham, being so much smaller than Whitstable, was a community where no doubt most people knew one another, hence the curiosity shown by the pub locals towards Pearl and McGuire. Robert too would be a comparative stranger, having worked for Simona and Jake in Italy until very recently.

Through the window, Pearl could see the shopkeeper handing some money to Robert and, as he now prepared to turn away from the counter, Pearl ducked quickly into the porch of the next doorway. From there she noted Robert leaving the grocer's to head further on up the road — and away from her. Then, coming out of the porch she took a step back towards the convenience store just in time to see the shopkeeper placing some jars in the window. They were filled with a clear amber liquid and labelled with a familiar image of a beautiful house on the banks of the River Stour, with the words: *Pilgrim's Honey.*

As Pearl was making her way past the village green and back to the villa itself, a few cyclists thundered past her, heading on the Great Stour Way towards Canterbury. Pearl, however, took her time, crossing the old iron bridge where she paused for a moment to look back along the river. The weather was still warm but the deep blue sky was now mottled with cloud and there was no sign of the family of swans she had spotted when she had been out with Nico on the river just the other day.

Crossing to the other side of the bank she approached the jetty, where she began to hear the soft murmur of voices. As she approached, it became clear that Layla Bright was talking to someone in the grounds of the villa, obscured by the weeping willow. 'I heard what you said but I still think we should call a lawyer.'

Silence followed before Steven offered a relaxed response: 'You're panicking.'

'I'm not panicking. I'm just being careful.' Her voice dropped to an urgent whisper. 'We were interviewed by the police, Stevie, for heaven's sake.'

'Routine enquiries,' he replied. 'We're not under arrest so there was no need to have a lawyer present.'

'Not yet,' Layla said ominously. 'But I like to stay ahead.'

'Layla . . . '

She cut him off abruptly. 'No, this isn't over. It's only just beginning. The police will be back. Pearl is a private detective, remember.'

'So what?'

'So what happens when they find out what we did?' Layla gave a long sigh. 'If any of this leaks to the press . . . '

'It won't,' Steven said, his voice determined. 'There's not a soul here who would want for that to happen — including that media tart, Nico.'

Silence. Pearl waited a few moments more before stepping closer to the tree. Parting the willow's branches she saw Layla and Steven at a distance as they headed back across the lawn towards the house. Then she felt a hand upon her shoulder and flinched. Reacting instantly, she turned to see who it was who had crept up behind her.

'Perla?'

It was Nico, who raised both hands in a gesture of surrender. 'I'm sorry,' he said quickly. 'I scared you again?'

'Startled me,' Pearl corrected him, still recovering.

He looked towards the willow tree. 'You were spying on something?'

'Yes,' she admitted. 'Two lovebirds.' Nico looked confused until she explained: 'A pair of nesting doves. But they've flown now.' She offered a smile. 'How about you?'

He gave a shrug. 'I just came out for a walk. There are worse places to be held prisoner but I still value my freedom.'

As he returned her smile, she dared to ask him, 'Is that the reason you haven't married?'

'Perhaps. And perhaps because I've yet to find the right woman.' He looked into her eyes. 'You and I have a lot in common.'

'Because I've yet to find the right man?'

'Maybe you have and you don't even recognise him.'

'And maybe you're right,' she said softly.

He smiled. 'Look, I talked to Simona this morning. While we have to stay here for the police investigation, we may as well make the best of it.'

'In what way?'

'Tonight,' he said, 'if the weather holds, we make pizza.'

' 'We'?'

'You and I, Perla. I even have *friarielli* for you. Look.' He handed her the brown paper bag he was holding. Inside she recognised the familiar yellow flowers blooming among the clusters of green florets that so resembled broccoli. 'How did you manage to find that here?' she asked.

He raised his shoulders innocently. 'I am Nicolò Caruso,' he said with a charming smile. 'I can do anything.'

For the first time, Pearl began to think he might be right.

12

Pearl was in her room having just showered before supper when she rang McGuire. 'So how was your meeting with Welch?' she asked.

'I survived,' came the reply. McGuire was in his office at the station on Longport, the desk before him covered in statements and reports which seemed to be a reflection of his disordered thinking on this case thus far.

'You said you had something to tell me,' he prompted.

'It's about the Bright-Sparkes.'

'The what?'

'Layla Bright and Steven Sparkes. The engaged couple. I understand they're in property development and have a company together. Can you find out what it's called and how long it's been in operation?'

'Why?'

'Because there could be a connection to the Villa Pellegrini, or Stour Manor as I think this place was once called.'

McGuire made a note. 'OK,' he said, awaiting more information. But Pearl had now fallen silent.

'What's on your mind?' he asked.

'Bees,' she said simply.

McGuire frowned. 'What about them?'

'I'm . . . not sure,' she confessed. 'But ever since I arrived here it's been difficult to escape them. Robert Bingley, Maria's husband, keeps them. He was telling us all about them just the other day.'

'Us?'

'Some of the other guests — Anemone, Frank and myself — but the bad weather intervened.' She confided, 'I've often thought about keeping bees myself. There's an old abandoned hive up at my allotment, and Robert's lent me a very interesting book which I've been reading. Do you realise you can simply lure a swarm? It's not as difficult or even as dangerous as it sounds because apparently that's the time when they're least likely to sting, because their main concern is trying to find a nice new place to live. You can even catch a swarm by putting a box or basket beneath it, though you have to be careful, especially if you're sensitive to bee venom, like Anemone. But that's why she has an EpiPen to administer an adrenaline injection if she ever needs it.'

McGuire waited on the end of the line for a relevant point to be made but Pearl merely added: 'If I can start keeping bees I might be able to use my own honey in dishes at the restaurant. A nice idea, don't you think? It links in with the whole idea of *terroir* cooking.'

'*Terroir*?' McGuire repeated, confused.

'Yes. It's a fancy French word for cooking with local ingredients. Rather like Nico using the San Marzano tomatoes for his Neapolitan pizza.'

McGuire felt no inclination to respond to her mention of Nico so Pearl continued, 'Well, Kent's always been known as the Garden of

177

England, remember? And rightly so since we grow hops and have plenty of orchards and fields full of apples, pears, strawberries and cherries — but we also have some great restaurants like The Whitstable Pearl and the Sportsman in Seasalter, where they make their own salt from the marshes and butter that's flavoured with local seaweed.' She beamed at the thought. 'With my own honey, made from local flowers, I could perhaps come up with a new marinade . . . '

'Pearl, please get to the point,' begged McGuire.

'OK,' she said. 'So today, I happened to notice Robert delivering jars of honey to a shop in Chartham.'

'And what's that got to do with Jake Rhys's murder?'

'I'm not sure,' she told him frankly, 'yet. But I have a feeling that in some way there's a connection.'

'To bees.' McGuire sounded unimpressed.

'Did you know that the pheromones of a queen bee are so powerful they can cause the female worker bees to become sterile? That way, only the queen remains fertile.'

'Pheromone?' McGuire was now completely lost.

'Chemical substances, in this case given out by bees. There's a whole chapter on this in Robert's book and it isn't just bee behaviour that's influenced by such things. There's another chemical called oxytocin that you could call the love hormone . . . for us.'

'Us?' McGuire echoed hopefully.

'Humans,' said Pearl.

Disappointed, McGuire asked: 'And is that all?'

'No,' said Pearl. 'I was wondering if you'd ever used the services of a psychic.'

'Are you serious?' he asked, incredulous.

'Of course. There have been plenty of police investigations that ended in cul-de-sacs, only for the services of a psychic to come up trumps. It's important to keep an open mind about these things, don't you think?'

'Look, Pearl . . . '

Ignoring his interruption, she pressed on. 'Certain police forces have used psychics to find missing persons but also to come up with clues to help other criminal investigations. There are lots of instances of this and the College of Policing actually issued a consultation document a few years ago with advice on how to proceed.'

'I read that,' McGuire said, 'but it also said there was no evidence to suggest that there's ever been any successful psychic involvement in a police investigation.'

Pearl quickly countered: 'Ah, but it also stated that any information received from psychics should be evaluated in the context of the case and that everything should be recorded and assessed in order to follow any vital leads. Surely you have a responsibility to consider any important evidence if it can prove or disprove a case?'

McGuire responded with silence, recalling a particular case of a missing person during which a psychic had come forward to wax on about the recurring image of a unicorn, only for the missing person's car to be found shortly afterwards near a rubbish bin that bore the local town council's emblem — of a unicorn. But McGuire decided to keep that to himself.

'Look,' Pearl was saying. 'Anemone Broadbent seems to have some kind of psychic sensitivity. Simona referred to it as a 'spiritual foresight'.'

'You mean she thinks she can predict the future?' said McGuire, unmoved. 'If that was the case, surely there wouldn't even have been a murder, as she'd have known about it before-hand and been able to warn Jake Rhys.' He went on derisively: 'Unless, of course, it was Anemone Broadbent who killed him.'

Pearl spoke quickly to scotch his scepticism. 'All things are possible,' she said. 'But there may be some way we can harness her skills to this case.'

McGuire said nothing, imagining the difficulty of trying to explain to Welch that he might wish to recruit the services of a fortune-teller for a murder investigation.

'Are you still there?' Pearl asked.

'Just about.'

'Well, think about it,' she said, 'because I have to go now.'

'Go where?'

'We're making pizza tonight. I've just prepared some toppings and . . . '

'We?' queried McGuire suspiciously.

'Nico and I.'

'I should've known,' he commented cynically.

'Yes, you should,' she said. 'After all, you're a

180

detective and he's a chef.'

'So why can't he prepare his own toppings?'

'Because he's making the dough,' she explained. 'And it's quite something to watch — a Neapolitan making pizza. He puts a tremendous energy into it — as with everything.'

As she spoke, McGuire found himself picking up the Villa Pellegrini brochure from the chaos of his desk and opening it at the page of Nico grinning as he proudly displayed a vast expanse of pizza dough in his hands. McGuire snapped the brochure shut and tossed it back on to his desk. 'Be careful, Pearl,' he found himself warning her.

'Of pizza?'

'Of Caruso.'

'Now why would you say that?' she asked with more than just a little mischief in her tone.

'You know why,' McGuire said soberly. 'Or you should — if you hadn't already dropped your guard. He's ingratiating himself with you. And there has to be a good reason.'

Pearl was instantly stung. 'There is,' she snapped. 'Though it's obvious you haven't recognised it.'

'Pearl . . . '

'I have to go.' Ending the call, she stared, peeved, at her phone for a moment before throwing it on to the bed.

McGuire, on the end of the line, realised she had hung up on him. Feeling increasingly stressed, he stared down at the hurried notes he had been taking throughout the call. They read: *'Bright-Sparkes, property, bees, chemical lovers, psychic forces, pizza, Caruso, Pearl'*. He didn't much like the look of this sequence at all.

Back at the Villa Pellegrini, Pearl was trying to calm her frustration by sifting through the few items of clothing that were hanging in her wardrobe, when her eyes fell on the red silk dress. It was the one she had bought for a special occasion — the one she had always thought she would wear for McGuire. She took it down and held the soft cool fabric against her cheek for just a moment, her eyes closed until the smell of burning wood from the oven drifted up from the lower terrace through the open window. She made a sudden and instinctive decision: she would wear the red dress this evening — whether McGuire was here or not.

★   ★   ★

'You look truly stunning tonight, darling.' It was Dolly who paid her daughter this compliment, on meeting her in the hallway as she came out of her room. She was right. Pearl's hair hung loose about her shoulders, and the silver locket was around her neck but the red silk dress still hung in the wardrobe because, at the very last moment, she had chosen instead to wear a vintage white crepe number that showed off her suntan. Dolly, by contrast, felt a little over made-up and suspected that in her fitted pink top and stretch denim jeans she no doubt resembled the badly packed parachute bag she had stuffed into the boot of her car before arriving here.

'I wish I'd thought to lose a bit of weight before this trip,' she said ruefully. 'With all the delicious food we've eaten I shall return as fat as butter, though I'm not about to pass on pizza after what we've been through lately.'

Pearl had just finished locking her door when she paused to look up at the name on it. '*Fiammetta*,' she said, before turning to her mother. 'Do you remember what Simona told us? The rooms and suites are all named after characters in *The Decameron*.'

'That's right,' said Dolly.

'Anemone's room is *Lauretta*,' said Pearl. 'And Simona's is *Pampinea*, the character in the book who suggests that everyone should head to the countryside.'

'Yes,' said Dolly. 'She was also the first to be made Queen of the Day, as I recall.'

They had just reached the top of the staircase where Pearl took a few moments to study the painting of Simona's father, Peter Cartwright. 'Simona lost both her parents,' she said sadly. 'And now she's lost her husband too.'

'Former husband,' corrected Dolly.

Pearl mused on this for a moment. 'You told me her mother had been unhappy in her marriage?'

'Well,' began Dolly. 'As I mentioned, Lucy was far younger than Peter and he was away so much with his work, she felt neglected, I think.'

'Neglected enough to have had an affair?' Pearl asked. 'Peter Cartwright reacted so desperately . . . surely only something like jealousy could have prompted him to do such a terrible thing?'

'Admittedly, it would have made his actions a

little more understandable,' Dolly considered, 'though not excusable, but yes, certainly many have been driven to murder from jealousy.'

'Like Othello,' mused Pearl. 'With Desdemona.'

'The same thing occurred to me all those years ago too,' said her mother. 'But there was no evidence at all of Lucy ever having been unfaithful to Peter. And certainly *not* with his best friend.' She added quietly but forcefully, 'I told you, Marshall is a man of duty — and of honour.'

Pearl gazed up at the pale blue eyes and the sensitive features of Peter Cartwright. It was hard to believe that this was the face of a man capable of murder, but the striking thing for Pearl in that moment was that his daughter should so resemble him.

★　★　★

The garden terrace was lit with lanterns when Pearl and Dolly arrived. The other guests were already assembled around a table decorated with flowers and tea lights, and the smell coming from the wood-fired oven reminded Pearl how hungry she was, having eaten nothing since her lunch with McGuire. The trout served in the local pub had been delicious, which was not at all surprising since so many establishments now boasted 'gastropub' status and certainly gave Pearl a run for her money in Whitstable. But they would hardly compete with the skills of Nico, especially where a Neapolitan pizza was concerned. Tonight he had parted with culinary tradition and prepared the pizza dough in a square format. In

184

minutes the pizza was ready, and with the addition of some bitter *friarielli*, he renamed his new creation *marinara alla Perla*.

He winked at Pearl as his glass met hers and she returned his charming smile, but nevertheless McGuire's comments about Nico ingratiating himself were hard to shift from her mind. She knew, without a doubt, that Caruso represented a challenge to McGuire as they were clearly both alpha males in their own territories. Now it appeared to Pearl that she was their common trophy. While she was sure some jealousy had been aroused in the detective about the picnic on the river, McGuire's warning that she had allowed herself to fall, unguarded, under the influence of Nico Caruso still irked her.

As Nico continued to entertain the assembled guests, together with Marshall and Simona, she recognised that even the shrewdest of women could become vulnerable in love — like Layla, who as usual was unable to keep her hands off her young fiancé over supper. Simona, too, had fallen hard for Jake and the result had been tragedy, as it had been for Peter, her own father. History had repeated itself, although unlike her father, Simona had survived and strangely, in spite of Jake's murder, she looked to Pearl to be less distracted than she had been in the days leading up to her former husband's unexpected arrival. It was clear Frank was helping in that, dutifully filling her glass and hanging on to her every word. And it wasn't only women who could fall hard for someone, thought Pearl, accepting the possibility that Frank could have fallen for Simona long ago at La Valle, when he could do little about his feelings as she was married to another man — a man 'with demons' who had failed to appreciate what he had.

Georgina yawned suddenly. 'Sorry,' she said. 'I don't know why I should feel so tired, as I've done almost nothing since I came here. It must be the country air.'

Frank piped up. 'I always find that it's sea air that helps me sleep.'

'Yes,' said Dolly. 'I usually find it a challenge to sleep at all when I'm away from home — but not here for some reason.'

'I know what you mean,' agreed Layla. 'I've got a butterfly brain and if I don't take one of my little helpers, the slightest thing can wake me.'

'But you've slept well here at the villa?' asked Pearl.

'Like a log,' Layla replied. 'The night before last, for instance, I thought I'd be awake all night after what had happened, but it was only the rain in the night that woke me.'

'The rain?' asked Pearl.

Layla thought for a moment. 'Yes,' she replied, but then she looked doubtful. 'Even then I was half asleep, so I may have imagined it?'

At that point, Maria arrived to serve dessert while Simona suggested, 'Perhaps we should have this course away from the oven? It's still so hot.'

'It certainly is,' Frank agreed, fanning himself with his napkin. 'What temperature did you say it reaches, Nico?'

'Hot enough for us to roast a joint of lamb

right now if we moved the ashes to one side,' he informed them.

'Amazing,' declared Dolly. 'And what do you burn in it?'

Robert replied, 'Any clean-burning firewood from trees like oak, maple, ash — all of which grow locally here.'

'Did I smell some pine earlier?' Pearl asked suddenly.

Robert nodded. 'But I'd stripped the bark so that there wasn't too much sap produced.'

'It's all very 'green',' Simona told them. 'The ashes go on the compost heap, which in turn is useful for the vegetables and herbs.' She glanced away to the herb garden and smiled.

The guests settled on the terrace away from the oven, and as the sky came aglow with a beautifully fiery sunset it was difficult to imagine that a man had died here only forty-eight hours before.

'Would you like me to make some coffee?' Maria asked her employer once the meal was over.

'Yes, please,' said Simona.

'None for me, thank you,' said Dolly.

'Or me,' chimed Layla.

'I'll have one,' said Marshall.

'Georgie?' asked Simona.

Georgina thought for a moment. 'Isn't there any more *grappa* left?' she asked.

For a moment, Simona's face clouded as though she had been transported back to the evening of Jake's arrival.

'I'm afraid not,' she replied.

'Then I'll have a coffee too,' said Georgina.

'I'll make a pot.' Maria was about to re-enter the house when Steven spoke up.

'I wouldn't mind some Chinese tea,' he said.

Maria turned back and Simona informed her: 'I think you'll find there's some loose leaves in a caddy in the pantry.'

Maria looked troubled at the mention of the pantry where she had come across the bloodied mallet and seeing this, Robert stepped forward. 'I'll get it,' he said. Taking the initiative, he moved inside as Maria followed after him.

Pearl now turned to Simona. 'I happened to see some jars of your honey in the village today.'

'Yes,' Simona replied. 'I believe Robert has found a stockist there and we hope to be selling our vegetables soon, too.'

'You were in the village today?' Nico asked Pearl.

'I went to meet Inspector McGuire,' she admitted.

'Have there been any developments?' asked Marshall. Then: 'Are the police any closer to discovering the truth?'

Pearl was guarded in her response. 'I'm sure they are,' she replied, trying to gauge everyone's reaction, but at that point the guests were distracted by Maria emerging from the house, carrying a tray containing a coffee-pot with milk and sugar, while Robert followed on behind with a tray of cups and saucers, a set of which he handed to Steven.

Not much more than an hour later, the guests began to file inside, though Dolly remained in

188

the grounds talking to Marshall while the table was finally cleared. Nico turned to Pearl. 'A good evening, considering,' he said.

'Yes,' she smiled. 'The food was delicious. I'll miss your cooking when I finally return home.'

'Is that all you'll miss?' he asked mischievously.

Rather than respond to this, Pearl remained silent before she asked: 'Your room is on the other side of the landing from mine, isn't it? *Panfilo* — that's another character from *The Decameron?*'

He smiled. 'That's right.'

'Tell me about him.'

Nico shrugged. 'Panfilo is meant to be the voice of Boccaccio himself. He's everyone's friend and a friend to all — that's what the name means in Ancient Greek. He's always cheerful and never down because he believes that love can fix anything.'

'And?' asked Pearl, intrigued.

'I think the character was in some earlier work by Boccaccio, together with Fiammetta — her name means 'little flame'. Some say she's based on a woman Boccaccio was in love with — a noblewoman.' He held her gaze.

'And Panfilo also becomes King for the Day?'

'And tells stories to amuse the others. But they are stories that give a warning.'

'What kind of warning?' Pearl was eager to know.

'That looks can be deceiving,' Nico told her. 'That we should search deeper beneath the surface . . . for the truth.' His voice lowered to a whisper. 'Why do you ask, Perla?'

She shook her head. 'Curiosity,' she said. 'Nothing more.'

He took a step closer, urging her, 'Come with me now, Perla. Down to the river.'

'Why?'

'To be alone,' he murmured. 'Together?' His dark eyes were willing her not to look away but she did so just in time to see Dolly glancing across and the moment broke the spell.

'Not now,' she decided. 'Not tonight.'

Disappointed, he shrugged then offered a smile. 'One day, Perla.' He pointed at her. 'One day.'

Pearl watched him enter the house as Anemone stood up and began to help Maria clear some of the cups from the table. She was just about to lend a hand herself when Dolly came back with Marshall. 'Are you coming up?' she asked.

'In a moment,' Pearl replied.

'Well, don't be too long,' her mother said. 'I don't like the idea of you hanging around out here after dark.' She took Marshall's arm and entered the house with him as Pearl approached Anemone, who was standing alone now on the terrace, looking thoughtful.

'Last night,' Pearl said, 'when you told me about *The Decameron*, I can see now that there's a resonance with its characters and all of us here, though we're clearly not fleeing the plague.'

'But we aren't free to leave,' said Anemone solemnly. She looked troubled but offered

190

nothing more, so Pearl decided to continue.

'I've also been thinking of what you said about us having a sensitivity to surroundings and each other. On the night of the murder, I woke at some time in the night with the sound of the balcony door having blown open during the storm. It banged against the frame in the wind and that may well have masked the sound of any disturbance taking place downstairs.'

'Indeed,' agreed Anemone.

Pearl was uncertain about proceeding with this train of thought but finally she went on: 'It was a warm night like this but nevertheless . . . '

'You felt it too?' asked Anemone quickly. 'The chill? I also woke and couldn't get warm, even after getting up to take a blanket from the bottom of my wardrobe. It didn't help at all.'

Pearl frowned at this. 'Could the temperature that night have dropped so much?'

Anemone shook her head. 'No,' she said. 'It was extraordinary — in the truest sense of the word. What I mean is, you and I experienced something that was 'out of the ordinary'. Very possibly we picked up on that poor man's condition, his fear at finding himself trapped in that room.'

'You think that's possible?'

'But of course,' declared Anemone. 'Surely you've known an instance of thinking about someone just before they call you? Or a moment's agitation just before discovering that a member of your family needs help? Twins experience similar responses, even when they are in different parts of the world. It is quite

191

inexplicable other than by understanding the shared awareness some of us have towards another's distress.'

'Like the alarm signal used by bees . . . the pheromones Robert talked about?'

'Precisely.'

'But Jake Rhys was a total stranger to us. To me in any case,' said Pearl.

Anemone nodded. 'I had met him only once before,' she explained, 'during my stay at La Valle. And he had little time for me. I was of no interest to him. Though he did spend some time with the lovely Georgina.' She glanced across at the latter, who was talking to Simona. 'She's a beautiful woman, after all.' Anemone paused. 'And Jake was clearly a troubled soul.'

'With demons,' Pearl said thoughtfully.

'A rather archaic way of putting it,' Anemone commented. 'Perhaps 'struggling with some addictive behaviour and possibly even a personality disorder' might be a more appropriate way of describing his problems. Nevertheless, I find it entirely possible that any one of us could have picked up on his considerable distress that night.'

'In the same way you sensed the negative energy?' asked Pearl.

'Yes,' said Anemone slowly. 'I found the atmosphere cloying, claustrophobic, as though something or someone was literally sucking the air from my lungs.' A hand lifted to her chest as she said hoarsely, 'Like drowning.' Her gaze was seemingly fixed on a point straight ahead of her but Pearl was unable to see what it might be.

192

'Anemone, are you all right?'

Pearl's question seemed to draw the other woman back to the moment, but she continued to look pained as she apologised: 'I'm sorry, Pearl, I'm feeling very confused. Something just happened, I do believe this death has affected me more than I realised. I need to rest and have a think about things.'

She picked up her bag and headed quickly into the house, leaving Pearl alone on the terrace and unable to see what Anemone could possibly have found so perplexing in the scene of the fragrant lantern-lit herb garden before her.

13

The next morning Pearl woke from a deep sleep, disturbed by a vivid dream in which her balcony door was banging noisily against its frame. When she finally got up out of bed to close it, she saw that Jake Rhys was standing there with ashen features and blood dripping from the gaping wound on his left temple as he held his hand out towards her. A nearby church bell began chiming insistently as though sounding a sudden warning and Pearl opened her mouth to scream but no sound emerged . . . Then she woke for real — and registered that the alarm on her mobile phone was ringing.

Reaching out towards her bedside table, Pearl switched off the alarm before noticing that Robert's book on bees was lying beside it. Picking it up, she began to thumb through the pages in an effort to shake off the memory of her nightmare with some suitably distracting images of hives. While she recognised that Robert's hives were of the more conventional 'framed' type with sloping sides, she read that bees weren't at all fussy and could be perfectly happy in something called a top bar hive which consisted of a simple box with sticks across the top — to which the bees attach their combs. Building such a hive was said to be as easy as putting up a few shelves, with the result that honey could be harvested one comb at a time while this seemingly low-tech method of beekeeping seemed to allow for little disturbance to the bees themselves as they went about their honey-producing business.

After a while, the interlude spent reading Robert's book had the effect of lifting Pearl's mood and she began to imagine keeping some hives herself, either in her sea-facing garden at Seaspray Cottage or at the family allotment in Whitstable — if the neighbouring gardeners had no objections. Then she sighed to herself as she acknowledged that it could be some time before she was home again, since the ongoing investigation had come up with little so far in the way of clues or other progress. It also occurred to her that she had no doubt missed breakfast, but at that moment her mobile phone rang — not an alarm this time but a call. She failed to recognise the number displayed and answered with a confused: 'Hello?'

'I'm so sorry to disturb you,' said the familiar voice at the other end of the line.

'Anemone,' said Pearl. 'How did you get my number?'

'Your mother gave it to me,' Anemone replied. 'I saw her a while ago. She had breakfast before heading off to the river with some watercolours but I didn't want to wake you too early.'

'Is something wrong?' asked Pearl, picking up on Anemone's tone.

'Yes. I mean no.' She decided to begin again. 'Look, Pearl, I'm calling because . . . well, it's all suddenly becoming clear to me.'

'What is?' asked Pearl keenly.

'What we were talking about last night: *The Decameron*. The plague, to be more precise,' she said, before adding more softly, 'It's not without, Pearl. It's *within*.'

At this, Pearl sat up in an effort to pay more attention. 'I'm sorry, I don't follow.'

'We aren't fleeing it, like the characters in the book,' Anemone explained, 'because it's right here among us. I felt it, last night when I was helping Maria.'

'Anemone?'

'No, Pearl. Please listen, I can't talk now.' In an urgent whisper she suggested: 'But I'll meet you in half an hour?'

'Where?'

'The herb garden.'

'OK,' said Pearl. 'I'll be there.'

★　★　★

Pearl took a shower in an effort to wake up properly as she considered the curious call from Anemone Broadbent. She was an eccentric character, a single middle-aged lady — with special powers, if Simona was to be believed. She seemed a gentle soul with the prettiest of names, although Pearl now recalled something Anemone had told her about her name on their very first meeting: '*People always assume that it refers to the wildflower but, infact, my mother was a marine biologist and named me after the sea creature.*'

Pearl reflected on what she knew about the sea anemone, remembering that it was a predatory animal which was related to the jellyfish. In its own environment it might look harmless enough, and its tentacles were certainly reminiscent of Anemone's own grey curls, but Pearl recalled now that the same tentacles were actually filled with venom by which the anemone captured its prey. A simple touch of a strand of sensory hair could trigger an injection of toxin sufficient to paralyse a small fish or shrimp while the anemone then proceeded to digest it. It was also known to live in symbiotic relationships with other creatures, like the hermit crab, on whose shell it might attach itself. In southern Italy, the sea anemone was considered to be a culinary delicacy, the whole animal being marinated in lemon or vinegar then coated in a light tempura batter and deep-fried in olive oil.

Pearl couldn't be sure if it was this thought that made the shower water seem particularly hot at that moment in time, but she switched off the tap and stepped out of the cubicle wondering whether she should perhaps take someone else along to the meeting. She didn't wish to disturb her mother's painting session, however, and decided against calling McGuire, knowing it would take too long for him to arrive.

Back in her bedroom, she checked the call log on her mobile just to make sure she hadn't dreamed the conversation. Then she put on a pale blue light cotton dress and sandals and ran downstairs to where the open doors to the lounge and Simona's study showed that both rooms were empty. The kitchen was similarly deserted as Pearl passed through it to the French doors. Once outside, the heat rose from the stone terrace and she put on her sunglasses before quickly descending the steps, admiring the Villa Pellegrini as the sun's rays splashed golden on its rose-pink walls. It promised to be a special day, both in terms of the weather and regarding the expectation created by Anemone's cryptic phone message. But on reaching the herb garden Pearl found her hopes dashed as Anemone had not yet arrived.

Taking a deep breath, Pearl inhaled the heady fragrance from a variety of long-stemmed French lavender that she knew to be used for perfume in Provence. There were beds filled with the culinary herbs of rosemary, coriander, fennel, sage and parsley, and also the 'strewing plants' of mugwort, lemon balm, mint and basil that, centuries ago, would have been cast among reeds and rushes on stone floors to banish unpleasant odours. Picking a leaf of fragrant Moroccan mint, she savoured its fresh taste, imagining she could use it in a dish at The Whitstable Pearl, marrying it with lemon oil to produce a sauce suitable for swordfish — if she ever found herself free to return.

She also now allowed herself to imagine taking an early-morning walk along the beach at Whitstable while the fishing boats headed out to sea and the bleached sails of the wind farm turned on the distant horizon. A cool breeze would be blowing in from the east across the rows of colourful beach huts that were spread across the grassy slopes of the neighbouring town of Tankerton. The porches of the wooden huts overlooked the coast and the spit of shingle which always appeared at low tide, stretching for almost a mile out to sea for tourists and natives to walk upon as the sea lapped on either side. Since she had arrived at the villa, Whitstable had seemed far away, though it was always close to Pearl's heart . . .

At that moment, her phone sounded. Pearl expected to hear Anemone's voice, but instead it was Nico on the line. '*Ciao*, Perla!' he said brightly. 'I didn't see you at breakfast this morning. Are you OK?'

'I'm fine,' she replied. 'But I overslept.'

'*Madreperla* is down on the bridge painting.'

'So I hear.'

'And you?' Nico asked.

'I'm in the herb garden.' She sat down on a bench, beside a bush of rosemary, its scent drifting towards her on the warm air.

'Are you alone?' he asked.

'Yes.'

'Then I'll join you,' he said quickly.

'I'm actually meeting Anemone,' Pearl explained. 'She wants to talk to me or I'd invite you along too.'

A pause followed as Nico took this in before he asked, 'And afterwards — you have something else to do?'

'I have some calls to make and I need to check on the restaurant.' Her gaze followed the flight of butterflies as they settled on the flowers of tomato plants. 'It seems impossible . . . ' she said softly.

'*Cosa*, Perla?' he asked.

'Impossible that someone should have been murdered here. In such a beautiful place. Under the same roof as us and while we all slept.'

'Not all of us were sleeping,' he corrected her. 'The murderer was awake.'

'Yes,' said Pearl. 'But you heard nothing?'

'Not a thing. Just the storm. Thunder . . . rain.'

'Me too,' she told him before asking, 'Your room is next to . . . ?'

'Steven and Layla's,' he replied. 'It's called *Dioneo*.'

'Another of Boccaccio's characters?' Pearl said thoughtfully.

'That's right,' said Nico. 'He's the good-time guy in the story. He does exactly what he wants. Why do you ask?'

'I don't know,' Pearl sighed. 'I'm finding it impossible to make the right connections.'

Nico cleared his throat on the end of the line. 'And what about your detective?'

'*My* detective?'

'You said you knew him.'

'I do, but maybe not well enough,' she said honestly before asking: 'Nico, the aria from the Rossini opera — *Otello* — you said it was . . . '

'Desdemona's aria.'

'Sung as she's sitting beneath a willow tree?'

'That's right.'

'And her husband was to murder her from jealousy?'

'Unfounded jealousy,' Nico pointed out. 'Remember, Otello was betrayed by another who told a lie about Desdemona.'

'Iago,' Pearl remembered.

'But Desdemona was never unfaithful. That was the tragedy.'

Pearl looked down at the rosemary bush, reminded that the herb was said to be 'for remembrance' — as another of Shakespeare's characters, Ophelia, had said in the play *Hamlet*. But she also knew that even before Shakespeare had written the play, the herb had been slipped into the pockets of lovers to help them remember their vows, and placed on the bodies of the dead, so that Ophelia's mention of the herb foreshadowed her own dramatic death. The thought sent a sudden chill through Pearl.

'I have to go now, Nico,' she said hurriedly.

'Anemone is there now?' he asked.

'Not yet,' she said. 'But she will be soon.'

'OK,' he said. '*Ciao*, Perla. *A dopo*.'

Having ended the call, Pearl looked back to the house but there was still no sign of Anemone and, checking her phone, she saw there were no new messages either. It was now more than forty minutes since the woman's call. She found Anemone's number on her phone, dialled it and listened as it rang on, unanswered. Then she ended the call. Replacing the phone in her pocket, she was just considering returning to the house when she heard the dog bark. It sounded as if it could be Toby, somewhere close by, perhaps in the meadow, chasing butterflies once more, as he had done while out with Robert on the day Jake's body had been found. But the dog's barking was insistent. It troubled her, so instead of going back to the villa, she turned in the direction of the arch cut in the tall box hedge that opened into the meadow.

As she approached the meadow, the barking grew louder and Pearl finally saw Toby framed in the archway, front legs braced straight out before him, head lowered and gaze fixed towards the pond. Pearl hastened on, and the focus of the animal's attention now became clear: something white appeared to be floating on the water — a bundle of clothing . . .

Pearl began to run through the long grass; blood-red poppies crushed beneath her feet as she raced to the scene. The young dog continued to bark but his tail now wagged at the sight of her, perhaps at the expectation of help for his master as Pearl noted the white beekeeper's veil worn by the figure lying face down in the water. Taking off her sandals, Pearl jumped into the pond, almost losing her footing as she slid on a pond floor of slime and weeds. Golden carp quickly darted away, diving deep beneath the moss green surface as she waded thigh-deep towards the centre of the pond, where she managed to tug Robert's body towards her.

Hearing only her own harsh breaths, she clumsily wrenched the veil from his head. It came away in her hand and she gasped in shock to see, not his thick chestnut hair, but a mop of wet grey curls resting like tentacles in the palm of her hand. A swarm of angry bees flew up into the air, finally escaping from inside the veil as Pearl turned the body over, recoiling as she saw Anemone's face before her, disfigured almost beyond recognition, eyelids swollen shut and lips bloated.

A flock of starlings took suddenly to the sky, scattering into the clouds, and the dog on the side of the pond ceased barking and began to whimper.

PART THREE

14

Two hours after the discovery of Anemone Broadbent's body, the meadow had been sealed off and the pond drained. Pearl sat with McGuire in the herb garden as officers went to and from the house to the crime scene, each appearing to perform a prescribed role as purposefully as bees in a hive or ants in a colony.

'Are you OK to continue?' he asked, noting that in spite of her suntan Pearl had lost her glow and was looking drained — and lost, the mischief gone from her eyes.

After a brief pause, she nodded. 'Yes,' she said. 'And I've gone over this again and again in my mind but I can't make any sense of it.'

'Think,' McGuire gently urged. 'She called you this morning?'

'That's right,' said Pearl. 'It was still early and I hadn't been awake long, but I didn't imagine it. The call is logged on my phone and, as I told you, she mentioned a conversation we had had last night after supper, about *The Decameron* — the book by Boccaccio. She wanted to meet today and tell me something.'

'But she didn't say what?'

Pearl shook her head. 'No. But we'd also been talking about how we felt on the night of the murder. We had both woken at some point during that night feeling chilled and unable to get warm. Anemone was sure it was some extraordinary experience we had shared.'

McGuire frowned. 'Experience of what exactly?'

'Of us picking up in some inexplicable way what had happened to Jake, the night of his death.'

McGuire looked away and Pearl read his thoughts. 'I know what you're going to think of this but Anemone was convinced she had some kind of powers.'

'And now you have them too?' he asked, sceptical.

She shrugged in defeat. 'I don't know. I'm not sure I know anything any more, except that last night Anemone was troubled and this morning she seemed to have reached some clarity and perhaps a conclusion of some sort. She had said she'd become aware of something not being right.'

'When?'

'Last night after dinner.' Pearl stopped to think. 'We'd been discussing the fact that our rooms are named after characters in *The Decameron*, and Anemone knew that the story was set during the year of the Black Death in Europe. A group of people flee the plague in Florence and take refuge in the countryside. There are parallels. But what she said to me this morning was that in our case, the plague was 'within'.'

'And what do you think she meant by that?'

'That's just it — I don't know.' Pearl shook her head in frustration. 'I thought she was about to explain it to me, there and then on the phone, but she suddenly decided she wanted to tell me in person.'

'Here, in this garden?' McGuire looked

around the borders of fragrant plants and herbs.

Pearl nodded. 'But not right away. In half an hour, she said. The time it took for me to get ready. But then I took a call from Nico.'

'Oh? And what did *he* want?'

'Nothing. He just called because he hadn't seen me at breakfast that morning. We chatted.'

'And you told him you were meeting Anemone here?'

'Yes, but . . . ' She broke off, eyeing McGuire with some suspicion. 'What are you getting at?'

McGuire put a curb on his personal feelings about Caruso. 'I'm just trying to establish the facts leading up to you finding the body. Where did he say he was?'

'He didn't. Look, I don't know what this has to do with anything . . . '

'You don't?' asked McGuire. 'Anemone was murdered some time after she called you at 9.41 and your discovery of her body around 10.26. This call from Nico seems to have kept you occupied during that time.'

'And from that you infer?' she asked spikily.

McGuire stopped himself from giving an honest answer. 'Nothing,' he said tightly.

'No. Go on — *tell* me,' she urged. 'Because it seems to me you haven't actually got very far with this investigation to date, and maybe that's because your attention is being diverted elsewhere.'

'Meaning?'

'You're concentrating on Nico and ignoring the other suspects. I wonder why that should be?'

209

He braced himself before responding, 'And you don't happen to think *your* attention is being 'diverted'?'

Pearl was stung by this. 'What're you talking about?'

'Leave it,' ordered McGuire.

'No,' she persisted, realising in that moment what he had just suggested. 'You mean you think if I hadn't been talking to Nico, I could have found Anemone sooner.'

'That's not what I — '

'It's *exactly* what you meant.'

He took a deep breath before replying. 'I'm not blaming you, Pearl,' he said softly. 'But it's a fact that this call from Nico arrived at a critical time and may well have been intended as a deliberate distraction.'

Pearl absorbed this. 'But you can't possibly be suggesting that Nico could have been speaking to me and murdering Anemone at the same time?'

McGuire's silence spoke more clearly than words. Pearl then answered her own question. 'No,' she said. 'Of course not. But it could have allowed him time to leave the scene. To create an alibi.'

Still McGuire said nothing and she continued guiltily: 'I *was* a little late arriving and, ironically, I thought Anemone had just been delayed so I used the time to enjoy the plants here. It was only when I heard Toby barking that I recognised something might be wrong. When I reached the archway I could see there was something in the pond, but it was only as I got closer that I realised it was the beekeeper's veil. I jumped to the wrong conclusion and assumed it had to be Robert. But it wasn't.' She then recalled something. 'Anemone came along to the talk Robert gave the other day because she felt she was protected from the bees by having her EpiPen with her at all times. That would have given her a shot of adrenaline if she'd been stung.'

'And she might well have been protected, if she'd been able to use it in time,' said McGuire.

Pearl frowned. 'Has it been found?'

He nodded.

'Close by?'

'No, in the long grass. And quite a distance away from the pond.'

Pearl was baffled by this. 'I don't understand. Why would she have gone to the meadow at all when she said she would meet me here? And why was she wearing Robert's veil?'

McGuire paused before offering: 'She could have been lured there.'

Pearl thought about this. 'In the same way Jake was lured to the kitchen on the night of his murder?' She then asked: 'It *was* a reaction to the bee stings that killed Anemone?'

'It looks that way,' said McGuire. 'Anaphylactic shock.'

Pearl took this in. 'And it was only the other day that Robert explained to us how vulnerable the facial area can be to bee stings . . . how bees are attracted to our breath.'

'Who else was there at the time?' asked McGuire.

'Just Anemone and Frank.'

211

'And you.'

She nodded slowly. 'When I lifted the veil, at least a dozen bees, if not more, were trapped inside. Anemone's body was floating face down in the water so they must have flown into her hair to keep from drowning.'

'There were a number of stings on her scalp too,' McGuire added.

'Yes,' Pearl said thoughtfully. 'I've been reading that bees have a natural response to burrow down, even through animal fur, to sting whatever they believe might be a predator.' She closed her eyes to block out the last image held in her memory of Anemone's hideously swollen features but McGuire tried to keep her on track.

'What do you think she meant by the plague being 'within'?'

'I don't know,' Pearl admitted honestly. 'But if Boccaccio's characters were fleeing something as deadly as the plague, then perhaps Anemone was trying to warn me that something equally deadly was among us . . . here?'

'For her, it was,' said McGuire.

A silence settled between them before Pearl eventually spoke. 'Has Robert been able to tell you anything?' she asked. 'About the bees?'

McGuire nodded. 'It's quite possible that the veil contained the trapped bees before it was placed over her face.'

'So the killer must have known how badly she would react.'

'How many people were aware of her allergies?' asked McGuire.

'Everyone here, I believe — except maybe

Nico. He arrived that first evening after a conversation we'd had on this subject.'

'That doesn't mean to say he didn't know.'

'True.'

'He was in Tuscany at the same time Anemone Broadbent was there. It could have been mentioned then.'

But Pearl had stopped listening and was gazing towards the archway in the box hedge.

'What is it?' McGuire asked.

'Last night,' she began, 'Anemone was looking in this direction when she seemed overcome by some . . . feeling of dread. That's what was written on her face, as though she had seen something terrible in that moment.' Pearl looked at McGuire. 'Perhaps she saw her own death?'

★　★　★

'I can't believe she's no longer with us,' Dolly said shakily. It was a few hours after Pearl's interview with McGuire and she and her mother were resting in their suite. Dolly shook her head to refuse the cup of tea Pearl had just made her.

'Please,' said Pearl, piling two heaped teaspoons of sugar into the cup, but Dolly was adamant: 'I honestly don't think I can.'

Giving up trying to persuade her, Pearl set the cup down on her bedside table.

Dolly looked at her in frustration. 'What on earth are the police doing about all of this?' she asked.

'As much as they can,' said her daughter gently. 'It's fortunate at least that the autopsy

213

results have come through so quickly, with the times and causes of death.'

But Dolly was not appeased. 'We're no nearer to finding out who the devil is committing these killings and why. For heaven's sake, Pearl,' she continued, 'when I heard there had been another murder, for one terrible moment, I thought the victim might be you!'

'And why would anyone want to kill me?'

'Because you're a detective yourself — and far more likely to solve this mystery than the Flat Foot. Also, it was you Anemone wanted to talk to.'

'Yes,' said Pearl, uneasy at the thought. Suddenly remembering something, she said: 'Anemone told me you went off to the river to do some painting?'

Dolly nodded. 'I did. It was such a lovely morning, I took my watercolours and sketch-pad down to breakfast and headed straight off afterwards. I didn't want to wake you so I told Anemone where I would be.'

'And where was everyone else?' Pearl wondered. 'When I came down, the house seemed to be empty.'

'All the other guests were there for breakfast — and Marshall and Simona. You were the only one missing,' explained Dolly. 'When I left the dining room, Georgina was making a call while Frank was talking to Simona. Layla and Steven mentioned going up to their room to change and Marshall was talking to Anemone. I told them both I was off to do some painting and they wished me good luck.'

'And which way did you go?' asked Pearl.

'Across the lawn to the river,' said Dolly. 'But I saw Nico on the terrace.'

'Doing what?'

'Talking to Robert. I guessed he was about to clear the oven.'

'The wood-fired oven, you mean?'

'Yes. He had a small shovel in his hand and a bucket for the ashes, but then Maria left the kitchen by the terrace. She said she was off home and Robert told her he'd walk with her.'

'Which way did they go?'

'Through the herb garden, of course. It's the quickest way to their cottage, isn't it? Straight through the meadow and down to the river.'

Pearl thought about this before asking: 'Did you see anyone else on your way to the bridge?' Dolly looked vague but Pearl urged her: 'Think carefully. It's important.'

Dolly looked helplessly back at her daughter. 'No one,' she said finally.

A soft knock sounded on the door and Pearl called for the person to enter.

Robert did so and greeted them both before addressing Pearl, saying tentatively, 'Would it be possible for you to speak to Ms Cartwright and Mr Taylor before dinner?'

Pearl and Dolly exchanged a look before Pearl replied: 'I'll be right down.'

★   ★   ★

Marshall Taylor was on his feet in Simona's study, leaning on his cane and observing Pearl

215

with the kind of look she was sure he must have given to many witnesses during his fifteen years as a magistrate.

'I must say, I am minded to ask exactly what the police are doing in this case. *Two murders?*' he continued, 'It's inconceivable that anything like this could possibly have happened here.'

'And yet it has,' Pearl said determinedly.

Marshall recognised her tone and nodded to acknowledge this. 'Yes,' he said heavily, 'you're right. But it hardly seems real, does it?' He looked perplexed. 'I can't help feeling that we're like characters in some play. What on earth is going to happen next?' He looked at Pearl for an answer then suddenly grimaced in pain.

Simona immediately stepped forward to help him, saying anxiously, 'Please sit down, Marshall. You were meant to be resting this week.' She looked back at Pearl as she realised. 'And so were you all. A holiday in the country . . . by the river . . . in my beautiful new home.' Increasingly distressed, her face crumpled.

Marshall reached out and took her hand. 'Don't worry,' he said, 'justice will be done and whoever killed that poor woman today will get what they deserve.'

'Yes,' said Simona, rallying at this, 'she was such a sensitive soul.'

'Perhaps too sensitive,' said Pearl.

Simona looked up. 'What do you mean?'

Pearl said starkly: 'I believe Anemone may have realised something very important relating to the murder.'

'Jake's murder?' asked Simona.

Pearl nodded.

'Like what?' asked Marshall keenly.

'That I'm not sure of,' said Pearl. 'Yet. But once the police have finished with Anemone's room, I'd also like to take a look.'

'You think you'll find something the police won't?'

'I'd like to try,' Pearl told him.

After a brief pause, Simona said, 'Very well. If there's anything at all we can do to help, just let us know.' She looked to her godfather for reassurance, but this time he seemed to be without a comforting answer.

In the next instant a text came through on Pearl's mobile. She saw that it was from McGuire.

15

Straight after supper that evening, Pearl slipped away. Making an excuse that she needed an early night, she darted upstairs to her room, where she exchanged the dress and heels she had been wearing for a pair of black jeans, a T-shirt and some flat deck shoes. From her balcony, she could hear the sound of voices in the lounge — Dolly's voice above everyone else's, seeking two partners to play a game of cards with Marshall. Pearl heard Frank and Simona agreeing to join the game — and then the French doors closed. A moment later, she heard another voice, this time from immediately below. Pearl craned to hear who might be there, before realising it was Georgina. She was speaking quickly on her mobile phone. It was impossible for Pearl to understand what she was saying since the conversation was conducted in Italian and only the odd word was intelligible: *dopo, disastro, polizia, non posso* . . . Finally, she signed off with, 'OK. *Ciao. Pronto.*'

At that point, Georgina began to speak in English — to someone else. 'You,' she said suddenly. 'Are you spying on me now?'

Pearl's heart beat faster at the thought of having been discovered, but it was Nico who replied. 'Don't flatter yourself,' he said, impassive.

Pearl edged out on to the balcony to hear more.

'Poor Nico,' said Georgina mockingly. 'You're *still* wounded I let you down?' Silence followed. Then she snapped: 'You may be a great chef but you are a hopeless businessman, to have run up all those debts and made such a mess of things with your rescue plan.'

'My rescue plan,' he repeated. 'By that you mean . . . you?'

'I was probably all you had left,' she sneered. 'But then you failed to satisfy me . . . that you wouldn't go and do it all over again.'

'I learned my lesson,' he said. 'A big lesson — about who to trust.'

'Yes,' said Georgina. 'And Simona is a very trusting soul.'

'When it comes to some people — *too* trusting.'

Tension entered Georgina's voice as she said spitefully, 'Don't worry, what she doesn't know can't hurt her.'

Creeping further out on to the balcony, Pearl could now see Georgina and Nico standing immediately below her in the grounds.

'But the truth could hurt *you*, Gina,' he said. 'I've been watching you since you arrived, all the little private conversations you've been having with Simona. You want to see if what she has here is worth being a part of, don't you?'

Georgina gave a shrug. 'I've been offering her some advice, that's all,' she said briskly.

'In exchange for what? A piece of the action — a share of the business? You like what you see here, don't you, Gina?'

'Don't *you*?' Georgina said archly. 'You're

here for one reason and one reason only.' She paused. 'Nico Caruso, you and I understand one another because we're really not so different, after all. In fact, the only difference is that I have more money than you, which is precisely why you found me attractive at La Valle.' Her voice stiffened. 'But I worked hard for every single penny I have, prancing along catwalks since I was practically a child, starving myself for photo shoots, being picked over by magazine editors, passed over by fashion designers. And I *earned* everything I have — unlike you. I respect money.'

Nico gave a sad smile before commenting, 'What a shame that respect doesn't extend to people, Gina.'

For a moment it seemed as if Gina was about to respond, but Nico spoke first: 'Threatening to get in your way, was he?'

'Who?' asked Georgina bitterly.

'Jake, of course.' He lowered his voice. 'No one else knew what he was talking about that night but me. Alcohol loosens tongues, Gina.'

To this Georgina said nothing, but as she walked away, he called after her: 'I'm watching you.'

A moment later, a door below was heard to close. Pearl froze, barely able to breathe for fear that Nico might discover her above. But he was too immersed in his own thoughts. His hand moved to his face as though to wipe it clean, then he braced himself before re-entering the house. Pearl remained stock-still, then allowed herself to exhale. She was just about to re-enter her own room when a door suddenly closed on the same floor and she realised that the Bright-Sparkes had just entered their own room — beyond Dolly's.

Layla's voice sounded. 'I feel like I'm in prison.' A pause then: 'Maybe I will be soon.'

Steven's voice cut in, betraying his irritation. 'Will you stop worrying?' Then his tone softened with the next words. 'Layla, we did nothing wrong. We were just looking after each other and our future, that's all.'

A pause followed before she said starkly, 'The police may not see it that way.'

'I've told you,' he continued, 'the police will never know. Trust me.' His voice became soothing. 'This has been a nightmare for everyone but things will look better tomorrow once you've had a good night's sleep.'

His next words were inaudible and the reflection of the light from their window suddenly dimmed as the curtains were drawn. Pearl remained motionless for a moment, still trying to make sense of everything she had just heard, when a text came through on her phone. Short and sweet, it read *Where are you?* She realised she was late for her appointment.

Before leaving her room, Pearl looked back at her four-poster bed and the connecting door to Dolly's room, and decided to carefully position a couple of pillows beneath the covers. With the bedside light on, it didn't look too convincing, but after switching it off she felt it might just fool Dolly if she should choose to look into her daughter's room later on. If all else failed and

Dolly discovered her ruse, Pearl decided she might just pretend she had gone to meet Nico — which would prevent Dolly from fretting about a late-night assignation with McGuire.

Walking noiselessly along the upper hall, Pearl passed the bucolic prints and the portraits of Simona's parents. Peter Cartwright's pale blue eyes seemed to follow her on her way downstairs, where she noted that the door to the drawing room was open on to the chequered hall. Simona, Frank and Dolly were concentrating on their hands of cards as Marshall dealt them a few more. Pearl slipped hurriedly out of the door into the grounds and ran silently across the lawn to the jetty. Safely hidden by the weeping willow, she now began to make her way along the riverbank, passing close to Robert and Maria's cottage, stopping in her tracks as she noticed a light in a window. A small garden ran down to a path by the bank, edged by a picket fence above which honeysuckle and delphiniums rose. As she neared this, Pearl heard the sudden growling of a dog.

'Toby,' she whispered urgently, trying to calm him. 'It's OK.' She continued to reassure the animal, who was duly silenced, but only for a few seconds more, after which he began to bark even more loudly and fiercely, alerting his owners to the presence of an intruder.

A door opened and Robert called sharply to the dog while behind him Maria asked fearfully, 'What is it?'

Pearl sidled closer to the water's edge, taking cover behind a tree on the bank. Toby fell silent but Maria's anxious voice was heard again. 'Robert?'

A pause came before he replied. 'It's nothing. Probably just the fox,' he decided.

A few moments later the cottage door was closed and bolted. Relieved, Pearl moved on to the old iron bridge, brought up short to see a figure silhouetted on the path on the opposite side of the river. As the figure turned, she saw with relief that it was McGuire who was waiting for her. She hurried across the bridge to meet him and whispered: 'I thought you wanted me to meet you at the railway station.'

'I did,' he replied. 'But then I didn't much like the idea of you making your way there, alone in the dark, when there's a murderer on the loose.' He looked at her and smiled, suddenly amused by something.

'What's so funny?'

'You.'

'Me?'

'Yes, you look like a cat burglar in that outfit.'

'I've sloped off secretly to meet a policeman,' she said. 'Would you have preferred it if I wore a red satin dress?'

McGuire considered this. 'I'd like to see that.'

'You should be so lucky.'

He slipped his arm around her shoulder and steered her away from the villa. 'Come on.'

Walking along the riverside path together they passed two lakes, once gravel pits, but now lined with reeds and wildlife. Across the river, at the tiny hamlet of Horton, another old manor became visible, its flint chapel stark against the night sky, and McGuire indicated for Pearl to share the same wooden bench with him that she'd shared with Dolly on their first day here. As she did so, she asked quietly, 'So, we're not headed to the station at all?'

McGuire shook his head. 'I only suggested it because the chances are we wouldn't have been seen. It's unmanned and there are no trains due for an hour.'

'So you've been doing your homework.'

'I'm a detective, remember?'

'So am I,' she replied.

'And what have you got for me?' he asked.

'Plenty,' she said. 'But you'll need something for me too.'

'I have,' he told her. 'For one thing, I checked on Marshall Taylor. He's booked in for an operation — arthritic knee, needs urgent replacement.'

'Right,' said Pearl, disappointed.

'But I also looked into the Bright-Sparkes.'

Pearl looked hopeful now. 'And?'

'The company check I did shows they've been in business for less than a year, so no accounts have yet been submitted, but you're right, it's a property development company.'

'And what's of interest?'

'A separate check on each of them turned up that Layla Bright's money is from a previous marriage.'

'To?'

'An Australian businessman, Eddie Bright, who made a quick dollar or two in the unconventional gas and oil industry.'

Pearl frowned. 'The what?'

'Fracking. Not too popular with the communities who have to live beside it, so he was Public Enemy Number One in an area in Queensland while extracting something called Coal Seam Gas. Then he went off to invest in shale in the US. It appears Layla didn't much like being the target of environmental group protests but she was happy to get a nice fat settlement from their divorce before Eddie Bright's company went to the wall.'

'You mean, the environmental groups won?'

'You could say that. It appears fracking's a short-term investment and a sharp drop in the oil price created problems with the financial viability of Eddie's plans. But Layla took her divorce settlement and made some pretty shrewd property investments with it instead, such as apartments in Dubai.'

'Where she met Steven,' said Pearl. 'By sheer chance. Though he was out there looking for an investment opportunity too.' She looked at McGuire. 'Perhaps he found it — in Layla?'

'The goose that laid his golden egg, as far as property's concerned. Their pad in Tunbridge Wells is worth a cool eight million. It's in her name but he probably persuaded her to buy there. It's his patch.'

'And it'll be worth considerably more once it's been restored,' Pearl said thoughtfully. 'As the Villa Pellegrini must be now — though, as I mentioned, it was once Stour Manor.'

'What are you thinking?' asked McGuire.

'Layla is a big fan of Nico.'

'You don't say,' said McGuire, unimpressed.

'But perhaps she's more a fan of the house,' she added knowingly. 'I overheard her and Steven talking. They're worried about something. Something that could incriminate them. But what?'

'I don't know. A check on Sparkes shows no criminal record but I managed to find out that there was a case some thirteen years ago when he may have been using a relationship with an estate agent to buy properties and turn them around for sale at a profit.'

'And that's illegal?'

'Very. If that's what he was doing, he got away with it,' McGuire went on. 'There was too little evidence for a conviction and it turned out the whistle had been blown on him by an old girlfriend, wanting to get even for him taking up with the estate agent — and when I say 'old', he was only twenty-two at the time and she was pushing fifty. Seems she'd set him up with a lot of nice toys: sports car, sharp wardrobe and a rent-free flat.'

'So she wasn't short of a penny or two?'

'Loaded. And smitten with Sparkes — a former public schoolboy — until . . . '

'She found out about the other woman?'

McGuire nodded. 'So she shopped him to the police.'

'Hell hath no fury . . . ' mused Pearl.

'But the evidence was limited, mainly circumstantial, and a vengeful lover didn't look too good in court.'

'I bet Steven did though,' said Pearl. 'He's an

attractive man. And there's something about him . . . '

'Like what?'

'A certain old-fashioned English charm.'

'You mean, the kind that Americans always fall for?'

'*And* some Australians,' said Pearl knowingly. 'Steven Sparkes is the player, not Nico.'

As she gave McGuire a pointed look, he responded, 'Doesn't mean Caruso can be trusted.'

'Well, I've discovered nothing yet to suggest he's anything other than a great chef and a poor businessman. Whereas Georgina . . . '

'What about Georgina?'

'She was a model, and from a young age, I think, though she now has a fashion company in Milan through which she may have met Simona. I heard her tonight talking to someone on the phone, maybe about business, because she was speaking in Italian.' She paused. 'I also overheard her with Nico.'

'You mean, you were eavesdropping.'

'I'm trying to help you with a murder case.'

'Nothing more?'

Ignoring him, she went on. 'Something Nico said tonight reminded me of something else said by Jake Rhys to Georgina on the night he arrived.'

'Well?' asked McGuire, impatient.

'Tonight Nico referred to the affair Georgina had had with Jake and how it might have impacted badly on her if Simona had found out.'

'Because they're friends,' said McGuire logically.

'Correct. But it seems Georgina might be keen to gain a share of Simona's business here.'

227

'Enough of a motive for murder?'

'Depends,' said Pearl. 'On how much Georgina might stand to lose if Simona were to find out.'

McGuire considered this. 'And what if Simona Cartwright already knows about this affair? That's more of a motive for her to murder her ex-husband.'

Pearl shook her head. 'I don't think she does know.'

'Why?'

'Because she would surely have used that as grounds for divorce? And she didn't. From what I hear, she paid Jake off — and with far more than he deserved by the sounds of it.'

Pearl fell silent. Staring across towards the other side of the river, she began to feel it was oddly fitting that she should be spending the evening sitting here with McGuire, going nowhere, especially with the case. She looked up to see the moon waning in a clear sky that was scattered only with a canopy of stars, but the dark shadow of the old mill still dominated the area. Old enough to be mentioned in the Domesday Book, it was still in production, though the old workers' cottages on Mill Lane had long been abandoned, their windows boarded, like sightless eyes still looking out across the Stour.

Sensing her mood, McGuire asked, 'What're you thinking?'

'About the river,' said Pearl. 'I think it had once been navigable as far as the town of Wye, but it wouldn't be possible now to get anything but a very small craft up to the villa.'

'That's right,' said McGuire. 'I got a report in today. There are two fields nearby, known locally as Ship and Port, that seem evidence of some kind of medieval shipping history. An ancient boat was even found during some building work, but apparently it disintegrated on contact with the air.'

'A bit like our forensic clues.'

Pearl got to her feet and stared towards the sound of rushing water which marked the point at Tumbling Bay where the mill's old leat rejoined the river. As Dolly had mentioned, the area was lined with signs for Deep Water, and Pearl thought about the young boy who had almost drowned here — and in that moment realised how much she was missing her own son.

McGuire spoke. 'Pearl,' he said softly.

She turned to see him standing close to her. In the moonlight his eyes looked as pale as those of the fox she had seen in the grounds on the night of Jake's murder, but there was nothing predatory about the police detective and, compared to Nico's dark good looks, McGuire's features seemed almost angelic — reliable and without cunning.

She found herself suddenly admitting: 'I know very little about you, McGuire.'

He held her gaze. 'What is it you want to know?'

In that moment she felt she could have all the answers she craved from him but part of her was too scared of learning them. Instead, she went to look away again but McGuire gently turned her

229

face towards his and kissed her — not a moment of passion but a tentative move towards recovering something he felt they were in danger of losing — trust and understanding. It was Pearl who broke away first. She looked at him, feeling vulnerable and vaguely fearful.

'I should go,' she said.

'I'll walk you back to the house . . . ' he began.

'No,' she replied — far too quickly for McGuire's liking. 'It's best no one finds out we met tonight.'

McGuire took this in and nodded slowly. 'OK,' he said, knowing it was best not to argue with her.

'I'll be in touch,' she said. 'Soon.' Then she turned to go.

'Pearl?'

At the sound of his voice, she turned back slowly. McGuire knew what he wanted to say but the words failed to form and instead he simply said: 'Be careful.'

She smiled. 'I will.'

With that, she took a few more steps away from him and disappeared into the shadows of the trees lining the path, but McGuire stood his ground, waiting until he saw her appear again on the bridge. Only when she had crossed over it did he look up at the pale moon above, feeling a sense of loss he hadn't known for some time — a reminder that his heart was still intact and that it was Pearl who always proved that to him.

★ ★ ★

Having reached the river's southern bank, Pearl took care to move silently past Robert and Maria's cottage. The night air had freshened and a cool wind rustled the leaves of the floodplain trees which provided roosting sites for birds and bats alike. A small splash was heard in the water, perhaps a shrew or vole, or even one of the many grass snakes that populated the river's clear waters, but soon she had reached the jetty where she realised she had been holding some tension in her chest. On another night, and without a moon to light her way, she might have felt the kind of fear she had known during other investigations — though she seldom experienced this by the sea — but here, inland, away from her home in Whitstable and the reassuring constancy of the sea tides, everything seemed unpredictable — and fraught with danger. She tried not to think of McGuire and his look as she had left him that evening. She felt dogged by confusion — about this case, but also about her feelings for McGuire.

Pausing at the weeping willow, she thought again of the Rossini aria — *Assisa a' piè d'un salice*, remembering the title well but not the melody, only the soaring note of a flute that had melded that day with Maria's scream. She froze as something passed close by — a tiny pipistrelle bat, heading towards the river like a night bird on the breeze. She watched it disappear before she finally turned back towards the house. As she reached the jetty, she parted the willow's branches, only to gasp with fear as she came face to face with someone.

'What are *you* doing here?'

'Waiting for you,' said Nico softly. 'I saw you crossing the lawn tonight. Where did you go?'

Resentful that he appeared to be stalking her, and continuing to head towards the villa, she said only, 'To meet someone.'

'The police inspector?' he asked, still following her.

'What does it matter who I met?' she asked, stung by this inquisition. But when he failed to reply she stopped and looked back at him. His expression was urgent.

'Perla, I ask because tonight I found something.'

She frowned. 'What?'

He placed his hand in his pocket and took out a small clear plastic bag, containing what appeared to be a metal tag from a zip fastener. She waited for an explanation.

'It was in the ashes of the oven,' he said simply. 'On the terrace.'

Pearl met his gaze then stared down again at the piece of metal. It was small though not insignificant for, in that moment, she recognised that what she was looking at was surely the first forensic clue found since Jake Rhys's murder.

16

'Why on earth have you arrested him?' Pearl was on the phone, furious with McGuire, as she paced in her room at the Villa Pellegrini, adding: 'Nico came to me straight away last night and I *trusted* you with that evidence.'

'Yes,' said McGuire, recognising that he had an important point he needed to get across to her. 'But you weren't doing me any favours, Pearl. You had a public duty to inform me about it. I'm the investigating officer, remember?'

'Thanks for reminding me,' she said tartly. 'You could have questioned him here.'

'I prefer to do things properly.'

'By arresting him?'

'I needed to question him at the station,' McGuire stated patiently. 'But he refused to co-operate.'

'To come voluntarily, you mean?'

'Exactly.'

'And that's the only reason you did this?' she asked.

'Nothing to do with you flexing your muscles and showing him who's in control, I suppose?'

'Pearl . . . '

'No. You know as well as I do that being the subject of a formal arrest always puts a witness on the back foot.'

'He's a suspect. As you all are.'

'And you also know that being arrested and

cautioned puts him in no doubt of that,' she said sarcastically.

'There are proper procedures to be observed,' McGuire reminded her. 'Some of them are for Caruso's benefit.'

'Has he asked for a solicitor?'

'No, but he's been offered one.' He counted to ten in an effort to calm his frustration before saying, 'Look, I'm investigating two murders here. Give me a break.'

'All right,' she conceded, 'but can you explain why Nico is suddenly under suspicion when he's just come up with the first possible lead you have?'

McGuire took a deep breath. 'For precisely that reason,' he replied. 'There were no witnesses to him finding that tag in the oven's ashes. We only have his word for that. And why was he waiting for you last night?'

'I told you, he said he saw me leave.'

'So why didn't he show this find to someone else? You said yourself there were other guests who were still up.'

'I don't know,' she confessed, wishing she did.

'Why didn't he call the police? This is a police matter.'

'So you keep saying. But has it occurred to you that he might have come to me first because he trusts me?' she asked. 'And maybe he simply doesn't trust the police?'

'Why not?' McGuire said testily. 'He seems to have spent plenty of time gaining *your* trust, but maybe it's not deserved.'

Silence followed as Pearl took this in before

McGuire made things abundantly clear to her. 'I have a job to do and I'm going to do it,' he said.

'Fine,' said Pearl. 'But just make sure you don't let jealousy get in the way.'

McGuire kept his cool, asking only: 'Do I have anything to be jealous about?'

Pearl resisted replying and ended the call. Seething, she took a moment to calm herself before leaving the room.

*   *   *

In his office, McGuire looked at the phone in his hand as he realised Pearl had hung up on him. He replaced the receiver and stared out of the window. The sky was masked with grey cloud, which seemed to reflect his mood. Having sat across a table from Nico Caruso that morning, he didn't much fancy returning to the interview room for more of the same. In his mind, Caruso had moved from the status of general suspect to specific suspect, classifying him as someone worthy of investigating further — but McGuire had little to go on other than a bad feeling; no significant evidence, just a copper's hunch that the man was not to be trusted.

He told himself that he had been a police officer for long enough not to allow his judgement to be skewed by personal feelings. Nevertheless he also knew Pearl was right; he was resentful of Caruso, of the man's dark good looks, his smug confidence and easy charm but, most of all, he resented Pearl's quick defence of him. It was perfectly possible that Nico Caruso had won her trust for reasons of his own and that he had manufactured the evidence he had given to her last night and maybe even spied on her with McGuire before doing so. But Pearl was also right about McGuire needing to feel he was in control again, if only of this case. Bringing in Caruso had at least achieved that for him. Having been cautioned before interview, a murder suspect could be held without charge for up to thirty-six hours in custody — and right now, McGuire felt every minute Caruso spent away from Pearl was a bonus.

★ ★ ★

'The police came very early this morning,' said Robert. He was standing on the terrace with Pearl, close to the wood-fired oven. 'It was a special team,' he explained. 'They sealed off the terrace to do tests and asked me how the ashes are usually disposed of.'

'On the compost heap?' Pearl queried.

'That's right. Wood ash makes a good alkaline mulch for the vegetables.'

'On the day Anemone died, my mother went down to the river to do some painting,' Pearl went on.

Robert nodded. 'That's right. I saw her go.'

'And where were you at the time?'

'Right here,' he replied. 'I was about to clear out the oven but Maria had finished the breakfast service and I didn't want her to go home alone.'

'So you went with her?'

236

He nodded again.

'And then?'

'I . . . went off to do some fishing.'

'With Toby?'

'Yes. I wasn't far away but the dog was restless and then ran off.' He stopped and swallowed hard.

'The dog alerted me to Anemone's body,' Pearl said.

'That's right,' said Robert, looking pained.

'And you cleared the ashes of the wood-fired oven later that day?'

Robert shook his head. 'No, the police arrived very soon after Miss Broadbent's body was found. Then we all had to give our statements and to be honest, I forgot all about clearing the ashes.'

'The oven has been used at least twice since I've been here,' Pearl remembered. 'The first occasion was on our second night here — Saturday. Was it cleared after that time?'

'No,' he said definitely. 'What ashes were left were just pushed to one side when the next pizzas were made.'

'Last night?'

'Correct. It's not necessary to clean out the ashes every time but Mr Caruso mentioned he was planning to use it for breadmaking — and that reminded me.'

'But you didn't get to do it?'

'I'm afraid not.'

'How would you normally clean it?'

'With a wire brush and a metal dustpan, which I empty into a small bucket.'

'And you use that to take the ashes to . . . '

'The compost heap — on the meadow side of the herb garden.'

'Thank you, Robert,' Pearl said gratefully. He had given her plenty to think about.

★ ★ ★

An hour later, she found Georgina seated at the table on the lawn. She was staring towards the river in the same way Pearl remembered Simona having done on the first day that she herself arrived — but Georgina had her vaping device in hand.

'Do you mind if I join you?'

Georgina said nothing but merely looked at the empty chair beside her before exhaling a long trail of vapour into the air.

'Can I talk to you about Nico?'

'What about him?' Georgina asked wearily.

'I just wondered what you could tell me about him, that's all. You know he's been arrested?'

Georgina gave an unconcerned shrug of her beautiful shoulders. 'He may well be a good cook but Nico's nothing more than an old ham. He loves the limelight and if he hadn't found fame with food, he'd have found it with something else. It's not even money he craves — it's attention.' She looked from Pearl back towards the river as she added, 'He could have made rather a good snake oil salesman, don't you think? Maybe he still could.' She met Pearl's gaze. 'There was a time I considered asking him to endorse some of my fashion lines on a

238

shopping channel programme. He'd have met some pretty models, had a camera trained on him for several hours and even made some money at the end of the day.'

'So why didn't you?' Pearl asked.

Georgina gave a slow smile. 'Because he was likely to say yes. I'm afraid Nico Caruso is a faded brand, unless Simona can rescue him with these culinary breaks. Although, in my opinion, she would do rather better by putting on some fashion shows here.' She glanced around. 'It's a good setting for a shoot, don't you think? But a string of murders won't do much for the Villa Pellegrini's reputation.' She paused. 'At least news of them hasn't leaked out to the press — yet. If it does, Simona might find herself having to go into the murder mystery business — and stage a few costume suppers.'

Pearl failed to respond to Georgina's sardonic comments but asked instead, 'Where were you on the morning of Anemone's death?'

'I already told that to some police officer,' Georgina replied. 'The good-looking blond CID inspector. Rather cool, isn't he? There's something of James Bond about him.' She took another inhalation of her vaping device and then decided to answer Pearl's question. 'I was in my room, on the phone to Marco.'

'Marco?' queried Pearl.

'Yes, he's my PA in Milan. Believe it or not, I'm launching a new line in less than three weeks and it would be rather nice if I could finally escape from here and get back to organising it. So . . . do you think you could get a move on and find the murderer soon? Surely it can't be that difficult? I mean, you're hardly short of suspects, as everyone hated Jake — apart from me, that is. As a matter of fact, I always found him entertaining, as well as rather attractive.'

'Until the other evening?' said Pearl pointedly. 'You accused him of being a bore.'

'Yes, well,' Georgina said tetchily, 'you saw for yourself, he'd had rather too much to drink and drunks *can* be rather tiresome. Nevertheless, I shall miss him.' She looked directly at Pearl as she added: 'And I'm probably the only person who will.' Exhaling a long trail of vapour into the fresh air, she gave her attention once more to the river.

★　★　★

On her way back to the house, Pearl saw Frank Ellis sitting with Simona on the terrace overlooking the herb garden. Simona was talking, an earnest look on her face as though she might be confiding in him, but Frank merely nodded encouragingly from time to time. Though Pearl was unable to hear what was being said she still felt uncomfortable observing them in this private moment; Frank's feelings for Simona were so abundantly evident, not only in the way he looked at her but in the displays of quiet attentiveness he showed, filling her cup with more tea and laying a hand gently upon hers in a gesture of warmth and protection.

At one point as Simona looked at him, Pearl felt he might be about to kiss her — but then her

240

phone rang and she disappeared inside to deal with the call. Pearl moved on and was almost at the terrace before Frank noticed her. 'I hope I'm not interrupting?' she said.

Frank realised that Pearl must have seen him with Simona. 'She just had to take a call,' he explained. 'The police, I think.' He sighed. 'So many questions to answer.'

'Yes,' Pearl said understandingly.

'And . . . Nico's still under arrest?' he asked.

'While he's being questioned,' Pearl clarified. 'He hasn't been charged and can only be kept in custody for a limited time.'

Frank took this in. 'Habeas corpus and all that?' He sipped his tea and furrowed his brow again.

'You're concerned for Simona,' Pearl ventured.

He nodded and said tenderly, 'She's had to put up with so much.'

'From her husband?'

Frank nodded again. 'And from her childhood. But I'm guessing you know all about that, being a detective?'

Pearl gave a sad smile of acknowledgement. Frank went on. 'Then you'll know that some people just attract rotten luck — although Simona's been trying so hard to turn things around.'

'And change her luck?' Pearl asked.

'If you like,' Frank conceded.

'Sometimes you need a bit of help to do that,' Pearl said gently.

'Indeed,' said Frank. 'Marshall's been amazing. He's always taken care of her as though she were his own daughter. Not that I know much about that,' he added. 'Family, I mean.'

'You don't have any?'

Frank shook his head. 'I'm an only child,' he declared. 'Ma and Pa long dead.'

'I'm sorry,' said Pearl.

'Don't be,' he told her. 'Not your fault, just life.' He sipped his tea as if it was any other summer's day.

'I take it you never married?' Pearl asked tentatively.

'Nope. Wasted a lot of time working and never found the right person.' He smiled bravely.

'Till now?'

He heaved a sigh. 'Is it that obvious?'

Pearl nodded. 'Just a bit.'

Frank winced. 'I . . . do try hard not to let it show.'

'Why?'

He gave a shrug. 'Because I don't want to embarrass her,' he said. 'To be honest, I don't want to do anything that might make her push me away.'

'I'm not sure she'd do that, Frank,' said Pearl.

'No?' he asked with some surprise.

'I think she needs someone she can trust — especially at this time.'

To this, Frank admitted: 'Yes, I feel the same. I'm just not good at negotiating relationships though. Give me a wine list and menu any day.'

Pearl returned his smile and Frank's mood instantly lightened. 'When all this is over, I'd like to come to your restaurant. I can write a review?'

'As long as it's a good one,' Pearl teased him.

Frank's smile suddenly turned to a frown. 'It

will be over soon, won't it? I mean, you and the police will finally discover who did this?'

In spite of all her doubts, Pearl replied, 'Of course.' But she now prepared to gauge his reaction as she added, 'It's always true that during any crime the perpetrator is bound to leave something behind — as well as to take something away from the scene of the crime.'

'What do you mean?' he asked, looking confused.

'It's one of the basic principles of forensics science,' Pearl informed him, 'and that is why I don't believe the killer can get away. Sooner or later, the clues to this crime will come together.'

'Like the ingredients in a recipe? Simona told me what you'd said about that.'

Pearl nodded slowly and Frank's expression seemed to cloud — but only momentarily.

'Well, I'm glad to hear it,' he said. 'For Simona's sake, this all needs to be over soon.' With that, he got to his feet, excused himself and entered the house, leaving Pearl to mull over his words.

★　★　★

It was after 8.30 that evening before Nico was released from custody and driven back to the Villa Pellegrini by a young Canterbury-based detective sergeant who had been newly pro-moted and sported the kind of keen expression that McGuire knew he too had once worn. McGuire had also gone along, and on arrival, noted that Caruso was greeted with a warm welcome from everyone but Georgina, who stood aloof by the French doors in the lounge, inhaling on her vaping device. When Nico met her gaze she pushed herself away from the wall she had been leaning against while declaring that she was heading for bed.

McGuire then asked to talk to Pearl outside. They walked down across the lawn towards the river, where she turned to him, saying, 'Well?'

He hesitated before admitting, 'You were right. Forensics are confident about their results. The good news is they were able to match the tag to a zip fastener on a particular brand of overalls.'

'For beekeepers?'

McGuire shook his head. 'Lightweight decorators' overalls available in builders' merchants all over the country. That's the bad news. There's nothing special about them so there's no lead.' He gave a small shrug.

Pearl frowned at this. 'Robert is presumably the only person here to have done any decorating — but if so, why on earth would he choose to burn overalls in that oven when he has a whole meadow in which to have a bonfire?' She had another thought. 'Were the overalls made from Tyvek, by any chance?'

'Why d'you ask?'

'Because that's the same material used for suits worn by forensics teams, isn't it? If so, it's possible the overalls may have been worn by the murderer to limit any forensic evidence being left behind — before being burned straight afterwards in the wood-fired oven. It's right outside the kitchen on the terrace, so — '

'No,' said McGuire, interrupting, 'they weren't made of Tyvek, which is actually inflammable. These were just a treated cotton fabric used in this brand of overall, and worn every day by thousands of people.'

'But it's still possible these were used that night for the same purpose as a set of forensic overalls — to limit the clues left behind.'

'All right, it's possible,' he conceded. 'The lack of any DNA at the scene *is* hard to explain.'

'And as you said yourself, it was a clean job. Perhaps *too* clean. Is there anything else from Forensics?'

'Nope. And none of this makes much sense.'

'But you also had nothing on Nico?'

'No, again. Every test result on that zip fastener pointed to him having told the truth. About this, at least,' he added.

Through the French doors, Pearl could see Nico himself looking towards her from the lounge. 'I could talk to him,' she suggested.

'I've done that all afternoon,' said McGuire.

'Well, something tells me I'll have more luck.' Then: 'Luck . . . ' she repeated. 'Do you know we actually found a horseshoe on our way here that very first day?'

'Maybe not all horseshoes are lucky.' McGuire smiled then noticed that the young DS who had driven him and Nico to the villa was waiting obediently, but somewhat impatiently, by the police car in the drive. 'I have to go, Pearl.'

She nodded. 'I know.'

McGuire paused — but said nothing more. As

he moved off, she watched him go, feeling that with every footstep he took, they were drifting ever further apart.

17

It was early afternoon the next day when Dolly entered Pearl's room to find her deep in thought. 'What is it?' she asked. 'What's troubling you so much?'

The truth was, she was as much troubled about McGuire as she was about the murders, but Pearl said only, 'That's just it — I don't know. I honestly believe that everything is here, right in front of me, but none of it is assembled correctly so I can't see a pattern.'

Dolly frowned. 'What kind of pattern?'

'It was something Anemone said on the day we first arrived. She said there are patterns in all things, and I believe she was right. But I just can't see what it was that she must have seen.'

Dolly took this in. 'Don't worry, love. This isn't your responsibility. You've done well with all your cases but you can't win them all. No one can, not even your Flat Foot. If you have to, let it go.' She gave a sigh. 'Perhaps coming here was a mistake — in which case, that was my fault. You're here because of me, no other reason. And certainly not to solve crimes.'

Pearl looked up and saw Dolly's considerate expression. So often, because of the amount of time they spent together, a certain tension existed between mother and daughter, but now there was only a tender moment of understanding.

'Yes,' Pearl said softly. 'Perhaps you're right.' Though she knew there was still one thing left unexplored.

A little later, Pearl went down to see Simona, who was standing near the window in her study looking out across the grounds towards the river as she had done on the day Pearl had first arrived. Her attention seemed similarly unfocused, as though she might be gazing back towards the past. Finally, she gathered her senses and said: 'The police seem to have finished with their immediate investigations at the house, at least for now.' She turned to look at Pearl as she went on, 'I suppose they'll be considering all the information they've managed to gather here so far?'

Pearl gave a nod. 'Though there still seems to be little in the way of forensic clues. Whoever committed these murders took great pains to cover their tracks.'

Simona shivered and came away from the window. 'Does that mean that these crimes are unsolvable?'

Pearl noted her anxious look. 'No, it doesn't,' she replied firmly. 'It just means we have to find another way of uncovering the truth.'

Simona took this in, nodding slowly before she confided, 'I have to say, this is all taking a terrible toll on my godfather. He's always been so brave about the pain he suffers, but in the last few days I see that pain written on his face. I do hope he doesn't feel compelled to cancel his operation because he thinks he should stay here with me. He's always been so protective of me but now I

Pampinea,' Anemone had said. 'Very apt since she's the one who persuades everyone to up sticks for the countryside . . . ' Pearl reflected on this. Nico's room was *Panfilo*: 'everyone's friend, and a friend to all,' he had told her. But Nico had also explained to Pearl that the characters' stories warned against being deceived by appearances.

Deceived. The word tolled like a bell in Pearl's mind — perhaps warning her that this was precisely what had happened. Had she been taken in by Nico's good looks? And could McGuire have been right in believing the chef to be capable of murder and deceiving her for his own ends — to distract her from the truth? She thought back to the day on the river. He had ordered in oysters especially for her, baked a cake, paid her so much attention — and yet previously, his competitive streak had been in evidence as he had sparred with her over dinner. What had brought about the change? Was it really — as he had said that day in the meadow — that he felt obliged to perform a role within a piece of theatre to keep his audience happy? If so, he was a good performer but Pearl was still not sure who the real Nico Caruso really was.

She saw him again in the boat, smiling as he rowed on the Stour that sunny day when he had told her: 'I talked to Simona last night. She tells me you are a detective.' Pearl asked herself if this might have been the first time he realised she was not just a chef to compete with, but someone capable of solving a crime. And could that have been the motive for the change in his behaviour to her? Perhaps McGuire *was* right. She had been charmed and for a very good reason — to blind her to the truth. But if Nico really had murdered Jake and Anemone, the question still remained — why?

Pearl opened her eyes, looked down at the book in her hand and moved to place it back on the coffee table. She wasn't used to admitting defeat and persevered in all things, but right at this moment she felt overwhelmed. As Dolly had suggested, she would have to let it go but, setting the book down, she hesitated. The room was as tastefully decorated as her own *Fiammetta* suite. *Fiammetta* — little flame . . . all of a sudden, something began to glow brightly in her mind.

What had caught her eye were some pieces of decorative china displayed on the shelf across the room. The storage jar was willow pattern, as was the small plate beside it — the distinctive Chinoiserie design that had become popular over four hundred years ago and remained so to the present day. The blue and white landscape pattern reminded Pearl not only of the real willow in the grounds that 'wept' into the river near the jetty, but also of Desdemona and her aria. But it was the china cup and saucer in this display which had captured her attention. She picked up the cup and examined it, noting it also bore the same willow pattern, but as she looked inside it, she suddenly felt she had finally been led to an answer — even though the cup was empty.

★ ★ ★

Shortly afterwards, Pearl located Nico in the grounds. Instantly registering her agitation, he laid a hand on her shoulder as he asked, 'What's wrong?'

'I need you to do something,' she said urgently. 'It's very important, Nico.'

He gave a quick nod of his head. 'Of course. Tell me and it's done.'

She calmed herself and explained: 'I want you to call the guests together for a final lesson.'

★   ★   ★

McGuire was in the shower in his Best Lane apartment, stretching his face up towards the hot spray in an effort to shake off the stiff neck that had dogged him all morning. He knew it was the result of sitting too long at his desk at the station, as well as the continuing tension created by this case which he sensed might have been less confusing for him if only Pearl hadn't been involved. He also knew he had made a big mistake in assuming that a woman as attractive and intelligent as Pearl might possibly wait around in Whitstable until he finally chose to call her. Having recognised that, he had also assumed he could easily put things right — but now he wasn't so sure, since the strength of Pearl's defence of Caruso had taken him by complete surprise. The man remained a suspect, as did all the guests at the Villa Pellegrini, but the one thing that separated Caruso from the rest was that he was also a clear rival for McGuire where Pearl was concerned.

McGuire knew he could never be accused of cutting corners with a case. He prided himself on following all important points of procedure in any criminal investigation, but he now recognised that he had failed to prioritise his relationship with Pearl. The more he thought about her recently, the more extraordinary she seemed. Having brought up her son single-handed while managing a successful restaurant, she was now trying hard to pursue an old ambition and for that she deserved his respect. But due to the conflict of interest with his own position, he had failed to give her this and his admiration for her efforts and skills had gone unsaid. Now she had moved on — and had clearly become involved with some half-baked celebrity chef who McGuire hadn't even been able to hold in custody.

Switching off the shower, McGuire stepped out and wrapped a towel around his waist. He paused to look at his reflection in the bathroom mirror. He was an attractive man but at that moment all he saw staring back at himself was a fool. Walking into the living room, he heard the oldest bell in the cathedral, Bell Harry, sounding for the closing of Canterbury Cathedral. So often the sound of the cathedral bells took him back to the chiming of the bells of San Marco in Venice, where he had spent a last holiday with Donna, but that evening the only image he saw in his mind was of Pearl and Nico eating pizza together in sunny Naples . . .

He moved to the open window and allowed the cool breeze flowing in from the Stour to ease his frustration. West of this spot, on another part of the same river, Pearl was still with Caruso — and that single thought made the unsolved murder case pale into insignificance for McGuire. Instead he paraphrased the lyrics to an old pop song — that it did indeed seem true that you don't know what you've got till it's gone. He put on a clean shirt and a pair of faded jeans, and had just slipped his watch on his wrist when his mobile phone began ringing. He answered it automatically, simply announcing his name, before realising that it was Pearl at the end of the line. 'What is it?' he asked, not expecting for one moment that she was about to say the three words he most wanted to hear: 'I need you.'

18

Just over an hour later, everyone was assembled in the lounge of the Villa Pellegrini to hear what Nico had to say. He had summoned them for a final lesson, as Pearl had requested, and the guests were now there, together with Simona and Marshall, as well as Robert and Maria. McGuire had also arrived just before Nico began to speak and stood in a corner of the room, ostensibly as an observer.

'This week has not progressed as planned,' Nico began. 'We all looked forward to a time of good food and good company, but it has been brought to a premature end — by murder. And so this will be the final session for our little group.' He paused and looked across at Pearl. 'It is a session that my fellow chef, Perla, will take because, as everyone knows, this week she has been more than a match for Nico Caruso and . . . ' he paused again. 'I'm sure she has been the same for Sergeant McGuire.'

He gestured to McGuire, who made sure to correct him. 'Detective Chief Inspector McGuire,' he said pointedly.

To this, Nico merely gave a casual shrug of his shoulders and smiled at Pearl, inviting her to join him. 'Perla?'

She got to her feet and moved to stand beside Nico, who took this as his cue to sit down. He did so, taking an empty chair beside Dolly, who was seated next to Marshall, while Simona and Frank were on Nico's other side. Georgina sat closer to Steven and Layla while Robert and Maria remained together. Pearl surveyed them all before she began.

'On the day I arrived, Simona happened to remark that while food and crime make strange bedfellows, I would certainly have a break from crime. But this wasn't to be.' She went on, 'One of the most important things I learned during my police training was that every contact leaves a trace. This was something I happened to mention to Frank only yesterday: during any crime, the criminal is bound to leave something behind as well as to take something *away* from the crime scene. This is a basic principle of forensic science put forward by a very knowledgeable French professor over a hundred years ago, and it remains true to this day. So I found it extremely puzzling that in respect of Jake's murder, no DNA, fingerprints or fibres had been found in the pantry or freezer room — other than his own — and Maria's, of course.'

Pearl glanced over at McGuire before she resumed speaking. 'As far as suspects for a crime are concerned, the three main things any detective always looks for are: method, motive and opportunity. But on the night of the first murder, it soon became clear that everyone staying at this villa had the opportunity to kill Jake Rhys — including Robert and Maria, who live very close by in their cottage.'

As everyone's gaze moved to the couple, Pearl quickly continued. 'The method was established by the results of the autopsy and forensic investigation, which determined that Jake had got up in the night, perhaps lured to the kitchen by someone in this house, and there he was struck on the left temple by a wooden mallet, rendering him unconscious or semi-conscious. He was then dragged to the freezer room, where he was left while the safety release and alarm system were dismantled. Jake died in that room, but not before he had gained sufficient consciousness to realise where he was — and that there was no escape.'

Pained, Simona looked away at this but Pearl steadily went on: 'Jake had the strength to pull down one of the plastic curtains at the doorway, perhaps to try to insulate himself from the cold — and possibly in the desperate hope that he might just be found in time. But time ran out on him and he died that night.' She paused. 'It was indeed a cruel death, a murder perpetrated by someone with little pity and no doubt a lot of hatred for Jake Rhys. Hatred may well have been the only motive, and Chief Inspector McGuire knows only too well that most murders are committed, not by strangers but, in fact, by close friends, lovers or family members of the victim — including spouses. Certainly, Simona had cause to be angry with Jake, who was her former husband. He had arrived that night, out of the blue — the 'uninvited guest', as Anemone put it — gate-crashing a private party and one which Simona hoped would be the first of many successful visits by future guests wishing to sign up to *Cooking with Nico* breaks at the newly

258

renovated Villa Pellegrini.'

Pearl held Simona's gaze. 'You were trying to put your unhappy marriage behind you in a brave effort to move forward, but then Jake arrived, not only to spoil this, your first week of guests here, but also to warn you that he was not about to be banished to the past. He caused you distress and disappointment that evening but also a great deal of humiliation from the drunken state in which he arrived. Significantly, he was not at all repentant and claimed that he would 'haunt' you and thereby blight your future.'

'That's true,' said Simona in a shaky voice, adding passionately, 'but that was no reason for me to want to kill him.'

'No?' asked Pearl. She pressed on. 'It's certainly true that in threatening to spoil this week, Jake also threatened others. After all, Nico was the figurehead of this new venture — the celebrity draw for anyone signing up to a course. There could be no *Cooking with Nico* week without Nico Caruso himself, but then . . . ' she turned to him . . . 'you were suffering a certain amount of humiliation and loss of face too from the demise of your own restaurant empire and bankruptcy. You were vulnerable, Nico, so perhaps you sought to do something out of the public arena while you rehabilitated yourself — and your name. Nico Caruso. A chef. A celebrity. You may not have been receiving too many offers lately but here was one you would gladly take up for all those reasons. You wanted to remove yourself from Italy and to simply be 'away', as you once put it to me. And so your

259

future was also threatened by Jake's arrival that night. How furious you must have been that this man whose 'dreams had gone bad on him' was now threatening to make your own dreams go bad. Frustrating? Certainly. But motive enough for murder?'

'No,' said Nico determinedly. 'Definitely not. It's true the man had demons but I would never have killed him for that.'

Pearl turned now to one of the other guests. 'Georgina had been Simona's friend for some time and had witnessed Jake's 'demons' in Italy. She had seen how he had become a liability for his wife, having drunk and squandered Simona's money while promising to make up for this once his writing proved successful — but that failed to bring any material success as his new project remained unfinished. He wasted his talent and his opportunities and yet, curiously, for Georgina, Jake held some attraction.'

'What do you mean, Pearl?' asked Simona with suspicion.

Pearl addressed Georgina. 'I mean that in spite of all Jake's inadequacies, you were drawn to him, Georgina. A moth to a flame. Why? Was it that in Jake's weakness you sensed your own strength? Or was it merely that you were jealous of your friend — kind, beautiful, gentle Simona, whose world you shared at La Valle and whose good nature you chose to abuse through your affair with her husband?'

Simona looked scalded at the possibility of such betrayal. 'Georgie?' she asked, appealing to her friend for an answer.

Georgina remained cool as she answered. 'Of course she's wrong,' qualifying quickly, 'about motive, I mean.' She then took a deep breath before admitting: 'All right, so I did sleep with Jake.'

'Why?' pleaded Simona, trembling with shock.

'Because I could,' Georgina replied flatly. 'Because you were so trusting, you would never guess — and because I always found Jake attractive, precisely because he was so bad.'

Simona recoiled and Frank put a protective arm around her.

Georgina gave Pearl a caustic smile. 'I'm guessing you would never have known, if *someone* hadn't told you?' She looked pointedly at Nico: 'He happened to walk in on us one day.'

Nico turned to Simona. 'I'm so sorry,' he whispered.

'But that gives me no motive whatsoever for Jake's murder,' Georgina said boldly.

'Apart from what was said on the night Jake died,' Pearl replied.

Georgina shrugged. 'I don't know what you're talking about.'

'I think you do,' said Frank. 'Jake said something about you having found him less boring another time. I wondered what he meant.' His expression hardened. 'Perhaps now we all know.'

Pearl took up the story. 'You were here ostensibly to offer help to Simona, but if this venture was to be a success, you also wanted to be part of it, didn't you, Georgina?'

Nico broke in. 'Just as you want a part of

everything — but giving little in return.'

'That's rich coming from you,' she spat. 'You were desperate for me to help you get out of debt, but as soon as I changed my mind about giving you a loan . . . '

'I wouldn't have *touched* your money after finding out about you and Jake.'

'That's enough!' ordered Marshall, as though he was disciplining a troublesome pupil or court witness. He turned to Pearl. 'Are you accusing Georgina of Jake's murder?'

Pearl said only, 'Method, motive, opportunity. There has to be a balance of all three. But this is why I found this case more puzzling than any.'

'Why?' asked Dolly, intrigued.

'On the night of Jake's murder, he said a number of things — to Georgina, as discussed — but also to you, Frank.'

'Me?' he asked in surprise.

'Yes,' Pearl said. 'It's clear you feel protective towards Simona.'

Frank searched for the right response before admitting, 'Why wouldn't I? Why wouldn't anyone? Like you say, she's kind, gentle . . . '

'True,' said Marshall softly, coming to Frank's aid. 'She's all of those things.'

Pearl went on. 'So while perhaps you, Frank, or Marshall, might be driven to murder to save Simona from the man who threatened to haunt her, why would either of you have murdered Anemone? And how on earth could Marshall commit such a crime when he is physically incapable of it?' She looked at him. 'For a time, I suspected that this might not be true, that

262

perhaps you were feigning your disability, but Inspector McGuire was able to confirm that your health and mobility problems were genuine as well as the upcoming operation and your reliance on a walking cane. No,' she said, 'Anemone had referred to something quite distinct in her message to me on the morning of her death.'

'What message?' asked Steven, confused.

'She had been telling me about *The Decameron*, as Simona has named several suites after Boccaccio's characters. I'd never read the stories so Anemone had to explain. She even offered to lend me a copy which she had in her room. She told me how it had been written at the time of the plague, the Black Death, about a group of people who take refuge in a country retreat outside the city of Florence, where they entertain one another by telling stories, as King or Queen of the Day. My suite is *Fiammetta*. Simona had already told me she was a strong and independent character, and Anemone was proud of being associated with *Lauretta*, representing justice, while Simona's room is fittingly *Pampinea* — the instigator of the trip to the countryside. She is also, as Nico once described to me, 'the queen' of this particular hive.'

She paused to reflect on this. 'Ever since I arrived here I've felt as though I was under a spell. This place is bewitching in its beauty but more than that, it also seemed as though I was being charmed, as if some kind of spell was being woven. I felt this first of all when I was out in the meadow with Nico — then again when I was on the river with him one day — but it was something more powerful than the charm of one man. It was the house itself, this enchanting place, as though I was not myself but a character in a play which was something you, Marshall, also mentioned one day. Then again, might it have been an opera?'

'Perhaps we were all simply performing a role, like the bees in Robert's hive: workers . . . drones . . . each of us acting under the strange influence of something like pheromones?' She sighed. 'For a time I even allowed myself to believe that I had something like Anemone's own sensitivity. I even asked Inspector McGuire to consider using Anemone's psychic skills in trying to solve this case.' She looked at McGuire. 'I'm glad he rejected this idea. But I had set something in motion — a train of thought with Anemone — to which she returned on the morning of her death.'

Dolly recalled, 'And she phoned you, you said, to meet up with her so she could explain?'

'Yes, she asked me to meet her in the herb garden because she wanted to explain what she meant by having told me 'the plague is within'.'

Layla looked perplexed. 'Well, what on earth was *that* supposed to mean?'

'I didn't know exactly,' said Pearl. 'And I would never find out from her as she failed to arrive in the garden that day. Instead she had been murdered by someone who knew just how powerfully she would react to bee venom without having access to her medication — the adrenaline in the EpiPen which had been thrown into the long grass in that meadow. But now I believe she was, of course, referring to *The Decameron* and how ten people came to a country house all those centuries ago to escape the plague, while ten others arrived at the Villa Pellegrini — Simona's newly restored country home — only to find the plague was indeed here among us.'

Pearl surveyed each of the guests. 'Something lethal — I think that's what Anemone was referring to as 'plague'. She understood that a deadly influence had invaded here — not Jake and his own demons — but one of the guests themselves. And she had recognised this precisely because of her activities. Remember how she clapped out the corners of the dining room on the night of Jake's murder in an effort to clear . . .'

'The negative energy,' Simona put in quickly.

'Yes.' Pearl nodded. 'She also felt the same chill I'd experienced during the night when Jake had been dying slowly from the lack of warmth and air. She was sensitive to her surroundings and to others in the same way that bees are sensitive to others in the hive. That's right, isn't it, Robert?'

'Yes.' He frowned. 'But what are you saying?'

Pearl carried on. 'Being sensitive to Maria and what she had gone through with the discovery of Jake's body, Anemone helped clear the table on the second night we ate outside using the wood-fired oven for Nico's pizza.' She addressed Maria now. 'You and Robert have been with Simona for a long time — eight years. You told me that on the first day we met, when you also showed me around the pantry and freezer room — all your idea, you proudly explained.'

'And what if it was?' asked Robert defensively.

Pearl looked between Robert and his wife as she spoke on. 'You both have an interest in the success of this venture, which set me wondering how far you might go to protect the queen of your *own* colony.' She took a moment to gather her thoughts. McGuire gave a nod of encouragement and she persevered. 'Poor Anemone died from anaphylactic shock caused by bee stings, the result of the bees having been trapped inside the veil. In their alarm they had stung her face as, one afternoon, we were to learn they would do most harm.'

Maria protested, 'Robert could never have harmed that woman.'

'Method, motive and opportunity — Robert certainly had all three because he was out that day, fishing on the river close by, though your dog sensed something was wrong and bolted back to the pond — yet another creature responding to the distress signal of one in danger.'

Steven threw up his hands. 'You've lost me. And it seems to me we've sat and listened to this for quite long enough — and for no good reason.'

'Other than the truth,' said Pearl. 'You see, Anemone mentioned something very important on the evening she helped Maria.'

Simona looked confused. 'Helped her with what?'

'Precisely,' said Pearl. 'I had almost forgotten when I saw the willow pattern china in her room — and suddenly I remembered. That night, everyone else had drunk coffee but you, Steven.

266

You alone asked for Chinese tea. Robert brought it to you — in a cup and saucer.'

'I remember,' said Maria.

'I don't understand,' Layla said tetchily.

'Neither do I,' Steven snapped.

Pearl looked at Maria. 'Anemone helped you to clear the table that night. But she picked up your cup, Steven, and I believe she read it — at least, the pattern formed by the leaves. She once said, 'There are patterns in all things, even in the murmuration of starlings in the sky. Nothing is chance.' And I think she was right. Do we always act with free will or are we influenced by other forces — like bees in a hive? Our invitation here was certainly not by chance, it was engineered.'

Dolly frowned in frustration. 'Pearl, for goodness sake. I explained . . . '

'It's true,' said Pearl. 'At some points in our stay it has seemed like a set piece of theatre. You even referred to that yourself, Marshall. It seemed that way because it *was* a form of theatre. The drama was, in fact, all plotted and predetermined. Why did Jake return that night, of all nights? Not because he was the 'uninvited guest' — quite the opposite. He had been tipped off exactly where Simona was and what she was doing. By you, Marshall.'

McGuire stepped forward, preparing to caution Marshall.

'No, Pearl!' exclaimed Simona, jumping to her feet. 'You said yourself: Marshall is physically incapable of having committed this murder.'

'Which is why he needed the help of someone else. An accomplice.' She turned to face Steven

267

while Layla instantly reacted to Pearl's damning look.

'Impossible!' she gasped.

'Layla,' said Pearl. 'You slept soundly on the night of Jake's murder because I believe the pill you took was not your usual one but another, much stronger drug. At a given point in the night Steven left you sleeping and came downstairs to meet Marshall, who lured Jake to the kitchen, where he was rendered unconscious. It was you, Steven, who dragged him to the freezer room and you who left him there.'

She glanced across to McGuire. 'It seemed impossible that there could be so little forensic evidence relating to this crime, but that's because you wore a set of lightweight overalls to commit the murder, Steven, similar to those used by members of forensic teams themselves, so that no forensic clues would be left behind. That night, after you switched off the alarm systems for the freezer room and left Jake Rhys to die, you went out on to the terrace and burned those overalls in the wood-fired oven. Nico was to find something that remained of them — a small zip tag in the ashes — and he therefore came under suspicion himself until being eliminated from the police enquiries. But on the night of Jake's death, you then returned to your room and showered while Layla was still asleep. She may have been slightly disturbed by the sound of you returning but, probably due to her sedation, she thought this was rain.'

Pearl concluded in a sombre tone: 'It took a black heart to leave Jake to such a death, but I

268

believe Anemone saw this in the pattern of leaves left at the bottom of a cup: something evil, lethal — the plague among us, the plague within.'

A silence fell for a moment before Steven finally burst into laughter. 'Absurd!' he said. 'You can't seriously expect anyone to believe this nonsense? Leaves in the bottom of a cup? You're out of your mind. This isn't evidence.'

'No,' said Pearl, 'you're right. But evidence was once heard in court concerning a young man who was intent on making as much money as he possibly could from property deals by charming older, wealthy women.'

'What?' cried Layla.

'It was Inspector McGuire who discovered this,' Pearl said. 'But what he *didn't* know was that you were already aware of this, Marshall.' Her gaze moved to him. 'You knew about the case because you had made it your business to check out Jake's friends since he had proved to be such an unreliable husband to Simona. You had been a schoolmaster in West Kent, and Steven is from Tunbridge Wells, so it may not have proved very difficult for you to sound out a few former colleagues from Steven's old public school who may well have heard about a local court case concerning one of their former pupils. The case hadn't led to a conviction so there was no disgrace to the school but, coupled with what you knew of Steven, and knowing he was a close friend of Jake's, perhaps you were planning to confront him with what you had learned of his past. But then something happened. You discovered from Simona that Steven had found,

269

quite by chance, the love of his life — on a plane returning from Dubai. What an extraordinary quirk of fate. Or was it? Layla is a very wealthy woman but as my mother puts it, when it comes to men, some women can be bad pickers. Layla was given a little help to pick Steven and it surely wasn't too difficult for someone like you, Steven, to arrange a seat beside her on that plane? It's a twelve-hour flight from Dubai. Long enough for you to have worked your so-called charm.'

Layla shook her head slowly. 'It's not true, what you're saying. We met by chance. That isn't how it happened.'

'I'm afraid it is,' said Pearl. 'It's exactly what happened. You were charmed, Layla, but perhaps 'groomed' would be a better word.'

'Continue like this,' said Steven coolly, 'and you'll find yourself in court for slander. Are you seriously accusing me — and a former magistrate — of murder?'

'Pearl,' said Dolly. 'Be careful.'

'I will.' Pearl addressed Marshall. ''A man of duty',' she went on, 'that's how my mother described you to me. And you'll know that she's so often right.' She held Marshall's gaze. 'So I'm sure it gave you no crisis of conscience to bring your own kind of justice to Jake Rhys, to redress the balance that you felt had been slanted against your beloved god-daughter for far too long.'

'That's not true,' Simona protested. 'We'd all moved on. There was no reason for Marshall to murder Jake.'

But Pearl was resolute. 'After Anemone's murder, it was telling that you spoke about how

270

'justice' must be done, and that whoever had killed Anemone would 'get what they deserve'. No mention of Jake, of course, who had already got *his* just deserts. But that day, Marshall, you were already getting what *you* deserved — a burden of pain, pain that has only increased ever since — and which Simona confided to me she has seen written daily in your face. Not physical pain, but a terrible weight of guilt for an innocent woman's death.'

Simona looked at her godfather but still he remained silent. 'Marshall?' she said. 'Tell me this isn't true.'

'*Can* you live with that burden?' Pearl asked him. 'Can you honestly allow Anemone's murderer to go unpunished?'

Still Marshall said nothing but Steven replied for him.

'It's pure speculation,' he said. 'Nothing more. Come on, Layla. There's nothing to keep us here.' He took Layla's hand and pulled her roughly to her feet. Confused, she went to follow him but Marshall's cane suddenly blocked Steven's path. Alarmed, Steven spun round to face him. 'What the hell do you think you're doing?' he hissed, trying to control his fury.

'I'm not going to lie any more,' Marshall told them all. 'Not now. And not to Simona.' He looked at his god-daughter, confessing, 'I invited Pearl and Dolly here for one reason only — to make sure that I could influence Pearl's thinking and divert attention for the police.' He addressed Pearl directly now. 'But it seems I underestimated you. And you're right: I have absolutely no regrets about what happened to Jake. He was given many chances — perhaps too many. But when he contacted me for money a few months ago, I knew something had to be done. Something final — to protect you, Simona.' He pointed to Steven. 'He agreed to dispose of Jake in return for the profits from the sale of my house — a considerable sum — but he also knew that Jake was now a loose cannon and liable to threaten his new relationship with Layla. Why?' He laughed contemptuously. 'Because even Jake knew what a sponge you really are.'

'Shut up!' said Steven menacingly but Marshall, liberated by the truth, continued to Pearl, 'Perhaps there's a dangerous hubris created by sitting in judgement over others. I hoped to rid the world of Jake Rhys but I never wished to bring harm to anyone else — least of all to Anemone. She was a decent human being who didn't deserve what happened. And for that I blame *you*,' he turned to Steven and struggled to his feet. 'You killed that woman after you overheard her call to Pearl that morning. *You* were the one who decided she had to die, that she had to be disposed of.' His gaze moved to McGuire. 'I surrender myself to your judgement, Inspector. I'll co-operate fully and I'll give you all the evidence you need to convict this man.'

'You fool!' Steven Sparkes lurched forward, knocking Marshall roughly to the floor as he made a bid for escape towards the French doors. But McGuire was ready and moved swiftly to tackle him. Steven was quicker and, in desperation, landed a punch that winded McGuire and gave himself another chance for escape. This time, Nico and Frank made to grab hold of him but in a split second, Steven had managed to dodge them both. He had almost made it to the French doors when he was floored suddenly, and completely, by a vicious blow struck hard to the back of his knees. As he collapsed to the ground, writhing in agony, several uniformed police officers appeared at the doors from the grounds.

All eyes now moved to Layla who stood, still clutching Marshall's cane, not by its heavy owl handle but with both of her hands at its tip. As though recognising what she had just done, she took a deep breath and pushed a stray strand of blonde hair from her face before she pointed to Steven and announced: 'I was taken in by that rat. He even made us put in a sealed bid to try and get his hands on *this* place, but I'm glad it went to you, Simona, and I'm even gladder I'm an ace golfer.'

Surrendering the cane now to McGuire she turned to Pearl and announced, 'Looks like you just did me a very big favour, Pearl Nolan.'

19

The next morning, while walking along the path leading down to the Villa Pellegrini, Pearl stopped in her tracks to consider the cars that remained in the parking space by the tall cypress trees. Georgina's Alfa Romeo had disappeared, having transported her away the night before, directly to the airport, where she had booked a first-class flight back to Milan. It was unlikely that she would ever again return to the Villa Pellegrini or have any further dealings with her old friend, Simona Cartwright. Dolly's Morris Minor had also left, a little over an hour ago, after she had said her goodbyes, explaining that she needed to return urgently to Whitstable in order to welcome guests to her own holiday property, Dolly's Attic — the charming little flat above her shop, Dolly's Pots, from which she sold the 'shabby chic' ceramics she crafted.

Pearl had seen her mother off in the car park before going for a walk to clear her head. The sun had risen brightly that morning as though any other summer's day was about to unfold, and yet, for those at the Villa Pellegrini, life would never be the same.

Steven Sparkes and Marshall Taylor had been arrested and charged by McGuire. Marshall's staid Volvo estate still sat in the car park, alongside the silver Mercedes belonging to his god-daughter, Simona — but not for much longer. His confession guaranteed that he would pay the price for taking the law into his own hands. In doing so, he had indeed helped to rid the world of Jake Rhys, but he had also set in motion a chain of events which had led to the death of a woman whose only failing had been to use a special gift — a sensitivity to her environment and to others — in order to discover the identity of a murderer in their midst.

A quirk of fate had proved to be the spur to unravelling the facts: something as simple as the pattern of a few leaves in the bottom of a cup. It was insufficient evidence on its own, as Steven Sparkes had well known, but a hunch from Pearl had convinced her it might be possible to tease out the truth from Marshall Taylor, the guilt felt by 'a just man' in that one last workshop she had contrived the day before. Now, with his confession, there was no doubt that a trail of lethal conspiracy would be uncovered by McGuire, and that this would lead to a long prison sentence for both men. The expensive Range Rover which had brought Steven Sparkes to the Villa Pellegrini would now leave without him, as his fiancée Layla would no doubt continue to reflect on her lucky escape.

Nico's vintage Fiat Spider was also still in place and, as Pearl gazed on it she smiled, recognising that while the model had been one of the coolest sports cars around in its time, it had also been a vehicle for those who aspired to owning a Ferrari but would never actually afford one. It was a fun convertible, both cheerful and charming, and its bright red colour guaranteed that it would always be noticed. The sleek Italian bodywork was still in place though a wing mirror had suffered some damage, but that hardly dented the overall handsome impression.

Pearl turned away from the cars and looked towards the house as she had done from this vantage point on the very first day she had arrived here with Dolly. The early-morning sun splashed across the rose-pink walls, and the terracotta window-boxes still sported red and white flowering geraniums. The window shutters were open but the house itself would perhaps never yield the full truth of what had occurred within it but instead cling on to this as Frank Ellis had once suggested ancient walls might be capable of doing. Frank remained at the villa and now seemed likely to do so, not as a great passion, as Jake Rhys had once been in Simona's life, but as a comfort and support to her — two things of which she would now be in need — and which Pearl was grateful she would finally receive.

Taking a deep breath of fresh air, Pearl prepared to return to the house to say her own goodbyes.

★ ★ ★

Nico was in the meadow, close to the wooden storage chest that contained Robert's beekeeping paraphernalia, and he was gazing towards the distant rapeseed fields when Pearl came up behind him. The startled look on his face transformed into a smile — not the famous grin he wore in the photos of the Villa Pellegrini's brochure, but one full of genuine warmth and affection.

'Perla,' he said softly, leaning forward to kiss her gently on the cheek, close enough to her lips to be temptation for them both. But he drew back and his dark caramel eyes scanned Pearl's features as if to make certain he would remember them for a future time.

'*Cosa posso dire?*' he whispered. 'What can I say? Yesterday was a *rivelazione* — as it was meeting you here, in this magical place.'

Pearl smiled at this but Nico looked instantly concerned as he asked, 'That was . . . 'cheesy'?'

'Yes, Nico,' she said. 'But I love you for it.'

His smile returned, broader than before, reminding her of another afternoon in the same spot when that same smile had seemed to enchant her, transforming all the preconceptions and resentment she had stored up against him into an attraction for the handsome Italian chef. The words to an almost forgotten ode by Keats had resurfaced in her memory that day:

My heart aches, and a drowsy numbness pains
My sense, as though of hemlock I had drunk . . .

But today, the spell was broken and Pearl's perspective was clear.

'So, today you will return to . . . ' Nico broke off, lost for a moment until she provided some help.

'Whitstable,' she prompted.

'Yes, Whitstable,' he echoed. 'The little village.'

'The small town.'

'Where you have your restaurant.'

'The Whitstable Pearl,' she said.

He smiled again, amused at this. '*Perfetto!* One day I will come and try those oysters which you promised were better than my own.'

'I'd be very happy for you to do that, Nico,' she said, before adding, 'And I'm sorry.'

'Sorry?'

'Yes. I pride myself on having good instincts for people, but I got you wrong. You see, part of me always felt that your efforts to win me round were calculated. That apology here in the meadow? The picnic — the special cake? I'm sorry to say I mistrusted all of this as much as Inspector McGuire did.'

Nico frowned. 'He told you that?'

She nodded, disclosing, 'He said you were ingratiating yourself, manipulating me for a reason.'

She expected some anger from Nico at this but instead he merely gave a philosophical shrug. 'Then perhaps he is as good a detective as you are, Perla.'

Pearl's eyes widened as he went on: 'It did cross my mind that a beautiful woman with her own successful restaurant and a heart big enough to respond to the operas of Rossini might help with the renaissance of Nico Caruso.' He raised his shoulders in a gesture of helplessness while Pearl's jaw dropped open at the thought, but before she could utter a word, he said quickly, 'But I'm pleased to say that even the greatest tragedies bring us lessons to be learned, and in the short space of time since the truth was discovered, I find I may even be offered a second chance.'

'At what?' Pearl asked, confused.

'Mangiamo number two,' he stated proudly.

'Your restaurant chain?'

'*New* restaurant chain,' he corrected her. 'The seeds of recovery are at an early stage,' he said in a hushed tone, 'and they need some . . . cultivation to be brought to fruition, but with the help of another — '

'Simona?' guessed Pearl.

But there was no time for a reply, since at that moment another voice sounded stridently. 'Nico?'

It was Layla, and she stood framed in the archway at the entrance to the herb garden. Today she wore a black and white tailored suit and designer heels while clutching a leather briefcase in her hand. Her blonde hair was gathered up into a neat pleat and her make-up had been expertly applied to conceal any possible evidence of tears. She appeared transformed and ready for business, sounding like it too as she called: '*Andiamo*, honey!'

Those two words were all that was required to summon Nico to her side. He raised his hand in a final farewell to Pearl. 'One day, Perla,' he said. 'One day.'

Layla's gaze remained on Pearl for a moment longer than Nico's, offering her a final look which seemed a complex combination of shame mingled with gratitude. Then she and Nico disappeared together, leaving Pearl staring towards the drained pond which she hoped would soon be refilled — and teeming with life.

Shortly afterwards, Pearl brought down the last few items of her luggage from the *Fiammetta* suite and settled them in the hall. Simona emerged from her study, followed by Frank. Her eyes were filled with sadness but there was also an air of quiet resignation about her. She looked pale but beautiful in a black crepe dress with the string of amber beads at her throat. An awkward silence fell before Simona finally offered her hand to Pearl, who took it, aware that this single gesture said more than words ever could.

'Your detective will be here soon?' Simona asked.

Pearl nodded.

'Good of him to offer to take you home,' said Frank reasonably.

For a moment, Pearl's gaze was held by the tiny bee captured in Simona's amber necklace. As though reading her mind, Simona said: 'I did consider trying to escape, leaving this place and pretending none of this had happened. Last night, it seemed impossible to stay, but then Frank and I spoke and he's given me hope that I can still make a future here.' She broke off and looked at Frank Ellis, who put a loving arm rather tentatively around her waist. Simona seemed comforted by this. 'I would like you to know that you and Dolly will always be welcome here, Pearl,' she said. And then, as though aware that she had now come to the end of a difficult speech, she took a deep breath and leaned in towards Frank.

Pearl said only: 'If there is anything we can do, you know where we are.' She shook hands with them both.

In the next moment the sound of tyres on gravel brought an end to further conversation. Pearl wheeled her suitcase outside to see that McGuire's car was parked on the other side of the path by the tall cypress trees. He saw her, got out and smiled as he walked over to meet her but then Pearl noticed Robert appear on the lawn, ferrying something in his arms. As he approached, she and McGuire saw that it was a cardboard box covered loosely with a towel.

'Robert?' she asked.

'Something for you,' he explained. 'If you want it, that is.'

Maria, carrying a bag over her shoulder, joined them, commenting: 'It's amazing, isn't it? He found the swarm today on the willow tree down by the jetty.'

Robert turned to Pearl. 'They're looking for a new home — and a good keeper.'

'Bees?' said McGuire, alarmed.

'I told you,' said Pearl. 'When they're swarming, it's the time that they're least dangerous.'

'That's right,' Robert confirmed. 'They'll have forgotten where they've come from and will re-programme their natural GPS instincts once they've found their new home. You could take them back with you right now?'

McGuire saw that Pearl, Robert and Maria were all looking at him for a decision but Pearl knew he needed some encouragement.

'Bees are having a hard time, you know,' she

began. 'There are pesticides, parasites, pathogens . . . But without bees, something like a hundred thousand varieties of plant would disappear — and then we humans might not be too far behind.'

McGuire could see they were all still waiting for his response. Finally, he gave it.

'OK, OK,' he said, accepting this. 'But you're not seriously suggesting we take them back in my car.'

'They'll be fine in the boot for the journey to Whitstable,' Robert said casually. 'I've given them some syrup, and that hive on your allotment will see them all right after that.' He smiled at Pearl while Maria lifted the bag from her shoulder and took out a pair of beekeeper's gloves, veil and smoker.

'It must be fate,' she said. 'A swarm on the willow tree like that.'

Pearl looked at McGuire. 'What are we waiting for?'

The detective heaved a sigh before taking Pearl's luggage and setting it on the back seat of his car. Then he opened the boot and allowed Robert to carefully settle the cardboard box containing the swarm of bees, along with the beekeeper's equipment.

'Are you sure this is safe?' he asked.

'Quite sure, Inspector,' Robert said politely. 'As long as you keep them with their queen they'll be fine, and I'll happily give you all the advice you need.'

Pearl smiled, grateful to him. 'Thank you, Robert. I'll take you up on that.'

McGuire closed his boot and then opened the

passenger door for Pearl before getting in, starting up the engine and completing an expert three-point turn back on to the road. Pearl lowered the passenger window and waved to Robert, who was now standing alone on the path as he had done on the day of her arrival — no longer welcoming her but bidding her goodbye, his figure slowly receding as McGuire drove away.

★ ★ ★

'The last thing I was expecting was a boot full of bees,' said McGuire.

'Robert knows his stuff,' Pearl replied. 'And you heard what he said, they'll be fine as long as the queen stays with them.' She smiled mischievously before adding, 'Of course, there *was* once a case of a car that was followed for two whole days by twenty thousand bees.'

McGuire glanced at her. 'You're kidding me?'

'Not at all,' she said casually. 'They'd become separated from their queen, who was trapped inside the boot.'

McGuire gave her a wary look but she smiled at him. 'Don't worry, I'll make sure they're made comfortable at my allotment — queen and all.' She leaned forward to switch on the radio and an unexpected blast of *Nessun Dorma* suddenly filled the car. Quickly turning down the volume, she asked: 'You've been listening to opera?'

McGuire seemed decidedly uncomfortable with her question. 'Someone must have changed the channel,' he lied.

The aria played on and Pearl was taken back to another day spent with another man in another place — a meadow filled with the lazy drone of bees. But before she could reflect further on that, she noticed that McGuire had begun rifling noisily in his dashboard for a CD. 'You know,' he began, 'I've been thinking of taking some time off.'

'Really?'

He nodded. 'I've got plenty of leave saved up and it makes sense to take it while the weather's good.'

Pearl considered this. 'So what will you do?'

He hesitated before replying. 'A staycation, I thought. Doing all the things you'd normally do on a trip away but . . . at home.'

'Home?' she asked.

'Staying around Canterbury. And Whitstable. A few days on the beach, some good food, maybe even some sailing?' He left a pause before asking: 'What do you think?'

Before Pearl could reply, the aria on the radio came to an abrupt end as they drove beyond the sign for the Villa Pellegrini. Approaching the old hawthorn at the end of the path, McGuire looked again at Pearl for an answer.

'Will it be . . . Italian food?' she asked.

'Definitely not,' he said firmly. 'Though I have been thinking of trying an oyster or two. After all, you do know your oysters, right?'

'Yes,' she said. 'I certainly do.'

He was now waiting for a space in the stream of traffic that was heading straight across their path along the old Milton Manor Road, but his gaze shifted to Pearl. Some American Country Rock began playing on a CD — perfect driving music for McGuire — but instead he kept his eyes on Pearl. He leaned in, tentatively at first, until she showed no signs of moving away, then he kissed her, long and hard — and as they broke apart, he admitted: 'I've been wanting to do that for a *very* long time.'

Pearl smiled. 'Good.'

McGuire was just about to turn the wheel to head out on to the main road when Pearl suddenly ordered: 'Wait!'

He saw she was rooting for something in her bag, quickly producing an old horseshoe which she contemplated for just a moment before tossing it from her passenger window on to the track leading down to the Villa Pellegrini.

'I'm sure they could do with it more than us,' she said softly.

McGuire drove on, knowing the city would soon open up before them and that they might now view it differently, as Pearl felt they might also view each other — not least because a change of scenery was apt to bring a change in perspective. She smiled and, as the music played on, she sank her head closer to McGuire's warm shoulder, knowing that for them both, the summer was just beginning — and in her suitcase was a red satin dress she had yet to wear.

Acknowledgements

It would like to thank beekeepers everywhere but especially Whitstable and Herne Bay Beekeepers and the Kent Beekeepers' Association.

Special thanks also go to Maureen Kelson for the very happy times I spent at her former summer home, *Es Collet*, and to Debbie Ellis for having once taken me to stay at a magnificent villa in Tuscany. From such things come inspiration . . .

I am also grateful, as ever, to Krystyna Green at Little, Brown and to Michelle Kass, Alex Holley and all at Michelle Kass Associates — as well as to Maria Cristina Nardini for help with Italian translation.

Thanks also to Dominic King of BBC Radio Kent and to Victoria Falconer of WhitLit and the most wonderful booksellers: Ruth Frost, Liz Waller and Henna Mattila for all their kind support — and to Phil Smith and A Casa Mia in Henna Bay goes my appreciation for introducing me to the wonders of a wood-fired oven!

Final thanks go to the Artichoke pub in Chartham, to Canterbury City Council for their upkeep of the Great Stour Way, and to pilgrims everywhere . . .

We do hope that you have enjoyed reading this large print book.

Did you know that all of our titles are available for purchase?

We publish a wide range of high quality large print books including:
Romances, Mysteries, Classics
General Fiction
Non Fiction and Westerns

Special interest titles available in large print are:
The Little Oxford Dictionary
Music Book
Song Book
Hymn Book
Service Book

Also available from us courtesy of Oxford University Press:
Young Readers' Dictionary
(large print edition)
Young Readers' Thesaurus
(large print edition)

For further information or a free brochure, please contact us at:
Ulverscroft Large Print Books Ltd.,
The Green, Bradgate Road, Anstey,
Leicester, LE7 7FU, England.
Tel: (00 44) **0116 236 4325**
Fax: (00 44) **0116 234 0205**

Other titles published by Ulverscroft:

THE COMPANION

Sarah Dunnakey

Billy Shaw lives in Potter's Pleasure Palace, the best entertainment venue in Yorkshire, complete with dancing and swingboats and picnickers and a roller-skating rink. Jasper Harper lives in the big house above the valley with his eccentric mother Edie and Uncle Charles, brother and sister authors who have come from London to write in the seclusion of the moors. When it is arranged for Billy to become Jasper's companion, he arrives to find a wild, peculiar boy in a curiously haphazard household where the air is thick with secrets. Later, when Charles and Edie are found dead, it's ruled a double suicide. But fictions have become tangled up in facts, and it's left to Anna Sallis, almost a century later, to unravel the knots and piece together the truth.

THE WOMEN OF BAKER STREET

Michelle Birkby

1889: Mrs Hudson, long-suffering landlady of 221b Baker Street, falls ill and collapses in her home, and is whisked off by Dr Watson to St Bartholomew's Hospital. Perhaps she has developed an overactive imagination thanks to her eccentric lodgers, but it seems she is surrounded by patients who all have skeletons in their closets — on a ward with an unusually high mortality rate. And was the quiet murder she believed she witnessed on her first night simply a hallucination through a haze of morphine, or something more sinister? Meanwhile, Dr Watson's wife Mary has another case in hand. Young boys have been disappearing unnoticed from London's streets for years, and the Baker Street Irregulars whisper morbid rumours of their fates . . .

A HIGH MORTALITY OF DOVES

Kate Ellis

1919: The Derbyshire village of Wenfield is still reeling from four years of war. Just when the village has begun to regain its tranquillity, a young woman, Myrtle Bligh, is found stabbed and left in a woodland, her mouth slit to accommodate a dead dove — a bird of peace. When two more women are found murdered in identical circumstances, Wenfield is thrown into a panic. With rumours of a ghostly soldier with a painted face being spotted near the scene of the murders, Inspector Albert Lincoln is sent up from London to crack the terrible case — but with the killer still on the loose, who will be next to die at the hands of this vicious angel of death?

have expected to stay in Scotland Yard for ever.

He was going back to Lancashire, where people didn't look at you strangely when you asked for black pudding. He would be able to walk up the hills he had walked up in his youth, to visit the lakes he had not seen since before he started shaving. It was a wonderful prospect, so he wondered why, even as he was savouring his return home, there was a part of him which was almost dreading it a little.